Advance Praise

"A man battling mental health challenges and homelessness seeks redemption and understanding in Bergen's novel. Caleb Taylor is first introduced to the reader in italicized first-person narration, describing the joys and pain of mania: "Mania courses through me. It flows through me, glows through me, goes through me." Having just moved to Columbus, Ohio, Caleb finds himself in yet another new town without a place to live. Carrying only a laptop (on which he writes short stories and poetry he hopes to publish), Caleb faces the daunting task of finding shelter. His adult life has been marred by mental health challenges; he confesses, "arrests, homelessness, and hospitalizations diminished my desire to try to get better." He applies to the Crossroads Men's Shelter and is eventually granted a bunk. There, he meets Malik, his assigned housing navigator.

The narrative then alternates between Caleb's and Malik's perspectives, providing insights into the experiences of seeking housing and the challenges of navigating the modern homeless shelter infrastructure. As the story unfolds, Bergen details the men's harrowing histories. Caleb is haunted by visions of his childhood tormentor, who later killed his own parents and frequently shows up in visions in the peaks of Caleb's mania, pushing him over the edge in dangerous ways. Malik uses his access to the shelter's database in his quest to find his long-lost father, a former addict with whom he lost contact years earlier. While Malik is the moral

center of the novel, he is not just a savior figure, but a complicated, rounded character dealing with his own anxieties. Caleb is likewise a multifaceted and sympathetic character as he struggles to outpace his dangerous visions, racing thoughts, and moments of mania when everything spins out of control. The novel may be difficult for some readers with its raw depiction of trauma and abuse, and detailed descriptions of the shelter systems that sometimes support and sometimes fail those like Caleb. For readers interested in realistic fiction that seems ripped from real life, with believable characters and distinct voices, this is a rewarding novel.
A poignant and memorable story of resilience."

— *Kirkus Review*

Waking Beneath The Chicory Flower

Waking Beneath The Chicory Flower

Joseph Bergen

First Edition

Casebound ISBN: 978-1-62720-618-1
Paperback ISBN: 978-1-62720-619-8
Ebook ISBN: 978-1-62720-620-4

Design by Jenna Mattern
Editorial Development by Olivia DiTroia
Promotional Development by Caroline Gerosa

Published by Apprentice House Press

Loyola University Maryland
4501 N. Charles Street, Baltimore, MD 21210
410.617.5265
www.ApprenticeHouse.com
info@ApprenticeHouse.com

This novel is dedicated to those who struggle with mental health.
I see you. I am you. Keep going.

INTRODUCTION

Caleb — Mania

I step beneath the brilliant, blinking blanket of the Milky Way, a display so bright it looks unreal. I feel as though I could sip from the tip of the slippery Big Dipper or blissfully kiss the mist on Orion's lips.

I sense the snipping of threads tethering me to reality. They fall, one by one, to the ground with no sound, now unbound. Mania is a jealous companion. She prefers me to be isolated and alone, strung up like a fanciful marionette dancing about the stage for all to see.

I bid farewell to the trappings of being tied down to one place. The open road is my palette. Walking into the night tastes tangy and sharp. Mania thrives beneath the frigid nighttime sky where ideas course from a source divorced from reality; they are new to me, through to me, a view too few pursue that is incarnate to me.

I walk through towns at 4:30 a.m. with just my duffel bag and laptop. The dark streets, vacant storefronts, and silent neighborhoods rest before waking, and I realize that the world devoid of humans is sublime. My footsteps move me in celestial syncopation with the stars. My toenails are bloody, and my ankles are blistered, but these pains only imbue my passions with the fuel to move forward, always forward, never peering back at the monsters that crawl through the folds of my mind.

These monsters were put there by hands that sought too much from a young boy. I looked at the world with moistened, wide eyes. Eyes forced closed so as not to see the violations put inside me, the fishhooks piercing skin, and gun barrels inserted into my mouth. And when I tried to communicate what was transpiring, I was told I was rude. I was silly. I was wrong. I was lying. Lying through my teeth, teeth that clinked down on pistols, clenching tightly shut when locked in the bedroom closet.

It's how, even now, walking beneath the stars, in the safety of anonymity, cloistered by the empty streets and unlidded garbage cans, he finds me. It releases adrenaline in me that saturates every cell in my body, knowing I cannot fight what is about to happen to my five-year-old self. He does things I know to be wrong. Things that make me turn my head away and slowly slip surreptitiously underwater. My conscious self departs from my body since my body cannot depart from what is happening. Imaginary waters envelop me in a cocoon of safety. My mind turns a blind eye as the water envelops me.

Pinochle is being played down the hall. I hear laughter emanating from the living room. I am in the closet, petrified with fears, in tears, for years, so my soul disappears. Time and time again, I succumb to the water, to the peaceful calm of the darkness and solitude, away from locked closets, cigarette lighters, and gun barrels. It's the thing that I do. I disappear in the waters. For too many years, I could not disappear. Now, when I see his face, a face that exists only in my mind, I feel the water rising above my ears. I disappear even though my conscious self tries to hold on, but the undertow is strong. It pulls me downward to safety.

This is how I happen.

Even now, as an adult, it's the thing that

I do. My mind perceives a threat, real or imagined, and I slip underwater. It's how I wake up in different cities, in strange train stations, in far-away bus depots unfamiliar to me. I wake up from zombie marches with bloodied socks and a frostbitten face, carrying the weight of my life in a duffel bag.

I am happening.

I flee, free, in perpetuity, because as a kid, I couldn't. Now I disappear, under the water, taking my mind away from what is intruding on my flesh because for so long my body had to stay.

I happen.

My mind sets course away from that which seeks to harm me, regardless of whether I want it to or not.

I happen...so nothing more will happen.

CHAPTER ONE

Caleb — Who. Are. You?

No one sets out to be the worst possible version of themselves, yet this is precisely what happened to me. I have become a caricature of myself. Symptoms of my illness are pernicious, like weeds slowly choking out a tended garden. Family and friends, weary of my behavior and lies, exited my life; and I theirs. The loss of family and the people I love is my own doing. Knowing everyone is better off without me cements my solitude in place. Having lost what is important to me, I often give in to the erratic comfort of mania. Its upward trajectory feels like I can move mountains. The allure of feeling lifted off my feet is the one good feeling I can achieve by myself, just by letting the mania flourish. So much energy. So many impulses. So many options. I am hungry for that seductive energy as I close my eyes to the chaos unfolding around me.

Feverish actions raised an alarm among those around me. This led to intervention by people trying to help, but mania doesn't work that way. Eventually, interventions by friends would be replaced by interventions by police, and oftentimes, arrests were made. Arrests and jail time translate into being fired from jobs or being kicked out of living spaces. Lack of income and housing parlays into homelessness. All of these red flags flap in the wind, but my surging mind doesn't see them. All I feel is the outpouring of my spectacular ideas as energy builds. Energy becomes an all-encompassing need to fulfill what my mind dictates as prudent. My notions are mercurial at best and nonsensical to say the least, even though they make perfect sense to me while gripped in mania.

I burn bridges to those trying to help. I spend money as I chase outlandish ideas. I pass on sleep because the energy of mania is intoxicating. Anything that places itself between me and my dysfunctional mind must be eliminated. All of this courses through me until some chemical change happens within the folds of my mind. When that shift occurs, I walk up to the precipice and plunge downward, like a lemming, blind to the perils of what lies at rock bottom. It's familiar territory. The deep depression, after the mania blows up my life again, weighs me down, like a stone settling at the bottom of a river, completely underwater and immobile.

Since I left San Diego and landed in Columbus, I am doing battle with the beast, what I call my depression. I have slept alongside a park gazebo, beneath bushes near a church, and behind wooden pallets in an alleyway. Long, dark winter nights afford me a few more hours of sleep before being found by the police and moved along. As temperatures continue to drop lower each day, I adjust. If winter comes gradually, it's easier to survive the nighttime frigidity. Tonight, however, the ice and snow of an early storm will barge in like a drunken, uninvited guest.

I don't know my way around the city very well, and the shelters I have found are replete with fellow wanderers. The beast yearns for me to abandon the notion of trying to improve my circumstances. I haven't had my medications since I left my last living situation two thousand miles ago, so I'm devolving. I can sense it. Even with mania lurking around each corner, my brain chemistry reverts to a feral state as the beast slowly consumes me. I catch glimpses of Craig. He's everywhere now, spurring me to keep moving as the waters rise.

The best weapon against the cold is to keep moving, even when my body burns with exhaustion. I shift the weight of my backpack and duffel bag. Each is packed haphazardly with the contents only a conflicted mind would think important. My muscles are fatigued from walking. My grip on life is waning. The more I lose grip, the less I care about gaining control over my life. I'm at that point, again, where I don't think about living. I only think about survival for the day, or by the hour, sometimes by the minute. Eventually, the depression will override everything until I yearn to lie down and simply forget to live.

Unaware of how many miles I've walked since arriving in Columbus, Ohio my body falls into something of a stupor. I'm endeavoring to find a shelter that popped up on Google Maps when I had a signal at a McDonald's a few hours ago. The shelter website states I must arrive by 6:00 p.m. to get a bunk. My phone says it's 5:30 p.m. I can walk about three miles per hour, four if I pick up my pace. I'm fairly certain I'm within a half mile of the shelter. If I can trudge forward, I should be OK for tonight. As the numbers on the lonely industrial street in the middle of nowhere keep rising, I'm confident I'm getting closer. My hopes are raised.

My hopes are raised. It is a strange feeling.

My earbuds play *Simon and Garfunkel's Greatest Hits.* I'm thankful every day for the albums and songs I downloaded years ago when I was well. Music is a rare salve against my many ailments. It can raise my spirits. I find walking to the rhythm of songs stimulates an internal metronome: 1 – 2 – 3 – 4 equals right – left – right – left. Music reminds me of various times when things weren't so dire. Music propels my feet forward toward a place of rest tonight. Music keeps at bay the pounding, apocalyptic scenarios that are the background to my everyday thinking. Music replaces thoughts, so when a song ends, life comes pouring back into my mind. I avoid that at all cost.

I can almost taste the meal they will offer tonight, no matter how simple it is. Food on an actual plate would be a welcome departure from the dollar menu at fast food joints. I've been eating fast food from a wrapper, spilling shredded iceberg lettuce on the floor like breadcrumbs on a hidden trail. When I am well, I would be embarrassed, but embarrassment doesn't register right now for me. Mostly, I am looking forward to setting my bags down and not having to lift them again for a few days while I rest inside, where it is warm and dry. Hopefully, I can bandage my blistered feet, and I can get my nose checked out for frostbite. The promise of rest, safe from the ice and hardness of the frozen ground, keeps me moving forward.

My reverie, however, is short-lived.

After reaching the small apex of a hill, I am stopped in my tracks. In front of me, stretching out for miles, is a sprawling eight-lane, concrete interstate highway peeling off in several directions. I'm less than a quarter mile from the shelter, but it may as well be a hundred miles. There's simply no way to cross the concrete and chain link monster impeding my journey to get to the shelter on time.

I peer across the eight lanes of highway toward the derelict section of town where this elusive shelter exists. I feel like a zoo animal behind a chain link fence, pondering freedom on the other side. My fingers lace into the fence, and I watch the cars soar by. I drop my head and accept the situation. I imagine for a moment trying to run across the highway. I know it would be dangerous. If I got hit, I might die, or even worse, I might live but be crippled. Dying doesn't dissuade me from crossing; it is the latter. Being homeless is hard enough. To be homeless and crippled seems unthinkable. A fleeting moment has me thinking about getting struck by a car. It would allow me to sleep in a hospital bed with food and attention to my illness for a few days. I ponder that scenario but decide not to do so. I'm not fearful of dying, but I am fearful of pain.

Shaking my head to dispel the thought, I walk south toward an onramp overgrown with weeds, bushes, and scraggly trees. There's a safety fence, but it is old and in disrepair. I slip through a broken segment without much trouble. I walk a dozen or so yards along the side of the highway through the tangled undergrowth, fast food wrappers, and ripped plastic bags. I close my eyes as I push through the undergrowth. I flinch as a branch draws across my face, leaving a bright red scratch, a reminder of my circumstance. The scratch over my sunburned face stings. It takes several minutes to heave my body through the matrix of branches and dried weeds. I finally break through to the slanted concrete below the overpass.

I assess the surroundings, looking for remnants of other homeless people who might be using the location as a place to sleep at night. I do not want to intrude upon territory used by someone else. That is how fights start. Homeless folks are protective of their private spaces, especially if they are tweaking. Meth heads are unpredictable and best given a wide berth. There's no sign of my peers. No burned-out fires. No collection of beer or booze bottles. No needles or smack bags. No overwhelming odor of urine or feces. No tattered clothing. No tarps hung with bungee cords into makeshift wind shelters.

I let the duffel bag fall off one arm, a dead weight finally released. My shoulder throbs as I take deep breaths, trying to dispel the pain. I allow my backpack to fall from the other side, catching it before it lands on the ground. In that backpack, I'm protecting the one possession I have, a small laptop wrapped in dish towels and a plastic shopping bag. I marvel at what this laptop has been through. I keep waiting for the fluids inside the monitor to freeze, but so far, it is still working.

I have no Wi-Fi, so I'm unable to check the temperature. The relatively clear skies of the late afternoon are harbingers of a frigid winter night that will batter people like me sleeping outside. The overpass will protect me from the snow and ice expected from the storm later tonight. I prepare for the night, ignoring the cold in my fingers and on my face. I clear a space on the ground where the weeds meet the concrete. I use my gloved hands to scrape away rocks and broken glass. One beneficial element of a frigid winter night is that the moisture in the ground is frozen. There won't be mud to seep into my clothing during the night. The only thing worse than being cold is being wet and cold. Tonight will be hard enough. I do not need to add hypothermia to my ailments.

Sitting on the concrete, a familiar feeling comes over me. Words like "ruddy" and "adrift" and "obsequious" crawl into my mind. Words are a salve to me. They help me understand the world when life doesn't make sense. It's my way of making a chronicle of my life. I take out my phone: 47% charge. I type with my thumbs as the words drop into place:

Cold, colder, coldest.
Ruddy cheekbones reflect
journeys of a body
loose on the wind
adrift with the current,
obsequious in nature,
unbound by logic.
Vast is the abyss
in which I dwell.

I sit down with my bags. My legs protest the overexertion. I've marched through neighborhoods with my laptop held beneath my coat and near my body to keep it from freezing. I imagine one day it's just going to quit on me. I keep hoping that day is not today.

I loosen my shoelaces, pull off my boots, and wrap my feet with the towels that once protected my laptop. I have twine in my coat pocket, which I use to bind the towels to my feet. I retrieve from my backpack a one-person hiker's tent. I haven't put up the tent. There's no place where I can punch the stakes into the frozen ground. On nights like this, I just unravel the tent and stuff myself into it like a sleeping bag. It acts as a windbreak and moisture barrier.

I unzip the front of my coat, pull up one of my sweatshirts, and push my computer under, so it won't freeze overnight. My laptop is the most important possession I have. When I'm presentable, I take it to a library or a coffee shop to continue working on a few projects I have. I've created a book of poetry I call *Chronicles of a Loser*. I know my endeavors are probably futile, but it's the one thing that keeps my mind going in a positive direction. I don't like many things about myself, but I like how I write. I've always loved words and language. I like how certain phrases, like "knock your socks off," or "apple of my eye," are understood even though they actually make little sense.

I listen to the cacophony of the highway as I lie down to battle with the nighttime cold. I remove my glasses and put them in my coat pocket. I sigh once and then commit my body to the ground for the night. It's a solemn occasion to lay one's body down on the frozen ground. Few events unite you with your mortality as this simple act of surrender, a submission to the universe. It is a tacit declaration of my brokenness. Death isn't just a figment of my imagination. It is a distinct possibility on nights such as tonight. Exhaustion finally wins out over the frigid air and unforgiving ground. I pull my gloved hands and hooded head into the body of the tent. With the roar of the traffic becoming white noise, I sleep.

Ironically, sleep comes faster to me when I'm homeless. Homelessness, contrary to what most people might believe, is all-consuming and exhausting. It's a life of constant walking. There are few places to rest throughout the day without the threat of police badgering me to move on. *Move on to where?* The constant weight of the backpacks. The burn from the sun. The frostbite from the cold. All these things create a life where so much work is done, yet relatively little is accomplished. If I can find a place to lie down, sleep is never far away. It usually will not last for more than a couple of hours though. Police, onlookers, or the elements will prod me awake, so when I'm sleeping outside, I'll take slumber when I can find it.

•••

I always have the dream. It's the same dream night after night. It starts simply enough, a pastoral field on a beautiful day. A young girl looks down at the lush grass with the keen interest only a child can possess. Despite being the only character in the dream, I have never seen her face. She's young, maybe four or five. Her white-blonde hair falls to her shoulders in a simple bobbed haircut. She is wearing a blue and white dress that ends at her two knobby knees. She's not wearing shoes. She ambles through the grass until she comes upon a white Shasta daisy. It may be because she is so small, but the daisy is immense. She walks up to it, and as kids do, she picks the flower. That's when things rapidly change.

The sky overhead, once brilliant blue with a golden sun shining down, darkens with jagged, dark, ominous clouds. The serene field turns into a carpet of dark-brown, dead grass resembling gnarled and rusted nails. The new terrain cuts her feet. She cries in pain. Scared to her core, she drops the flower, which is now dark and brittle. The edges of the field surge with clouds of dusty rubble churning into a metallic, twisted sky. Military tanks and low-flying aircraft hurl shrapnel across the field. Gunshots, sounds of heavy machinery, and military warfare grind in the little girl's ears. The only light is that of reflections off hard, metal surfaces. A metallic, mechanical army closes in on the little girl, closer and closer, until she is overtaken in the catastrophic melee of anger, pain, and despair. She is paralyzed with pain, and the last thing her little tearful eyes see and hear is a morbid, macabre face smiling down upon her with sharp golden teeth saying, "Bad girl. Very, very bad little girl."

And then she dies...

•••

I wake up startled and sweaty, despite the bitter, raw temperature. Disoriented and cold, I curse loudly into the roar of traffic, an admonishment to the nightmare that has plagued my sleep since childhood. The ever-present yellow halogen lights cast absurd shadows upon the underpass as my mind searches wildly for some kind of marker to indicate where I am. I breathe in sharp, cold breaths. My heart rate eventually starts to slow down as the reality of my circumstances is evident.

Oh, to wake up in a bed, in a home, with heat, with food in that simple kind of life I took for granted for so long. I brush aside the notion of normalcy, as I cannot afford to indulge in wishful thinking right now. It's still below freezing, and the dampness of my sweat becomes icy around my face. Still wrapped in the layer of my tent, I unzip my coat and fumble for an interior pocket, withdrawing my phone. Twelve percent battery remaining. It reads 7:12 a.m. I slept fitfully, but I did sleep. And more importantly, I made it through another frozen night during this unseasonal cold snap. On mornings such as these, I wonder if I hadn't made it through the night, if a homeless guy dying from exposure would make it into the news. Would it even be a blip on social media? Would anybody care?

I unzip myself from the tent, and the sting of cold touches my face. I open my eyes in the direction of the rising sun. My breath appears like apparitions dancing in the breeze. My glasses are still in the interior pocket of my coat. A small object, though, is bobbing up and down, defying gravity, in the tuft of grass growing through the cracks in the concrete. Squinting doesn't clarify what I'm looking at. The whole morning is blurry until I wipe my glasses clean and put them on my face.

A small, colorful shape comes into focus. A starburst pattern about an inch across in a periwinkle hue, slowly nodding up and down, with the pale light of morning behind it. It's an angelic sight. A respite from the trash and weeds of the underpass. A beautiful, simple greeting of the morning swaying in the wind, in such stark contrast to the brittle, dead flower in my dream. It steels my heart and gives me the courage to rise, with the pain of a long journey and cold night's sleep still deep within my bones. I must find a way to navigate the concrete labyrinth before me.

I stand upright despite the complaints from my joints and muscles. I check my nose, cheeks, and fingers for frostbite. My hands are OK, but my nose is tender to the touch. I hope it's just sunburn from walking yesterday and not frostbite from last night. A frostbitten nose, reddish and ruddy, is a trademark many homeless people wear on their faces. So far, I've managed to avoid it. I pull my laptop out from underneath my sweatshirt, pull the towels from my feet, and reassemble my makeshift computer carrying case.

Over these past few days, my body has become putty. My neck, shoulders, back, legs, and feet are strained near their breaking point. Standing up, I turn toward the dirt and gravel and unceremoniously relieve myself. I manage to swing the duffel bag back up onto my shoulders even though they roar in pain. I accept and settle into the ache while hauling the smaller backpack up onto a weary shoulder. It takes deep breathing and concentration, but I put the pain aside.

Walking through the barrier of brush and branches, I emerge onto the shoulder of the highway onramp. A blue BMW idles at the red light. The driver awaits her turn to enter the freeway. She's engaged in a lively conversation on her phone. A young child is strapped into a car seat in the back, playing with a doll. She watches as I climb out of the underbrush onto the side of the highway onramp. The little girl looks at me for several moments, uncertain as to what she is witnessing. I can imagine she might think I'm Sasquatch. But would Sasquatch have earbuds and be listening to *La traviata* by Verdi?

The little girl's expression is one of childlike interest. I wave at her. The young girl waves back, breaking into a smile and creating a momentary connection between her warm place in the car seat in her mother's BMW and the world in which my scruffy character dwells. I wonder if the little girl is thinking about *Alice in Wonderland* and whether I look like the Mad Hatter. I wonder if, in her head, she is thinking about the big blue caterpillar asking, "Who. Are. You?"

CHAPTER TWO

Malik — Good Morning

I open my eyes.

Tap. Tap. Tap. Tap. Tap.

Alexa is set to turn on at 6:30 a.m. with The Too Live Crew talk show streaming into my bedroom. I figure if I can immediately start thinking about what the show hosts are talking about, I may be able to skip over the fixation on what is wrong.

The clock says 6:12 a.m. I assess. *Dammit – I woke up too early.* I spend the next eighteen minutes taking stock of things. I stare at the ceiling, taking note of my level of anxiety. *Did I finish that report at work? Did I RSVP to my cousin's wedding invitation? Did I lock the car door? Did I make that deposit? Did I finish reading that memo?*

Eighteen minutes. Not fifteen. Not twenty. Eighteen minutes. There's no going back to sleep, and I know better than to break my routine.

Tap. Tap. Tap. Tap. Tap. *Over and over.*

Finally, Alexa allows The Too Live Crew to broadcast into my bedroom. Commentators are discussing Barack Obama's speech yesterday at the HBCU convention. *Does he ever wake up staring at his ceiling? Does he have stress the moment he wakes up? Does he know about morning dread? Does he worry about climate change? Is it hard to do his job?* I close my eyes.

Tap. Tap. Tap. Tap. Tap.

I say my mantra five times. *I don't have control over this, but I can get control of myself.*

I assess.

It's not bad this morning. I tap my index fingers and thumbs together five more times to finish that thought. My jaw doesn't hurt from being clenched all night. I don't recall any bad dreams. I didn't have to take Xanax yesterday. I feel rested.

I assess, tapping my thumb and pointer finger five times. No, wait, ten times.

It's not bad this morning. I'm going to take that for a win. It's exhausting to wake up and not want to get out of bed because I've spent the night obsessing over the minutiae in my life. *Did I lock my car? Did I prepare the coffee? Did I remember to get cat food? Did I get my dry cleaning? Did I change the oil in my car?* Nine times out of ten, no wait, ninety-nine times out of one hundred, I've done the things I obsess about. I try to put it out of my mind, but the more I try not to think about something, the more I actually think about it. I answer yes to the questions popping into my mind and decide they're not so bad this morning. I actually feel good. Today might be ok.

Tap. Tap. Tap. Tap. Tap.

My cat, whose name is Moose, sleeps next to me atop the comforter. He's fluffy like a cat but acts more like a dog. He even carries his favorite toys around in his mouth. He will hunt for his toys at night and bring them onto the bed. This morning, there are three balls and a toy squirrel. Looking at me, he rolls onto his back and yawns his protest about getting up so early. I pet him, and he purrs. Apology accepted. His reluctance to get up is erased by my scratching his belly five good strokes. He responds by stretching out his arms and legs to his nearly three-foot length.

Sitting up, I reach for my sweatpants on the floor and pull

them on, tapping each foot on the ground five times. I go for my glasses on my bedside table. I ask Alexa to shut down. Silence settles down upon my bedroom. Yawning, I pad my way to the kitchen, still wearing the socks and t-shirt that I slept in. I turn on the electric kettle for my morning French press of extra dark roast. *See? I did remember to prepare the coffee.* I click the TV on to the *Morning Show* to catch local news.

Moose eventually follows me out and sits by his food bowl, patiently waiting for me to be done boiling water for my coffee. I retrieve his can of food from the fridge and scoop out a teaspoon, tapping it five times on his bowl. He gives a short meow of thanks and sets about eating. I sit at my dining room table with my iPad, swiping through the national news as my coffee steeps. More people were shot to death, this time in Miami and a small town in the northern part of Colorado. Politicians are falling into their predictable positions. Nothing ever gets done, and the shootings continue. There was a recent shooting in the Short North neighborhood of Columbus, just west of where I live, so the subject is a bit raw for me still. I then do what most people in the US have been conditioned to do—I swipe away from the news of the shooting. Russia's aggressions. Swipe. Hamas in the Gaza Strip. Swipe. White nationalists threatening a synagogue. Swipe. A labor strike. Swipe. And a missing girl has been found unconscious, but alive, only six miles from where she lived. Five swipes is enough national news.

Five minutes have passed, and I set my iPad down. I pour the magical elixir into my favorite mug. Nothing adjusts my attitude in the morning more quickly than this ritual of making coffee: ¼ cup grounds, 2 cups boiling water, five minutes to steep, pour, and five minutes to cool. Neat and tidy. I don't have control, but I can get control. I can control the coffee, which helps control my day. I take five sips, and the day becomes a bit more tolerable.

My phone chimes, alerting me to the in-service training I have to take as a part of my ongoing education. I'm a social worker at the Crossroads Men's Shelter. Today's training is about creating safe spaces in our shelters for marginalized communities, such as LGBTQ+ clients and clients with developmental delays. I don't recognize the name of the woman leading the training, which is good. The County desperately needs to invest in training the trainers, because the classes are quickly becoming a laughingstock. Few of us want to attend these trainings, but they are mandatory for the shelter to maintain its licensure. You would think that the program director would screen instructors who can really teach a subject rather than just read aloud to the class. I ponder volunteering to teach a session but quickly reprimand myself for thinking I need to fix every problem I encounter. *I don't have control over this, but I can get control of myself.*

Tap. Tap. Tap. Tap. Tap.

As I sit at my dining table, the TV news breaks a story about the cold snap gripping the Midwest. We could have snow before Thanksgiving. It was below freezing last night, which means we'll probably get a rush of people clamoring for the limited spots available at the shelter. Shortly after Thanksgiving, we will go to an emergency status, which means everyone can come inside out of the cold. We roll the dining room tables up after dinner and put down one-inch foam pads on the floor. It's not comfortable whatsoever, but it can save lives. I wonder if we lost any clients to the cold last night. There is talk about the shelter administration making an exception and opening up emergency spots early.

Moose, having finished his breakfast, jumps onto my lap. His favorite spot is between me and whatever device I'm working on. He looks at me and utters an impatient meow, indicating I have forgotten to pet him, so I stroke his head and ears. Cynically, I'm happy to have the training today so I don't have to deal with the hassles of my office. I share an office with two other people, whom I enjoy very much, except for the fact that they are both pretty sloppy around the office. I keep my area relatively clean and try to plan my day to be out of the office as much as possible. *I do not have control over my office, but I can get control of myself.*

As I swipe through news and give Moose attention, I'm reading about tonight's forecast for a cold snap. There is a whole community of homeless people who survive outside throughout the winter. Most of them are people with open criminal cases, are currently abusing hard drugs, or are on sexual predator lists. Getting a bunk at the shelter means you've been cleared through the state police. Those who don't approach shelters for emergency placement run the serious risk of freezing to death. There was a woman, back when I was at a shelter in Marquette, MI, a few years ago, who fell into a shallow river. She suffered from hypothermia. The fact that she was drunk didn't aid her situation. By the time her friends found her and called 9-1-1, she was dead.

I say softly, "She was dead. She was dead. She was dead. She was dead. She was dead."

There are jokes told quietly by staff comparing the shelter to *The Hunger Games.* We joke about which of the shelter guests would die from living on the streets. Dark humor and compartmentalized thinking about the shelter are coping mechanisms. It's easy to get jaded in my line of work. Truth is, any one of the guys in the shelter would make it further than me if it came down to being homeless. There are a million little things homeless people contend with that make them strong. I think about this morning and the fact that I was chilled when I got up. I am in my heated apartment drinking hot coffee after getting out from under my flannel comforter. *When did I become such a snowflake?*

At 7:30 a.m., I lower Moose to the floor and head back to my bedroom to shed the sweats and t-shirt in exchange for my khakis and a button-down shirt. I don't need a tie today for the training, so I can wear sneakers instead of loafers. Moose watches as I get dressed. He washes his face with a paw until some noise from the other room gets his attention, and he proceeds to investigate. In the bathroom, I glance in the mirror and use my boar brush to smooth down my hair. I keep my hair short because I don't like spending time in front of the mirror in the mornings. I put my watch on, tapping the face of it five times. Finally, I put a dab of lotion in the palm of my hand and apply it to my dark skin until it's absorbed, and I smell lightly of patchouli.

Tap. Tap. Tap. Tap. Tap.

I don't know why the tapping helps, but it does. It makes me feel like I've finished something. If I don't tap, things seem undone. Tapping makes me feel like I can get from one moment to the next. I feel stuck if I don't tap. It's the difference between a good day and a bad day. So far, today is good, so I'm thankful I can tap. It gets a little uncomfortable when I must be in public. Today's training is one of those times. I can feel my apprehension rise as I think about sitting in a room with other people. I always bring a scarf or a coat or a backpack with me that I put on my lap. I can tap underneath whatever I brought. It just makes things feel right.

Looking out my second-story window, I take in the view of the street outside. Trees along the sidewalk still cling to some of their leaves. Cars amble their way along. Several people carrying satchels walk down the sidewalks toward work or coffee dates. Moms with strollers carrying babies wrapped in fleece jog down the sidewalk.

A block away, I see a figure with a sign that reads, "Anything helps." Most people walk around the man sitting cross-legged on the sidewalk. A few people bend down and put some change or a dollar in his cup. Beggars often make people nervous. They can't imagine what could have befallen a person who begs as a way to make it through life. He isn't an aggressive panhandler, so most police officers allow him to sit on the sidewalk and collect change. Some days, he can make seventy-five dollars. He keeps stuffing the bills into his pocket, so it never looks like he's made much money so that potential donors might give him more.

I happen to know the figure sitting on the sidewalk. He goes by J.J. He's a resident of the shelter where I work. He's a good guy. He stays out of trouble. He's a former meth addict. He has the telltale sign of eroded front teeth. Drugs, and eventually prison, really changed his life. He was a middle school teacher at some point in his life before he began using meth. He says it took a good year before he got fired. He kept using and eventually ended up being convicted of possession with the intent to sell. He received a four-year prison sentence, during which he got clean. He came to Crossroads on the advice of his parole officer, and he's slowly been making his way back to a life beyond drugs. A lot of the money he collects goes toward cigarettes, but the rest he is saving to get a studio apartment somewhere, anywhere.

The guys at the shelter are survivors and hustlers. I think of them as "honest con men" who have or are overcoming tremendous obstacles. For the most part, they are recovering from drug and alcohol abuse, bad deals in divorce settlements, getting their bearings after incarceration, or struggling with mental health issues. All of these factors disqualify them from most jobs. Crossroads provides these individuals with a safe space to explore until they find their niche in the world.

I move away from the window, pulling my comforter up and putting my pillows back into place. Moose is back from his investigation and jumps onto the made-up bed, rolling onto his back for his goodbye belly scratch. I oblige. Thank God for Moose. I understand why people have emotional support animals. That stupid face of his makes my whole body and mind feel better. His even-keeled temperament makes me feel at peace. I finish his morning attention session, take one more glance in the mirror, and I'm set to go to the training. I pour the rest of the coffee into my travel mug and head for the door. It starts at 9:00 am, so I have time to grab an egg croissant sandwich from Starbucks.

Tap. Tap. Tap. Tap. Tap.

I grab my key fob and wallet from the ceramic dish by the door and head down to the street. There are seventeen steps in the staircase leading down to the street. I always skip two steps to make it fifteen steps down to the sidewalk. Today is good.

As I walk to my car, I consider that my life is opulent compared to the guys at the shelter. I wonder what life would have been like if I had taken a different path, a path like many of the kids I grew up with. My mom kept me on track. I wonder about what kind of family life the guys at the shelter came from. *Is it just a matter of luck that my life turned out differently? What if my dad were still in the picture? What if Moms and Pops stayed together? What if Pops really hurt Moms, like killed her? Would I have been placed in foster care?*

I don't have control over this, but I can get control of myself.

Tap. Tap. Tap. Tap. Tap.

There are so many variables to consider when contemplating why a person can become successful. My mother protected me from many things. Perhaps her fear served as a buffer between our little family and the neighborhood. No matter how bad it got in the neighborhood, inside our home felt safe; I mean, after Pops left. I never really understood how much Moms worked to keep me safe until I got to college. Five times I say softly, "I got lucky."

Tap. Tap. Tap. Tap. Tap.

Today should be all right.

CHAPTER THREE

Caleb — Finding Shelter

I've done my best to pick the leaves and twigs from my clothing. I must look comical to the casual observer. I walk several miles to find an overpass with a pedestrian crossing leading in the right direction to the shelter. My feet are throbbing, but I don't slow down. If you stop while you are sore, chances are it will be far more painful to restart walking. The lack of water for the past twelve hours also helps exacerbate the effect of lactic acid in my muscles. I lumber forward, hungry and exhausted, like a bear from hibernation.

I walk across the overpass, down a new industrial road, and finally to the address where the shelter is. The past few days, I feel like I've been walking in a desert chasing a mirage. There's a large, weather-worn brick wall. There are a few windows on the second floor and just one metal door beneath an entrance sign: Wel ome.

The "c" is missing.

A few men hang around outside smoking home-rolled cigarettes with their shoulders braced tight against the cold. *I guess this is my new home.*

"Is this the shelter?" I ask.

"Yep," one guy says. "You new?"

"Yes, I am."

"Probably won't get in. Got cold last night, so all the idiots came looking for a warm bed. Got so cold my beard froze." He laughs a laugh of a thousand cigarettes. The men are silent, no doubt having heard their friend's joke many times over by now.

"Weren't you inside last night?"

"Nope, got here late."

"Well, I gotta try. I don't want to be outside again tonight."

"You got that right. But be careful with dinner. I chipped my tooth on the soup last night." His laughter peels off again, sounding like he is gargling chainsaws.

I smile curtly and make my way to the door, taking in the brick building's worn façade.

Looking back to the frozen trio, I ask, "Is that where I go?"

"Yep. Good luck. Tonight is burritos." More bulldozer laughter.

Good Lord, burritos in a homeless shelter.

I walk over to the door, find the buzzer, and press it. The door unlatches with a click. I spot a few more of those little flowers growing in the cracks of the cement. They're pretty little flowers growing at the ends of scrappy little stems. I go inside, and the sudden warmth of the shelter is soothing. There's a short hallway leading to a large glass window, the bottom of which is open enough to slide paperwork back and forth.

"Hello."

"Hello," answers a woman, not looking up from her paperwork as she gives her memorized greeting. "Welcome to the Crossroads Men's Shelter. We are here to serve men in the homeless community. If you wish to have a bunk in our facility, you will need to not be on any sexual offender registry in the state. If you are on a sexual offender registry list, we can refer you to a shelter that accepts men in that position. You will need to bathe and wash all clothing before entering the bunk area. Any belongings you bring with you will be stored in cold storage to minimize the risk of introducing bed bugs or roaches into the shelter. You are allowed access to your belongings once a day, so be aware of what you want and when you will need it. There is no smoking in the building. There are no drugs allowed, and this includes marijuana, even if prescribed by a doctor. You are not to have sexual contact with any other client of the shelter." She pushes a stapled collection of papers through the slot. "Here are the application and the shelter rules. Read them. Sign at the bottom that you understand the rules." She paused and then said, "If you have any outstanding warrants, you will not be permitted entry. We can refer you to another shelter that allows entry for those individuals. Do you want a referral elsewhere?"

"No, ma'am."

"Do you want to apply for a bunk at our shelter?"

"Yes, ma'am."

"All of our bunks are full, but we do have a limited number of emergency spots available. If you are awarded a spot in our emergency shelter, you'll receive a mat for sleeping in our cafeteria after dinner. You will be up and out of the cafeteria by 6:00 a.m. each morning. You can have dinner before your mat is put out in the evening, and you can have breakfast here after your mat is put away in the morning. You can have access to our showers and washing machines..."

A shower...what a luxury. I've been walking for days, so the thought of a warm stream of water over my tired muscles sounds wonderful. I know that my blisters will sting, but I won't complain. Hopefully, I can get some gauze from the staff to wrap around my feet as the blisters heal.

"Leave any medications with our staff for distribution."

I know I have a list of meds in my paperwork. I hope they can help me get connected with a psychiatrist to get new prescriptions for them.

"Do not bring medication into the living quarters for any reason. We have a zero-tolerance policy for drugs, alcohol, violence, or any shit talking that can lead to a disturbance."

No problem.

"You may use this address to receive mail. Do you still want to apply for a place at our shelter?"

"Yes, ma'am, very much so."

For the first time, the woman behind the glass looks up and gives a slight smile. "Well, good. Fill out your forms over there in one of our waiting chairs. Bring them back to me. It's first-come, first-served for the emergency mats, and spaces are limited." She pushes a pen through the slot. "Welcome to the Crossroads Men's Shelter."

I drop my bags to the floor by the chair and begin filling out the paperwork.

Words like 'broken', 'refuge', and 'calm' swirl through my mind. One by one, they drop into place as I work to get entry into the shelter.

> A stranger at your door,
> broken, tired, and bent.
> Knocking knuckles now,
> all energies spent.
> Refuge from the madness,
> calm respite now sent.
> My footsteps fairly falling
> where they were not meant.

I put the words into my phone.

Perhaps a by-product of suddenly being so comfortable in the warmth, my mind drifts a bit, thinking about my current situation. I'm fifty years old and have made more mistakes than any five people combined. I changed my name a few years ago to start over, but starting over doesn't do much good if nothing in your mind or behavior changes. I have moved from city to city, but geography makes little difference to the loop of self-loathing playing in my mind.

•••

I have tried to end my life four times, twice just for attention, but twice because I wanted to be off the Earth. I stepped in front of traffic. I swallowed the contents of a bottle of sleeping pills. I tried cutting through my wrists. And once, I stole a gun from someone I knew and sat for four hours just looking at it, trying to muster the courage to pull the trigger. But as with almost everything else, I failed at the one task my mind truly wanted: To cease being.

When I was in Glens Falls, NY, my depression overtook my life, and I slipped into catatonia. The staff at the shelter I was staying in could not get me out of bed. I missed meals and didn't drink any water for three days. The director of the shelter decided I needed to go to the ER to be checked out by the medical staff. EMS was able to get me upright. I walked, with their support, to the gurney.

In my mind, I had gone to bed at the shelter, and when I woke up, I was in the Warren County Hospital. After two days of rehydration, being fed by a tube, and being stable on a heart monitor, I was delivered to the Behavioral Health Unit for an involuntary seventy-two-hour monitoring period. There I was examined, questioned, reassured, and finally convinced to surrender to an inpatient hospital admission. My responses to questions and treatments were extremely sluggish. It took me longer than usual to respond to questions. I had broken out of catatonia and landed just a level above being frozen. I wallowed in a major depressive mode that was typical for me after an extended period of mania.

For the better part of two weeks, I languished with little progress. Still, it was also there, after several different counseling and medication protocols could not break through my depression, that I met Dr. Clark, a psychiatrist. He dug deeper into my past. He pieced together a mental health evaluation from other hospitalizations in my history. It was Dr. Clark who coaxed me into allowing 440 volts of electricity to fire through both temples as I clenched down on a rubber mouthpiece. I did this every other day for two weeks, in what is called bilateral electroconvulsive therapy, aka shock treatment.

The shrink told me that ECT causes changes in brain chemistry that can alter neural pathways and make symptoms of severe mental health issues lessen in severity in a short amount of time. And with there being over ninety billion neurons firing in my three-pound brain, that can be a lot of change. Or at least that's what psychiatrists think. They are not entirely sure how it works, but they know it can be effective most of the time. I couldn't help but think, how did this treatment come *into being? Did someone electrocute themselves and suddenly have a sunny disposition?*

At the end of my treatment schedule, the staff and the psychiatrist agreed it seemed to have made a difference. It was not a cure-all, though, and it wasn't without side effects. I noticed gaps in my short-term memory, especially when it came to numbers. I had trouble remembering my Social Security number. Phone numbers slipped from memory. General lapses in memory occurred, too. I'd get up to do something and forget what I got up for, probably a dozen times a day. These were all things the psychiatrist said may happen after ECT. They were all things I was ok with in exchange for a mind that was more at peace.

•••

I finish the application and slide the form back to the woman. She takes it, flips the pages, reads my name, and then says, "OK, Caleb, I checked with our placement staff, and you can have an emergency mat. I'll buzz you through to the intake area, and we'll get you cleaned up, your laundry washed, and checked into the emergency shelter. My best advice for you is to come in, mind your own business, and don't let any of the guys get under your skin."

"Yes, ma'am. Thank you." *Under my skin? Where did that come from? It's kind of the same as making my skin crawl. Idioms are so weird.*

"My name is Tracy Miller, but everyone calls me Trace."

"OK, Trace. Thank you. Do you have some gauze I can use to cover blisters on my feet?"

"Yes, we can help with that. Ask the staff member who helps you get your belongings into storage; they can grab some supplies for you."

She gives me a wink and then returns to her paperwork.

I'm inside...I would probably cry if I weren't so tired.

The mention of dinner, breakfast, and emergency mats has me in a state of anticipation that would give Pavlov's dogs a run for their money. I'll ask tomorrow if they have referrals to psychiatrists. I'll need the medication if I want to stay in the good graces of the shelter. "Manic me" or "depressed me" won't last long in such a controlled environment as a shelter. I need the beast to be gone. I need "medicated me."

Desperately.

CHAPTER FOUR

Malik — Bootstraps

All the usual suspects attend the training. Over time, I've gotten to know other social workers in the city, or at least in my part of the city. Trina, with the huge red, curly hair, is here with two others from Intake Services at the hospital. Malcolm, who seems only to have one sweater, is here from the Belkin Women's Center. Mickey, a very tattooed and rough-looking addiction counselor, is here from county-wide NA/AA organizations. There are about a half dozen social workers from the various shelters around town, all of whom are just as happy to be out of their offices as I am. The rest are unknown faces.

The information at the training is good. I learn a great deal about working with transgender men and women. From time to time, we do get a trans woman living at the men's shelter. The system is not set up for gender diversity, so if someone is a biological male, they are placed into a men's shelter. There's one such person who goes by Melly. I see her around town at various establishments that assist the homeless. She wears a lot of makeup, women's outfits, and some undergarments, giving her the appearance of breasts. Before she comes back to the shelter, she removes her wig and makeup, changes her clothes, and takes off whatever is making her breasts. As a woman, she appears confident and strong, but when dressed as a man, she seems unsure and nervous. She is barely recognizable when dressed as a man.

There is little compassion from the guys at the shelter and from the staff for what she must go through, especially being homeless. I don't know this for sure, but I believe she is a sex worker. I haven't seen Melly in a while, which brings about feelings of trepidation. I've heard many accounts of trans women being killed in the sex worker trade by johns who didn't get the memo that they were having sex with a biological male. I think about Melly, being homeless and trans, how dangerous her life must be, having no real protection from those who might seek to harm her.

I can't say I understand what being trans is all about. Still, I can recognize that they face rejection on many fronts: conservative religion, uncaring parents, an untrained medical community, lack of employment, and so many other things. I have my own barriers being Black. I can't fathom what trans people face each day.

Tap. Tap. Tap. Tap. Tap.

Another relevant point of the training concerns individuals with developmental delays. They are often targets of thievery because most receive some disability income. Unscrupulous guys in the shelter befriend them, tell them they'll help them, and end up taking their money each month. For the most part, the clients with delays never say anything because they are fearful of losing their newfound "friend." We have two social workers who can act as guardians at the shelter, and the city also has some people available for them. The tragedy of clients with developmental delays is they've fallen through the cracks. Usually, they aren't addicted to anything, and even though they have delays, they are often free of mental issues. They're just vulnerable. It's heart-breaking.

Tap. Tap. Tap. Tap. Tap.

The final speaker discusses different theories about

homelessness. She touches on Conflict Theory, suggesting social issues like homelessness are an individual's shortcomings rather than flaws in the society itself. That does not go over well with the twenty-three social workers in the room. They know better. I know better. None of us says anything. It's too bad the theory is still discussed. It's a cop-out. The "better off" see individuals struggling with homelessness as lazy, dim, and a drain on society. What we do at Crossroads is get them off the street and then move them as quickly as possible into housing of some sort. After their placement, we get them nourished and hooked up with some type of employment. It's the Housing First model. It works well because retaining employment and following through with health care is infinitely more successful when doing so from the safety of a simple apartment.

Employment is more sustainable if a person can sleep where it's warm and dry, shower regularly, and eat before work with help from food stamps and food pantries. It's similar to the argument behind providing school lunches to kids—they learn better when they are nourished. Newly homeless people are more likely to be successful in securing and maintaining employment if they have the basics. People on the street can't visit food pantries because they cannot store or cook the distributed dried goods. It may seem like an extravagance, but dollar for dollar, it is cheaper to house someone than to provide long-term shelter services. The one obstacle we have as a shelter trying to place people is the lack of apartments that meet the minimum standard of the health code.

I look toward the door and see a familiar face, my friend Keith. I say to myself, "*Hello Keith. Hello Keith. Hello Keith. Hello Keith. Hello Keith.*" We went to OSU together and graduated from the same social work program. During the break in the training, I walk over and say hi. He is surprised to see me. Normally our agencies don't frequent the same training. He's with the City, and I work for a private non-profit. He's in administration, and I'm in client services.

"Hello, my brother," I say.

"Malik. Hey, man, good to see you." Keith, I, and two other guys went through OSU together. We've remained friends. We get together once or twice a month for beer and Chinese food, usually at my place because I'm the only adult in the group whose home isn't a disaster. My house is immaculate. It has to be, otherwise I can't relax. Everything has its place. "Are you slumming today?"

"Yeah, my boss wants me to have these trainings under my belt so the shelter can say they are current."

"How are things at the shelter?"

"Same ol', same ol'. We opened for emergency placements when the temperature dipped below freezing, but I don't deal with that end of it, so things are normal for me except for generating files on the newbies."

"Did you read the Point-in-Count numbers for this fall? There are now over two thousand homeless people in Columbus."

"Wow, that's up quite a bit from last year, isn't it?"

"About 27%."

"Where the hell are we going to put all these people?" I think my mantra five times. *I don't have control over this, but I can get control of myself.* Keith respects the few seconds it takes me to complete my phrases.

"That's what the City is trying to solve. Even with all the shelter space available, we can only house about half of the PIC."

"I can't find enough housing for the people we already have. I don't even know where to look for a 27% increase in numbers."

"The City is looking into building a permanent shelter, like the one they have in Des Moines. They can fit several hundred under one roof, with a social service staff just for the residents at the shelter."

Tap. Tap. Tap. Tap. Tap. And then I laugh a little. "Yeah, I bet the fair citizens of Columbus will be thrilled about that."

"Ya never know. It might work. The one in Des Moines is located on the edge of town. It helps keep the unhoused out of the downtown area, which is the problem we're getting here. All of the services are in the damned county buildings in the center of downtown."

"Yeah, someone with the City didn't think that one through. Typical."

"Nice little jab there." We both chuckle a bit, even though it's true.

The training instructor steps out into the hallway where many of us have congregated. She lets us know we are about to start again. An image of Pops comes to mind. *Was he someone with a hidden disability? Was it just addiction? Did he create such dire circumstances because he was weak, or was he strong as hell because he fought addiction and some mental illness and managed to survive? Is he just languishing somewhere? Has he survived?*

Tap. Tap. Tap. Tap. Tap. Nope, ten times. Nope, fifteen times.

I feel the urge to skip the rest of the training and dive headfirst into another search for him in our agency's databases. I found a glitch in the system. Occasionally, our agency contracts with outside sources for technical support. They are given access codes and passwords. For some reason, the agency never deletes the information. Essentially, there are about a dozen codes and passwords that are accessible and assigned to a person other than me. There aren't any cameras in the admin wing, so if I use the outdated passwords, I can gain access without revealing who is accessing the system.

I turn to Keith, who has been looking at the syllabus to see what's next in the training. "Hey, would you take notes for me? I have something I need to do." Under my breath, I say, "Need to do. Need to do. Need to do. Need to do. Need to do."

"Sure," Drake says, understanding that my repeating that phrase means I'm dealing with an OCD urge. "Like what?"

I turn my mantra over in my head. *I don't have control over this, but I can get control of myself.* Only I don't feel like I'm in control. I feel like my compulsion is controlling me, but I can't find the wherewithal to fight the feelings.

"Just some personal stuff I forgot to take care of." *Forgot to take care of. Forgot to take care of. Forgot to take care of. Forgot to take care of. Forgot to take care of.*

Drake looks at me with concern but doesn't pry. "Right on. I'll email the notes to you after we're done."

"Thanks."

I leave the training and drive back to work, tapping in groups of five. I reach seventy-five and then stop as I pull into the shelter parking lot. Several staff members are out of the office for training, so the administrative section of the shelter is relatively empty. Thankfully, the conference room is empty for the day. There's a computer connected to the network in there, so I head to it before anyone sees me slip back into work. I retrieve the codes I found and enter them into the system. There are some preliminary steps to go through: putting in my "name" as Karen Walker, my username "kwalker," and the password "1248da&p." This links me to the agency's main menu. There are searches available by criminal record, social services, shelter logs, housing placement history, client reports of incidents, and financial guardianship.

I enter his legal name, Walter Arons, his birthdate, and the last four digits of his social security number. I click through the departments. Nothing. Again. I try Walt Arons, W. Arons. I try his middle name, Clarence Arons, C Arons. W.C. Arons. Walter Clarence Arons. Nothing. Since I started doing these searches, I've called nearly every morgue in the state, too. I begin to feel the stress of not knowing where he is.

I don't have control over this, but I can get control of myself.

"Where are you, Dad? Where are you, Dad? Where are you, Dad? Where are you, Dad? Where are you, Dad?" I say softly as I stare at the screen, trying to think of something I've not thought about previously. I've done this probably twenty times. I've tried every combination of his name and initials, and I never find anything. He must have moved out of state. That's the only thing that I can think of. Or he's dead. I know that's probably the real reason he doesn't show up. Addicts who aren't receiving care and are on the streets don't last forever.

Drugs do that to people. They change people, almost at a DNA level. Their thoughts, their behaviors, and their decisions are driven by the substances they abuse. Everything that creates self-esteem in a person, drugs take away. The pleasure of drugs slowly wanes, leaving just addiction. Addiction is the result of seeking pleasure in a substance that, over time, morphs into the person only seeking to avoid the pain of withdrawal. Imagine how distraught someone would become if the one thing they counted on for pleasing them became the single focus of their misery.

I wonder if Pops got to that point.

Tap. Tap. Tap. Tap. Tap. Nope, fifteen times. Nope, twenty-five times.

CHAPTER FIVE

Caleb — A Cold Toast Buff

A few weeks at the shelter have done a great deal of good. I got set up with an agency psychiatrist who was able to prescribe the medications I'd left behind in San Diego. I feel much better in my skin now. My social security disability was auto-deposited for the month, so I have seven hundred dollars in my bank account. I buy clippers so I can shave my head. I bought a couple of flash drives to store my writing in case I lose or break my laptop. I splurge and get some deodorant, lotion, lip balm, and a good pair of gloves. I also use a few bucks to go to Starbucks and order my Americano. I usually go right after doing laundry and shaving my head. This way I don't look like someone living at a shelter. And that's the point. I'm in disguise as one of the normal people I see out and about every day. I receive meals and rest at the shelter, so I save the rest of my disability benefits with the hope of finding housing outside the shelter.

Once I got moved off the cafeteria floor into a regular bunk, things really started turning around. Going from a one-inch mat on the hardwood floor to a four-inch mattress on a bunk with a box spring is a game-changer. Such trivial things make the most significant difference. It reminds me a bit of college, where we slept in bunk beds in small rooms. Thirty years ago, when I started college, my symptoms were becoming apparent. I was enrolled at a Lutheran university in Southern California, approximately 400 miles away from home. My parents knew I had been struggling, but they weren't interested in counseling. Instead, they steered me toward prayer and encouraged me to speak with one of the many pastors on campus. Thankfully, once I was in college, I found my way to a pastor to talk about things, and she referred me to their counselling services. I had my first sessions with a real therapist who, in turn, connected me with a psychiatrist for diagnosis and medication, if needed. Counselling went well except for the fact that I was still only at the beginning stages of fully recognizing what had happened to me as a kid. With the help of the counseling center, I managed to make it through one year at college...barely.

•••

It was the last two days before the summer break of my first year at university when I had my first out-of-control manic episode, and it all centered on furniture of all things. Students moving out were told to leave any unwanted furniture on the sidewalk outside of our dormitories, and the university would collect it. My mind latched onto this opportunity. I couldn't let all of this furniture go to waste. After obsessing over the matter, I made a connection with a guest speaker in my Spanish class who worked with impoverished people living south of Tijuana, near dump sites. They made their living scouring the mountains of garbage for things to sell. With all the intensity that mania brings, I managed to arrange for the university to provide a truck and a driver through campus ministries to deliver the used furniture to their small, ramshackle town. By sheer manic persistence, I soon had a plan. I hadn't slept much in the past few days, but the idea I had had merit. The university assigned a professor of sociology to lead the expedition to Mexico.

The man from my Spanish class provided a map and offered to accompany me in the truck. I would follow behind in my beat-up Pontiac Ventura. With the map, I informed the small team of helpers that I would go down first and arrange parking for us using my rudimentary Spanish skills. I barreled down the I-5 to the border—this was before you needed a passport to get in and out of Mexico—and spent the day driving around on sandy dirt roads until I got to a town called El Dumpe, translated literally as The Dump. When the truck arrived, I unloaded the furniture with the help of a few locals. It had been almost a week without sleep, and since this was my first episode, I had no idea what was coming for me. My mania started to crash. I was exhausted. I told the folks with the truck that I would stay to visit with the few friends I had made that day. I ended up staying at The Dump for almost a week. I'm sure it was confusing for the people who lived there to have this depressed gringo residing in his car, eating tacos made with intestines, and drinking orange Fanta soda because Lord knows I wasn't going to drink the water.

This is how it went for me after that first episode. Usually, the upward swing into mania helps me succeed in things. The university was impressed with how I organized the trip to El Dumpe. No one knew it was because of my mania that would soon lead to a depressive crash. I could study for days on end. I could work extra hours to help pay off tuition. I could organize events, work on committees, and participate in various activities. I underwent significant changes during my freshman year as I transitioned into adulthood. This is when the mania began to grow into full-blown episodes. My work in college became erratic. I had several complaints from other students that I was acting strangely. I was drinking a lot. I had a lot of sex, and this was in the late 90s, right when AIDS was a pandemic. I don't know how, but I made it out of college with just one case of chlamydia.

•••

My eyes cringe shut, a reflex from the sudden glare of overhead lights. Muffled complaints arise throughout the room when this happens. I turn over on my foam mattress away from the interruption of the early morning lights and press my hand against the cool, smooth layers of paint on the concrete block wall. It feels good, stable, comfortable, and grounding.

I'm in bunk six. Twenty-three is going to work. I don't know his name. He's a small Black guy. He hardly says a word to anyone. He's focused, not one to participate in the shenanigans around the shelter. He's across the room from me. Guys come and go so often from the shelter, it's easier to remember numbers rather than names. To see in the darkness, you must turn on the overhead lights for the entire room because there are no individual lamps by the beds. The ceiling lights broadcast an intense, unnatural light. Thirty guys in a room means the light goes on and off frequently. Some guys are careful, using them sparingly; others don't care, turning lights on just to put on their shoes. When you've been here for a day or two, you learn to get dressed in the dark. Turning lights on for shoes is an overt act of contempt. Contempt hangs in the air around here. It's contagious. Living here hones it. There is always someone ready to chastise someone else, and all of this negative energy simmers around the shelter.

I pull out my phone as the words fall into place:

> Beneath consideration,
> struggling between
> worthiness and worthlessness.
> I stir in my bunk,
> pining for reprieve

from the scorn I feel
for the sin of being homeless.
Unknowing faces convict me anew,
for living the sentence meted out
by the contempt of passers-by.

I try my best to write down these passing thoughts. I'm a lot of things: mentally ill, homeless, depressed, nuts. It's almost cliché to say that I'm a writer—what writer isn't all those things? I'm not famous, so in my case, mental illness, homelessness, and depression aren't eccentric; they're just that: mental illness, homelessness, and depression.

When done, I place my palm against the wall again. I find it grounding like therapists in the past have said specific actions can be. I always did the grounding exercises, claiming they worked, when I was biding my time to leave the session. But here, at the Crossroads Men's Emergency Shelter, despite the sharp and jagged edges of my peers, I find a modicum of calm in the hardness of the concrete wall.

Sleep is difficult for me, even with medications in dosages large enough to lull a horse to sleep. I swallow pills every night, and every night, I settle into bed, lazy with chemical fog. The drugs get me to sleep, but I generally get about four or five hours. People talk about going to sleep shortly after their heads hit their pillows and sleeping through the night. That makes about as much sense to me as swallowing a watermelon whole. It just seems impossible, yet I've gotten used to going back to sleep after the lights wake me.

The shelter helped me find employment. They have a relationship with a few large local businesses. They hooked me up at a place called Barron's Lines, a warehouse specializing in gift baskets of lotion, cream, soap, and perfume. It's nearing Thanksgiving, which means the holiday shopping season is beginning. This place would hire anyone, including me. I work from 4:00 p.m. to around midnight. This gives me time to catch the last bus back to the shelter. It is nice to have a schedule again and make a little money.

The shelter helps residents achieve financial stability. There is no cost for having a bunk or for the food. Since I have a small income, I let my disability accrue. The warehouse pays us on prepaid debit cards, so I use that for expenses. The eight-hour shift at minimum wage may seem paltry to most. For me, it's a game-changer. I stand and fidget with pretty little bottles as the assembly line burps them out, hour after hour. Ex-cons, the homeless, and erstwhile ruffian types put the fancy little bottles into fancy little boxes to be shipped to fancy little stores where they sit, perched as thinly veiled ostentatious tributes to overconsumption. I'm quite sure lovely ladies opening their presents on Christmas morning haven't a clue about who has manhandled their pretty little treasures.

Twenty-three turns off the lights. I move my hand again to the surface of the wall and float between slumber and wakefulness for the better part of an hour.

•••

...the early rays of morning filter through the last remnants of leaves still clinging to the twigs of brush along the freeway overpass. My face, left exposed by a scarf falling away during the night, is bright red with chill. My body, likewise, feels inflexible from the cold, hard ground of a frigid November night. I feel for my bag. It's there, containing the entirety of my life. I blink into the sun as I focus my eyes on a singular, poetic feature: the periwinkle starburst of a wildflower moving in the early morning breeze. I think for a moment about God sending a rainbow as a promise to the faithful. Despite the pain of waking up beside a highway, beneath the shrubs and amid the trash,

I think to myself, "Is there a lonesome deity out there floating about in some alternate version of heaven who is watching me? Did they send this flower?"

•••

The dream of the wildflower dissipates as the sublime voices of Anna Netrebko and Elīna Garanča sing "The Flower Duet" in French through my earbuds. It's just like when Andy Dufresne played the piece over the loudspeaker during *The Shawshank Redemption*. It never fails to lift me up. They're set to sing at 6:25 a.m. in my ears, so I'm ready for the Cold Toast Buffet.

Breakfast is served at 6:30 a.m. by two very orderly vets. One wears his Korean vet cap, and the other wears his from Vietnam. Veterans occupy a sizable portion of the shelter. The two vets take pride in having everything ready on time. The readiness, unfortunately, is problematic. The bread is toasted so far in advance that there is no viable chance of it being served hot. The kitchen, by some administrative rule, closes promptly at 7:00 a.m., creating a half-hour window to serve the Cold Toast Buffet to more than 60 residents. Waking up at 6:25 a.m. to my angels of song gives me enough time to don my slippers over my socks. Everyone sleeps in their clothing so there's not much to do to prepare yourself for breakfast.

Each morning the fare is identical: cold toast, one yogurt, one packet of oatmeal, one pint of milk, and one piece of fruit. It's not a diet well-suited for my diabetes, but adherence to a diabetic diet is hard to come by in a shelter. You cannot have doubles on anything, another administrative rule. Each piece of food is offered on a plate the size of a tea saucer. You compile the little saucers on your tray and move to the beverage kiosk. Don't take much time, and don't make any fuss; if you do, you are subject to the verbal harassment of everyone else waiting for coffee.

The coffee kiosk looks like something rescued from a 1950s motel. It's large and complains with a mechanical whine whenever the spigot is used. You can pour coffee, decaf only for some godforsaken reason, from one spigot and hot water for your packet of oatmeal out of the other.

Next to the beverage kiosk are several jars of peanut butter and bottles of squeezable grape jelly for the toast. The story goes that when the cold toast and the cold butter met, the guys were tearing their toast apart and getting riled. The Golden Rule of the Crossroads Men's Shelter went into effect: remove anything or anyone causing a problem; hence, no more butter.

A few days ago, I saw a guy steal a jar of peanut butter. He was a skinny white street kid with low-slung, baggy pants and facial hair trimmed into an Art Deco design. I admired his grooming tenacity. Being in a men's shelter diminishes your desire to look prepared for the world. The skinny white street kid was prepared. He held the jar down by his hip and left the cafeteria. He kept his eye on the kitchen in case someone looked his way as he left with the jar of stolen nut paste.

Neither of the vets looked up as the skinny street kid was leaving. That didn't surprise me. The pair started breaking down the cafeteria line and putting the dishes into the commercial dishwasher. Odds were in favor of the street kid. I didn't say anything. There are enough ex-cons here who believe ratting out fellow residents is a sacrilege. If you are found to be reporting something, you may not get your ass kicked like in prison, but everyone will know it was you. You will feel that at any moment you may indeed get your ass kicked. The second reason is, like I said earlier, they will take it away if you complain about something. And I like peanut butter.

Living in a homeless shelter, I'm granted the honor of being called a "client." This phenomenon humors me. I'm the furthest thing from what I would think of when describing a client. It's a term created because the state pays the shelter a certain amount of money per homeless person in a bunk. Technically, I am the client. I imagine the shelter will find a way to extract more funds for us sleeping on the floors.

I remember John Irving's novel *The World According to Garp*. The main character said that because of her gender, she was a sexual suspect. Here, because of our status, we are societal suspects, because no one ends up in a homeless shelter on purpose. Many have just been released from prison and don't have any support network in the community. Many battle serious addiction issues and aren't welcome in homes where they once were. Many of us have serious mental health issues. We're part of suspect groups. These suspect groups share a common element: bad decision-making. Most walk around with their fists closed, shoulders tight, and brows furrowed. Hardened faces disallow any show of emotion. Friends are hard to find here.

It's no one else's fault that I am living here in a shelter. My bad decision-making is part and parcel of my mental health, but I still made the decisions. I'm guilty of that. Most guys here will list five or six reasons other than themselves for being in a shelter. I have only one reason: me. It's complicated, and then again, it's not. If I'm honest with myself, psychotic behavior is easy to explain, yet impossible to understand. My psychosis has a PTSD chaser, and some shrinks have included a side of bipolar disorder. My mind comes and goes on its own schedule. I am seldom consulted. It's challenging to be honest with yourself when your mind plays tricks on you. It's probably the reason I became an exquisite liar. I learned early on to make up stories.

I'm on anti-psychotic, anti-depressant, anti-seizure, and sleep meds when I have access to medication. I'm also on medications to control diabetes. I always take my medication, with no exceptions. When I'm stable, I am not one of those patients who thinks, *"Hey, look at me. I'm stable, I don't need the pharmacy anymore!"* I've seen enough cell phone videos of my mania, read enough police reports of my psychosis, and swallowed enough pills during suicidal depression to understand that me without drugs is not an option. I see many in the shelter who are too prideful to accept that their conditions warrant taking medications, yet they wonder why they can't get things together.

"Better living through chemistry" is my motto.

We are not allowed to keep our medications with us. There are serious addicts in this shelter. It's simply too tempting for them to buy, steal, or inflict pain to get narcotics. As a result, we get our medications from the staff at specific times throughout the day. We must put them in our mouths, drink water, swallow them, and open our mouths to ensure we've taken our pills.

On my days off, I stand in the early morning line, eat breakfast, and leave right after The Cold Toast Buffet. I always leave the shelter. I'm grateful for the bunk at night. The shelter, though, is a toxic environment. The feelings of anxiety and discontent tend to concentrate in the hallways. The anger is palpable. I would much rather be at a reasonable distance from the shelter than surrounded by the infectious nature of my esteemed colleagues.

And the words drop into place:

Oh brother of mine
with passion in your heart,
exhume from your mind
the broken, broken part.
Oh brother of mine
with anger-littered mind,
dig deep down for peace

for a healing, healing heart.

The swearing and unkindness echo throughout the building. It reminds me of how Craig used to mutter obscenities and jumbled sentences to himself, as if he were talking to someone else in the room. He never made sense unless he was instructing me to do something. Oftentimes, I wouldn't hear him until he slapped my face, pulling me back to a place my mind had carried me away from for my safety. The slap would bring back the darkness of his closet, the mottled light beneath the door, and his confused voice whispering in my ear.

•••

I can hear laughter from the dining room. I can hear the 8-track tapes my brother Mikey is listening to with Lauren, Craig's sister, in her bedroom down the hall. I'm inside Craig's room. I'm inside Craig's closet. He is supposed to be teaching me how to tie a fishing lure. The fishing lure excuse is used often. My dad doesn't fish, so he wouldn't know the difference between a lure I had made or one that Craig had randomly selected from all the lures he had made. My folks thought that my playing with him might be pacifying since Craig was having a tough time emotionally. It was, just not in the way my folks thought it would be. Craig is smart. He is familiar with the dynamics of our families. He knows how far he can push me. He always has an excuse ready for my parents. If they asked, "Hey, what are those red lines on your arms?" Craig was prepared with, "Sorry, Mr. Taylor, he held the fishing wire too tightly when he was tying a difficult knot. I should have noticed."

My dad would reply, "Not to worry, Craig. Thanks for watching Caleb."

•••

"Hey, are you gonna move or what?" It's one of the clients on his way out of the shelter to grab a smoke.

"What?" I say, startled. I find myself standing in a doorway to the cafeteria. "Oh, sorry, man." I step out of the doorway, and he heads outside. *How long was I standing there?*

I hate it when I lose time. I shake my head to clear away residual thoughts about being in Craig's room. I set about leaving the shelter. I'm eager to go because some of the folks in charge make no bones about telling any of us, at any given moment, that if we get out of line, we can lose our bunk. I don't think I'm in any jeopardy of losing my bunk, but still, it is harsh to be reminded that my residency here is so tenuous. There are individuals here who appear to engage with the monitors daily. These arguments often arise when clients are asked to do something like chores or another item of responsibility. Arguments also arise when the monitors feel their small pond of power is being questioned. It's an impossibly complicated job, and I'm almost certain they are only paid minimum wage. The clients and monitors seem equally trigger-happy.

The final reason for getting out of the shelter every chance I get is that I fear being here. All I want to do is take my laptop to the library and write. I need the predictability of a haiku. I need the meter of a sonnet. I need the page, filled with words, leading me away from the life I lead. Writing is about the only thing keeping me tethered to this world. I fear that if I can't write my thoughts down each day, I won't have any thoughts at all. The simple workings of my mind die when images evade words, and the blank page taunts me. I'm not exactly in control of my mind all the time, so when I am, I like to record it.

And the words fall into place:

> I don't hear voices.
> I hear past conversations

replaying in my mind,
venturing places never traveled
when they first transpired.
As if the person chastising me
gained free rein to speak,
in feral terms,
with the vitriol of savage beasts.
I am the recipient
of my own mind's toxic condemnation.

My mind has been at relative peace, so I've been trying to get myself situated to finish some projects before I happen again. Getting my medications through the shelter is working out well. I'm generally good at taking my meds until hypomania sets in. It feels wonderful, like you've gotten the best night's sleep, and you have energy for the day. The feeling improves steadily; meanwhile, I require less sleep. The decreased need for sleep and the surge of creative energy are intoxicating. It's how I write operas in my head, books on my laptop, or create businesses online. It's like that movie title: *Everything, Everywhere, All at Once.*

The lack of sleep is taking a toll on my body, but it doesn't seem to register. Mania propels me forward. My actions and language become more outlandish and more unpredictable. At least here at the shelter, if I start skipping medications, they'll let me know right away. Part of keeping my bunk at the shelter means I must be compliant with my medication. I've seen several guys get the boot because they've spiraled out of control again. We're heading into the colder days of November, and I do not want to sleep outside. Spring and summer are different. Winters can be deadly. Despite wrestling with suicidal ideation, freezing to death sounds excruciating. If I end my life, I want it done quickly, not over hours of deepening pain. No thanks.

CHAPTER SIX

Malik — The Columbus Kid

I stand in the doorway of my office. It's ludicrous.

Tap. Tap. Tap. Tap. Tap.

Boxes upon boxes of case files create towers of paperwork from our agency, partner agencies, the City, County, and the State. The boxes occupy all available desk space, resembling a monster game of Jenga. The only relief from the paperwork is the area in front of the computer monitors, our points of entry into the endless bureaucracy of our municipal government.

Two other social workers and I cram into this office, a space most likely built for one person. Making matters worse, my two co-workers, Dex and La Rae, are fat — like round fat. Over time, we have learned how to make things work. The organization of the office, no matter how you look at it, is a hot mess. I come in early, so I have a few hours to myself. When my office mates arrive, I have meetings in the cafeteria with clients. These two things help, so we don't have to rub bellies all day. I'm sure it's not true, but sometimes I wonder if part of my getting hired was due to my being slim and short. I decreased the critical mass in the room.

The disorderly nature of our shared office used to be a real issue for me. I do not like chaos. I like a predictable quality with things that impact my life. I almost quit after a few weeks because my tapping and mantra recitations were becoming a nuisance. I couldn't get work done in the office because all I could focus on was the mess. Over time, though, I learned tricks like arriving early, using the office as a drop-off point, and working in the cafeteria or conference room. Dex and La Rae caught on pretty quickly to my mannerisms and let me work out my routine.

One area that still bothers me is the printer that we all share. It's under one half of a six-foot folding table. The other half of the table serves as a desk for La Rae. If she's here and we need to get a copy, she's gotta get up out of her desk. I try to retrieve my printouts while she's on break or early on when I have the office to myself. I hate crouching down while she stands over me, waiting to sit back down. There are at least a dozen other examples of how our office is chaotic, but as a branch of city government located in the inner city, we do the best we can with the space and resources we have.

Tap. Tap. Tap. Tap. Tap. Nope, fifteen times.

I've been here for about six years, but I'm still considered the new kid on the block. I plan on staying here too. No matter how bad the work conditions are, the benefits of a city job, at least for the time being, are dope for a social worker. I could have gone into counseling, but I don't have the stomach for listening to problems all day that are out of my power to solve. I'd likely start smacking clients. And hell, if I don't do anything monumentally stupid, it is nearly impossible to get axed from a city job, so I decided against the private practice work of counseling. I landed this position with my bachelor's degree and a less-than-traditional master's degree. I say 'less-than-traditional' because I earned the degree online. What the hell, it was quick and accredited.

I knew about the shelter where I now work because several of my family members stayed here from time to time over the past two decades. My family was straight out broke growing up. We did it all: food stamps, emergency cash, social security disability, Medicaid, shelters, food lines; you name it. I was raised on W.I.C., the food subsidy program. Growing up in a poor neighborhood, you are an expert in these things by the time you are in middle school. The food bank at St Vincent's was the best because they let you pick out what vegetables you wanted to take with you. If it weren't for that pantry, I might still not know what a carrot is.

More than once, as I sat at my desk, I paused to dwell on the concept that the homeless shelter system that housed several of my family members is now contributing regularly to my 401(k). I'd gone from the food bank to the actual bank. Not bad for a hood rat.

I open a drawer in one of the file cabinets and take out one of several ties I have on hand and put on the office noose. Too many times, I've left work and gone out with friends, only to lose ties after untying them during the evening. So now I have several basic ties in the office to wear, office dress code and all. I take them off before I leave work unless I'm going to visit Moms. When I see her after work, I make a point of keeping my tie around my neck. She loves seeing me in a tie. Not many in my family wear ties, and it always makes her proud. Every Christmas, her present to me is a new tie, from Nordstrom, a nice one. She says it is the best shopping trip she takes all year long.

Moms had me young, at fifteen. It was completely unexpected, even though she knew the risks of unprotected sex. To her credit, though, she pulled it together. She made sure I kept my nose clean, too. I've never tried cocaine or any other drug, for that matter. They were everywhere during the '80s when I was coming up. In large part, I kept clean because of my Pops. He was a cocaine addict, and when cocaine wasn't around, anything would do to get his mind out of reality. He'd be around long enough to spend their food stamps. He never paid for anything. He and Moms were always yelling about money, or him having drugs in the house, or his never working. At least that's what the fights I overheard were about. And as an only child, I heard most of them.

The little I know about him trickled down from eavesdropped conversations late at night when Moms thought I was asleep. Pops had been to this shelter several times. I parsed together enough stories from different aunties and uncles to understand that my Pops was involved in a lot of bad things. As a kid with no knowledge of what drugs can do to a person, I kept trying to pacify him so he wouldn't get upset with Moms. Pops had it bad. Satisfying his need for drugs was his primary endeavor. When he couldn't find a fix, he became brutally angry at the world and physically angry with my mom.

When he was sober and trying to get his life together, I saw him for a few weeks at a time. His role as a father eventually took a back seat to his role as an addict. His visits were sporadic and put us all on edge. Moms would phone the police when he showed up unexpectedly, especially if he showed up high. The courts had granted her full custody, and the local police were aware of this. When they arrived, the routine was usually brief. It nearly always led to Pops going away in the back seat of a police car. I remember the fights and the yelling. Each time he showed up, I would resent his presence. Each time he left, though, of his own accord or in the back seat of a squad car, my desire to find and help him remained.

His appearance in my life ended abruptly when I was seventeen. The gist of the story goes: he was tweaking, a guy owed him money, and Pops killed him for twenty dollars. According to court transcripts, he hit the man over the head with a Jack Daniel's bottle. Several times. Until the bottle broke. The transcripts detail a grisly scene. The guy's face was just gone. Pops got twenty years instead of life, due to mitigating circumstances: vagueness of the assault, lack of witnesses, and lack of a lot of things except circumstantial evidence. And of course, the State's attorney wasn't going to waste a lot of money on a junkie vs. junkie murder. His life of addiction and lengthy arrest record worked to his advantage regarding his mental acuity. His mental health gave him a shortened sentence.

This single situation has nearly broken me into pieces. It is definitely one of my triggers, the not knowing. Aside from my forays into hacking our system with old passwords and usernames, I also casually ask other social workers, housing navigators, and monitors about my father. There's never any news. A few of my father's incidents made it into the digital record, but the paperwork stored before 2000 was destroyed when the overhead sprinkler system was activated in response to a fire in a different part of the county building. The destroyed records would have told me more about his life.

Tap. Tap. Tap. Tap. Tap. Nope, ten times. Nope, twenty times.

Early on, while I was in grade school, I toyed with the idea of becoming a cop. I held onto an idealistic notion that I could right the wrongs of my father that way. But this was Columbus, OH, and since I was young, there had been a hesitance from family members about becoming involved with the police force. Columbus was the city where Tyre King, a 13-year-old playing with a toy gun in the park, was shot by police. That's just the modern incarnation of racial tensions that have existed in Columbus since before I can remember.

The DOJ had investigated Columbus several times. Each time the investigators came to Columbus and did their investigation, it brought more tension to the city and to my poor, but beautiful-in-my-eyes, Four Corners neighborhood. The problem with the local police occurred well after the investigators left our community.

The cops remained on high alert for negative reactions from the Black community. One of the places investigated was Cliff's. Cliff was an older man who ran a mom-and-pop shop down the street on Sullivan near Souder just around the corner from the shelter.

Cliff's store wasn't under investigation, but the nightly activities taking place in the parking lot and vacant lot next door were. It was a hotbed of solicitation and illicit drug sales. Crack cocaine was becoming popular in our hood then, and users were buzzing all over Cliff's parking lot at night. The sad irony of that situation was that Cliff himself lived a life straight as an arrow. He hated what happened around his place at night. He put up cameras, but they got smashed. He told police, but Sullivan wasn't exactly where cops like to spend time. Ironically, the miscreants hanging out in Cliff's parking lot never robbed Cliff. In a weird show of community, the junkies took care of their parking lot at night, as long as Cliff kept up his habit of not calling the police about the activities that took place there.

His proximity to a vacant lot, which in turn was next to an abandoned house, made it a perfect location for illegal nighttime salaciousness. The police in the area were not overly familiar with Cliff, his store, or the neighborhood. This was before community policing was established. There were hardly any Black officers at the time. The patrol of neighborhoods where the crime took place equaled no more than a few drive-throughs each night unless something went down. If that happened, damn near half the police force would show up. It was an all-or-nothing response from the police, and no one could ever determine what kind of response was coming.

The incident that broke the neighborhood went down just before Easter one year, when I was still a kid. On a random Saturday night, things were in full swing at Cliff's. Drugs flowed from car windows to tweaking clients. Prostitutes tricking johns took up residence in the abandoned house nearby. One of the prostitutes, also high on crack and making terrible decisions, brought her three-year-old daughter with her to the abandoned house. The little girl's mother, high from a pieced-up eight-ball, locked her daughter in a room off the hallway from where she was turning tricks. The mom's confused logic was that she would be safe nearby. Well, she wasn't. After paying to have sex with the little girl's mother, the john found the daughter. A john who had all the energy of someone high on crack raped that little girl. He raped her so violently; she died sometime that night after he left.

Upon finding her daughter dead in the decrepit room, the mother, still high on crack, lost her mind. Having taken payment for her services all night in the form of cocaine rocks, her reaction was cataclysmic. With the pistol she kept as protection, she began shooting. She began shooting anyone. Everyone in her path went down as she made her way out of the house.

Her shots were fired in such proximity to the drug dealers in the parking lot that soldiers for the drug pushers drew weapons. The street lit up. The volley lasted almost twenty minutes before the cops arrived on the scene. Gunfire extended for another thirty minutes with every available unit arriving locked and loaded. The only thing I remember about that night is Moms holding me and telling me it was just a thunderstorm outside. She said we were going to stay there in my bed together until the thunder ended. I slept through it for the most part.

By the time the sun rose, fourteen people were dead, all of them people from the neighborhood, including a nine-year-old boy sleeping in his bedroom in a house across the street from Cliff's. No cops were injured. That night drew the full wrath of the Columbus police force. The handling of it did little to quell the neighborhood fears. Tensions rose to a boiling point. The Feds were drawn into the mess again. They did their investigation. No cops were punished, but more than thirty arrests were made in our neighborhood. The lines had been drawn, and for the better part of a decade, cops were on one side and everyone from the neighborhood was on the other.

On a night of devastation like that, where the police sustained no injuries, it didn't matter if their response to the incident was by the book. My hood was roiling with anger at what was perceived as an example of no police accountability. Blue Columbus was incensed because they had done their job again with no thanks from the Black community. Black Columbus was outraged, too, thinking they had been overlooked yet again. And true to form, when Blue is pissed at Black, Black loses.

During my first year of college, NWA put out their hugely enormous blockbuster of a song *Fuck tha Police*. A side result of the release of that song was to muster up a lot of feelings of resentment that had died down. It became the anthem for many young Black kids. It seems foolish to think that a song by a rap band could affect the trajectory of my life. But it did. Whatever notions I might have had about becoming a cop got squashed beneath NWA's infectious rhymes and my neighborhood's response to those lyrics. It prompted me to explore other opportunities for contributing to my community. Growing up west of downtown in the Four Corners neighborhood put me in the shadow of the Crossroads Men's Shelter. So, as my first real adult decision, I gave up the idea of becoming a cop and focused on the entity that still had a good reputation in my city and in my neighborhood: social services.

So, here I sit. The nameplate on my office door, beneath my two counterparts, reads Malik Arons, Social Worker. Within my profession, I'm what is called a housing navigator. I work with clients here at the shelter to find housing in Columbus. The clients here present challenges to the usual process of finding an apartment. Fifty percent of them have prison records. Having a felony is an obstacle to jobs and housing. Many are currently abusing drugs or alcohol, despite multiple attempts at sobriety. Thankfully, as a navigator, I don't deal with the day-to-day enforcement of policy set up at the shelter. Just like I couldn't deal with patients as a therapist, I don't think I could deal with the daily interactions I hear monitors going through. Clients I deal with have steered clear of most of the day-to-day drama. They've been with the shelter long enough for us to get a sense of how they will present in interviews. We conduct a preliminary background check to understand the challenges they face before referring them to someone like me, a housing navigator. By the time we've had our meetings and done the checks, we can, for the most part, gauge who will be successful in securing permanent housing.

Some of the clients I deal with don't fall into the category of criminal or addict. Their records are clean, and they appear to be good candidates. These guys generally are dealing with some type of mental illness. People can be placed in our shelter for many reasons. Many come after psych admissions. Some experience severe manic episodes and are placed under arrest for being a public nuisance. Some simply succumb to depression and lie down in a hidden alley to die. When psych wards are done tuning their meds, they come to us.

Despite all this, we do have clients who succeed. It's great to witness. It does the heart good. And truly, I'd love to say it is enough to keep me going, but I've been here long enough to be professionally jaded. What keeps me going is the paycheck, not the client victories, although I do relish them. I think it's common among social service agencies. At one time, early on in our careers, we may have been idealistic. I'm sure we all felt that our work in our chosen fields would make a difference in society. And we do, from time to time, make the difference we once thought would ground us in our profession. But it's the relentless nature of dealing with people. As soon as you have a success, five more unsuccessful ones will take their place.

Always.

The problem is larger than any one person; so is the solution. If I'm being totally honest with myself, the one prospect, even beyond the paycheck, which brings me back to this office, is the fantasy that one day, Pops will come back into the program. It's foolish. I know it's foolish. But there it is. I'm still the high school kid thinking my dad is going to come walking through the door. It's ridiculous. He's a junkie. He left the family repeatedly. He killed someone, for God's sake. But despite all that, I keep harboring in my mind the idea that there must be some story he can tell that will explain away all the bad decisions he made, and that we will start a new relationship.

Sitting here, alone in the office, I shake my head. There is no reason a Black man with all those strikes against him is alive. There it is. My dad ain't nothing but a nigger in a woodpile. I think about that phrase and why I use it. I'm not entirely sure what it means exactly. My mom said it had been used in early movies. She used it a lot. To her, it meant a person so relegated to nothingness that they are simply cast off, like a nigger in the woodpile.

I chastise myself for thinking about my father in such a manner. Truth is, he could have moved to Cleveland or even another state. The further truth is, I'll probably never know. Maybe he moved away knowing he had burnt bridges with Moms. Maybe he needed a fresh start in a neighborhood where his reputation wasn't known. Homeless people are notoriously hard to track, especially if they are not plugged into the welfare system somehow. From what I can tell, my dad has never been a part of Medicaid, Medicare, disability, food stamps, housing, or cash assistance programs in the counties where I have access to data. I volunteer during the holidays when various organizations distribute food, blankets, socks, and other essentials directly to homeless camps, hoping that maybe I'll see him or hear about him. The ultimate truth in this whole obsession of mine—Pops is probably dead.

I chastise myself for thinking this way. Maybe I had seen my father and didn't recognize him. Perhaps he lacked the capacity to recognize me. I shake my thoughts from my head and sit down at my desk. It's 7:30 in the morning. We don't officially start until 10 o'clock. There is a stack of files, approximately ten inches tall, to the left of the computer. This is the caseload to get through today to stay caught up on my duties. Each file takes about half an hour to go through, so I grab the top folder: Caleb Taylor.

I think I have seen him in the cafeteria: a tall, white guy. I flip open his folder and see that he has no negative interactions with staff. Not unheard of, but most of the guys have some run-ins with another client or with a staff member. It says he's buried deeply in psych medication, too, but still no run-ins. Guess the medication is working. Consistently taking medication is a good sign.

As I look at Caleb's file, I must admit a racist line of thought percolates. I am looking for the reason he's homeless. I come from a place where if you are white, you have certain privileges people of color don't get. White folks must have something extraordinary happen in their lives to have them wind up here, as opposed to Black folks from my neighborhood, where this may be a common step in getting an apartment, leaving a dire situation, or using the shelter to save up money. I hate that I think this way, but I do.

I flip through his file. He's working too. A guy on all this medication is still holding down a job—that combination creeps into the rare category. This should be an interesting meeting. Looks like he's working the night shift, so I should be able to catch up with him at breakfast before he grabs his bunk. I look at the clock and see that the 8:00 a.m. roll call will take approximately ten minutes. I grab one of the yellow half sheets of paper and scrawl a note for the roll call monitor. It reads, "Please have Caleb Taylor see me for an introduction."

I get up from my chair and take the note with me. I walk out of my office and down the hallway lined with other similarly cramped offices to the security door leading to the cafeteria. I turn my key in the lock, and the heavy deadbolt thunks back into its receptacle. Pulling back on the door, I enter the cafeteria, which is loaded with guys still drinking coffee and chatting at the tables. They're waiting for the roll call. Breakfast is a pretty calm time.

I have the note ready to hand over to the monitor who will perform the roll call duties that morning. I see Caleb ahead of me at a table. He's by himself, reading. He always comes across as polite, if I remember correctly, almost professional. He's alone. He is much of the time. Instead of handing the note over to the monitor, I decide to introduce myself. I maneuver my way through the tables and chairs. Caleb has his head down in a book and doesn't look up, even when I come to stand by the side of his table.

"Good morning, Caleb," I say.

Caleb looks up at me and says, "Hi." His answer is neither friendly nor grumpy, just a response.

"My name is Malik. I'm a housing navigator."

Caleb brightens slightly at that introduction. "Good to meet you," he says, extending a hand.

I hate shaking hands. In my mind, I instantly imagine everywhere a hand at a men's shelter could have been recently. Hopefully, none of that shows on my face as I shake his hand. "Do you have a moment?"

"Yes," he answers. Not "yup" or "yeah" or "uh-huh," but yes.

"Great," I respond. "I've been given your name to add to my caseload. I assist clients in finding permanent housing within the community. Is that something that interests you?"

"Yes," Caleb says. "That's something I would like."

"Well, I can see you as early as 8 o'clock. That will give you a chance to get some breakfast, and then you can see me. Today is Monday. Would this Wednesday work for you?"

"Absolutely," he responds. "Wednesday morning at eight. I'll be right here."

"Perfect," I say. "I will come get you here in the cafeteria, and we can spend about an hour getting you registered for placement, and we'll see what we can get started for you. Sound good?"

"That sounds more than good, Malik," he answers.

This guy may do OK, I think to myself.

CHAPTER SEVEN

Caleb — Wet Sock

In Northern California, where I grew up, summers are typically hot. Temperatures consistently remain in the 90s, with many stretches of triple-digit heat. One day, my folks decided that we would go next door to our neighbors' for a swim after church. We all changed out of our Sunday clothes into shorts and T-shirts. My mom packed up a great lunch for us to eat. She always said to never go anywhere without something to share. The neighbors had a daughter, Lauren, my brother's age, which could be hard sometimes because they were just old enough not to want to be bothered by a little squirt like me trying to play with them. But I loved swimming, so I wouldn't be bothering them today. I ran out the front door, skipping with excitement, my feet barely touching the ground in the way that only small children can move.

"What's for lunch?" I asked.

"I packed summer sausage, Ritz crackers, potato chips, sodas, lemonade, and Oreo cookies."

"Yum!" I roared.

My brother punched me in the arm, and I looked at him, confused.

I helped Mom carry the ice chest over. The neighbors hadn't made it home from church yet, but they'd told us to go ahead and jump in because the church council was having a meeting. I was so excited because that meant Craig wouldn't be there yet.

But I was wrong.

Craig didn't go to church with his parents and sister. He was 19 years old and did as he pleased when it came to going to church. He was standing in the kitchen window when we entered the backyard through the side gate. As my dad put it, he was an Eagle Scout and was confirmed in our church, but he was always a bit off. This was in the early 70s, and not much was known about treating paranoid schizophrenia, personality disorders, and psychoses. We often prayed for Craig at the dinner table. Craig was starting to show some severe symptoms, and the family's response to that was to pray harder.

Seeing Craig in the window changed everything for me. I used to love swimming in that pool. Things are different now. I sat next to my mom, who was a bit bothered that I was clinging to her side. I reluctantly got into the pool, sitting on the steps in the shallow end. Craig watched my brother and me closely from the kitchen window. I heard the phone ring from the kitchen. That was when telephones were as large as bricks and tethered to the wall by a long curly cord. I heard Craig's voice on the phone through the open kitchen window. A few minutes later, he came out onto the back patio and said that his folks wouldn't be home for another hour.

After some time, my mother decided we should get out and dry off. We got out of the pool. She packed up what was left of the snacks she'd brought. She gave Craig a large Tupperware pitcher filled with lemonade for his mom. The phone rang from our house, so Mom took the ice chest and scurried over to answer. This was before answering machines, so it would be fine if it rang fifteen times.

As Mom headed out, she said, "Craig, I'm going home. Let the boys dry off and then send them home, would you?"

"Sure, Mrs. Taylor."

There were towels in the bathroom, so my brother and I got them to dry off. As we were done drying ourselves, Craig says to my brother, "Hey, Mikey, why don't you go on. I want to show Caleb my new model train. Tell your mom he'll be home shortly." My brother was not interested in trains, but I always was. Well, I was curious when Craig's father showed me the trains. Craig showing me the trains meant something completely different.

"OK," my brother said to Craig and then headed out to go home.

Even though I was inside, the water started to rise in my mind.

"Do you want to see the train?"

"OK," I say quietly.

"You're soaking wet," he says.

"OK," I answer.

"Take your suit off and let it dry."

"OK." I pulled my swim shorts down.

Craig approached me and knelt. He had fishing lines and fishhooks in his hand.

"This might hurt."

"OK."

•••

...later this summer, I will be going to South Dakota for a few weeks with my family to visit relatives. I think about leaning my head against the window as we drive along the highway. Rows of corn pass by at a dizzying speed. The car hums. It's hypnotizing. It's comforting. It's safe. I feel protected as we drive away from California. Craig doesn't come to South Dakota. I'm free to roam my grandparents' farm, explore the barn where the kittens are born, and watch the

cattle as they all come in from the pasture to drink from the well at the base of the windmill.

My grandmother seems to be permanently perched in the kitchen, cooking up magic in her oven or cutting pastries out on the cutting board. She lets me take all the scraps of food out to Patches, the farm dog, who loves to run and play with my brother and me. My grandpa, dad, and brother enjoy going goose hunting. I don't like to go. I don't like guns. I don't like the way they taste or feel. My mom notices this and finds something else for me to do while they are gone. There's a weekly newspaper that I like to look through because they have puzzles and cartoons.

I can also run upstairs to look out the window. From there, I can see acres and acres of sunflowers gleaming gold in the sun. The fields of flax shimmer indigo blue. Everywhere else, there is corn. This is my version of heaven, and it's where I go in my mind when the water rises. I think about the old-fashioned clothes wringer my grandma used to press out the water before she hung them out to dry, flapping and moving in the breeze. I think about the hallway coat rack where my grandpa hangs his fedora. When he's gone, I wear it around the house and pretend I'm an adult. I think about the crocheted lace curtains. If you push your face against them, you can see outside where the hawks are circling over the corn fields as they search for mice and snakes.

South Dakota is my safe place.

•••

When I arrived in Columbus, I was a stranger to the city. I left my last place quickly, chaotically. When I am manic, everything makes sense to me, and anyone not understanding what I'm experiencing is simply too inept to recognize the sheer elegance of my ideation. I'm intimidating, too, because I'm a big guy. When I am underwater in my thinking, anything goes. The most insipid part of having manic swings is that I never know when it's happening. Despite considerable changes in my behavior, my mind doesn't register the change. When it's over, I'm left to pick up the pieces, should any pieces remain.

As is so often the case, once I am manic, I pursue avenues that exacerbate the effects of my behavior. Craigslist is at the top of my list of destinations. I wish that damned list had never been created. But it was. And I go there. I always go there. I have a vague memory of looking at a post for a job in Columbus and knowing I would be perfect for it. I obsess over it. I read into the job description. I create a whole imagined alternate reality about how this posting on Craigslist is there to change my life; it may even change the world.

That's where my mania really thrives, in the hyperbolic state of chaotic imagination and boundless energy. Mania creates fantasies in my mind when I'm too far gone to reel myself back to rationality. I know the fantasies I create are the most brilliant, the most astounding, and the most creative thing of all time.

Ever.

Ever. Ever. Ever.

In my elevated state, I imagine the staff at my new job with a sign saying "Congratulations." They are ecstatic to see me, really over the moon. They're wearing party hats. They have tears in their eyes. There's even a cake with my name on it. My vision is so comforting. These people want me. I needn't send my resume. I don't even need to talk to anyone at the workplace. I know it will be perfect. I just need to show up, and all will be perfect.

I tell my friend, who has been letting me sleep on his couch, that I'm going. He begs me to stay.

'*Asshole,*' I think.

The few people I do call to announce my exciting, sensational, phenomenal, stupendous plan all plead with me not to leave. *More assholes*. What do they know? Screw them. My new friends where I'm going are waiting for me. They are dying for me to arrive. They'll see the second I walk through the door that I am the ONE!

I get on a Greyhound bus with two bags of essentials. Upon boarding, I begin to work with my laptop, paper notebooks, and all my files. On the bus, I start creating my new life. I'm going to have a new job waiting for me. The ad says the job pays forty-five thousand dollars, but I'm sure they'll pay me more, so I begin budgeting for a life at one hundred thousand dollars. I'm sure someone at work will let me stay with them, so I probably don't even need to budget for an apartment. They'll probably even help buy me clothes because they'll be so thankful when I arrive. Everything will be taken care of, and everyone will be so happy. I will be happy. It will be perfect.

On the bus, passengers are so polite. They obviously see how busy I am, how important I am. My earbuds are thumping out the rhythms of Dee-Lite. Piles of crumpled papers, my notebooks, and my bags keep spilling into the aisle. It's awesome to be in the groove. I'm really cranking out the ideas now. I'm busy in my seat for nearly thirty hours. Then somewhere about Denver, Colorado...

I fall asleep.

I fall asleep hard.

I fall asleep for several states.

Upon waking, I'm disoriented. People are getting off the bus. The beast rummages through my mind, pulling me down.

"This bus is going out of service, ladies and gentlemen. Everyone must get off the bus," a disembodied voice pronounces.

I'm painfully thirsty. I'm surrounded by a flurry of papers with my wild, incoherent scribblings. My computer has lost battery power. I can't really make sense of what is in the seat next to me and on the floor in front of me. And then the bus driver is telling me in no uncertain terms that I must get off the bus.

"Where am I?" I ask.

He rolls his eyes. "Look at your damned ticket," he says.

"My ticket?" I'm confused, but then again, I'm not. I'm not clear where I am, but I've been here before; not physically in this city, but here regarding trying to figure out where I am after mania rocks through my life. I know also that now, in these teetering few hours after mania, my footing will begin to fall over the cliff into depression, deep depression because I'm here...again. Hello beast.

I shove paperwork, cords, files, and garbage I've created into the bags I've brought. I stumble down the aisle of the bus, paper and wrappers trailing behind me. The steps down to the parking lot end in a blast of cold air. It takes my breath away but snaps me into alertness. I walk toward the Greyhound terminal. I have recreated my own disaster once again because, once again, I happened.

I step into a shallow, icy puddle in a small pothole in the parking lot. My left boot, the one with the sole peeling away, fills with water. My foot becomes frigid and wet. Perfect. I'm used to being homeless. For the most part, I can handle it. There are circumstances, though, that break through the veneer of readiness. The combination of winter and water is one of them. They can be dangerous. They can be deadly. A wet foot is no big deal if you live in San Diego, where I came from. But I'm no longer in San Diego.

I enter the Greyhound depot and scan the waiting room. It's one large rectangle with bathrooms on one end and a small cafe on the other. There are rows and rows of wire metal seats. I walk toward the side of the waiting room where the bathrooms are located. I lay one of my bags at the end of a row of seats. My body is stiff from being seated on a trek halfway across the country. I undo the laces on my boot, pull off the sock, and refit my boot onto my foot. Unceremoniously, I wring out the sock and flop it over the back of one of the metal chairs.

I struggle to get my body down to the tile floor. Once there, I lay my head on the bag containing my few clothes. I pull the strings on my hoodie, drawing it around my face. A tag on my bag indicates to Greyhound staff that I have, or have had, a ticket. It will be a day old soon, but they won't look that hard. I can probably get some sleep here while my sock dries.

And the words drop into place:

> Greyhound station
> pavilion of impecunious travelers
> hop-scotching the country
> confused by circumstance
> seeking emancipation from their past
> blind to the future
> anticipating freedom
> despite all signs to the contrary.

I fall asleep to the mélange of thoughts in my mind until something startles me awake. Not remembering when I got into Columbus, I fish my phone out of my front pocket. I have seven percent left on my battery; my laptop is completely dead. My phone reads 3:50 a.m. My foot is sore. I remember I must get my sock into the bathroom to dry under one of the automatic hand dryers. I'm also hungry and have a relatively urgent need to use the bathroom. With all that on my mind, I still don't get up. I can see the bathroom at the other end of the depot from where I am lying. My solitary thought upon waking is a simple one. I have nowhere to go. I know nothing about anything or anyone here.

And the words drop into place:

> All he wants is a place in the world

to be found and be bound,
after so long lost.
To be tethered by insight,
awash in verse,
words creating steppingstones,
like graveyard bones
to the skeletons of my past.

The words reverberate and soon slip from my mind, lost with the rest of the poems and thoughts that stray through. I sit up. The need to go to the bathroom increases exponentially. I get up with the agility of the Tin Man in The Wizard of Oz before he gets oiled. The arm I slept on is somewhat asleep, but I manage to pick up a bag with each arm. I make it to the bathroom. I hang my bags on the hook on the door inside the bathroom stall. I stand in front of the toilet, unzip, and for several satisfying moments, I empty my bladder. My eyes are closed as I enjoy the relief throughout my abdomen. Feelings of relief will be very rare going forward.

Posters hang on the bathroom stall walls for various organizations, including the Homeless Action Network, Addiction Recovery Services, the Runaway Youth Hotline, Domestic Violence Prevention, and several other agencies in town that address the needs of the homeless. At first, I think how odd it is to have a bathroom stall as a place to advertise, but then I realize it's the perfect place. One poster reads: "In need of clothing?" It goes on to specify a place where you can go once a month to receive free clothes. The poster also indicates a Lutheran church providing three meals a day, every day. I grab the poster, sending the thumbtack flying. The poster has a bullet point for something called "The Sandwich Line," where anyone can go get a few simple sandwiches and help themselves to whatever donations of food were collected that day.

I pull my phone out of my pocket. I start putting numbers on the poster into my phone, and then I remember I never plugged it in to recharge. I sling my bags over my shoulder and leave the bathroom stall. Walking back into the depot on my still soggy boot, I scan the walls for outlets and see a few, all filled with the chargers and phones of fellow travelers. Walking by the wall with the vending machines, I spot an open outlet next to an "Out of Order" Gatorade machine. I slump down against the wall and plug my charger into the outlet. Mania is exhausting when you come down from it.

I wish the ECT had a more pronounced effect on my mania. I'm eternally grateful that it helped cure me from major depressive mood swings, but it did little to affect my mania. Mania is horrible, especially when it comes with a slow buildup. I'm not able to recognize it when it happens. One thing I am thankful for is that my mania doesn't lead to suicidal ideation like my depression can. That being said, I always have a little voice in the back of my head saying, "*It's OK if I die.*" It's almost like a Plan B, a mantra playing deep in the background. I don't dwell on suicide, though, which is a beautiful effect of ECT. It allows me to dwell more in the present. That is, until Craig shows up again and I go underwater.

•••

I'm awakened by someone tapping my foot. One of the depot attendants is tapping my foot with his own. He's a large Black man wearing a crisp white Greyhound shirt with the little dog logo on the breast pocket.

"Hey, bro, can't sleep here," he says. I'm about to argue with the guy when he says, "I don't mind if you hang out, just can't be so obvious you sleepin.'"

"Fair enough," I say, realizing this guy is trying his best to be helpful while still doing his job. His nametag reads Rick. "Thanks, Rick."

I look at my phone after half an hour or so. It indicates it has 47% power. Keeping the phone plugged into the outlet, I pull out the crumpled flyer and dial the 800 number. There are a multitude of options, and as I'm waiting for the free clothing prompt, I hear, "Press seven for Emergency Shelter." Could I be that lucky? I press seven. A nice woman says hello. She takes my name and a lot of information including my social security number. She asks how long I have been a resident of Ohio. She asks if I am in danger of physical harm. She asks if I have been in a shelter before. She informs me that she needs to check if I am on the sexual offender registry. She puts me on hold and runs her check. She comes back saying she has everything she needs and that I am on the list to receive Emergency Shelter.

My number is thirty-seven. The shelter in San Francisco had a similar system to the one described by the woman on the phone. You are given a number on a first-come, first-served basis, with preference given to youth and veterans. As they put people into beds, your number decreases. When you are Number One, you're next on the list to get a bed. When I was in San Francisco, my number was two hundred fifty-six, so thirty-seven seems good to me.

The mania has left me now. My body registers the fatigue that mania had kept at bay. The high energy, the explosive thoughts, and the imagination on overdrive have subsided. In their place comes the slippery slide down into depression. It's almost as if the impending depression takes on shapeshifter qualities. I look forlorn and quiet, yet what roils in my mind is chaos and crippling guilt. The chaos is found in the newly arrived city where I am without friends, support, or medication. The guilt is for all my mistakes and the ones I continue to make as I sit on a Greyhound station floor with a wet sock and no idea what comes next. I imagine I may look like I'm just lazy. No one would suspect that my mind is starved for the right neurotransmitters which I can no longer manage without medication. I probably have a few days until it really sets in. It's a miserable way to exist, but that, indeed, is my reality. When I am treading water and the water is lapping at my face, things get dicey.

If Craig shows up, it makes everything worse. It's subtle at first. A person disappearing around a corner whose face strikes a resemblance. He's in aisle five of the grocery store, so I close my eyes. When I open my eyes, he's gone. The man on the other side of the street turns his head just as he enters a store. Sometimes it's a voice on the PA system at Walmart asking someone for customer service. Other times it's just the hair on the back of my neck when I see something unexpected. I can look into a storefront window and see his face reflected in the glass behind me. I turn around to face him, and nothing's there.

I know it's happening. I know it's not real, but before I can draw a rational conclusion for what I'm seeing, or not seeing, I'm already slipping into the water, waiting for whatever is to come. Wherever I am when it happens, I become still. Even though now, as an adult, I am probably bigger and taller than Craig, he looms large in my mind with his imposing stature towering over me as it was when I was a kid. I feel the water rising. I see his face in my periphery. The water is still rising. I catch a snippet of his voice. I draw in a breath, but the water covers my mouth, then my nose, and then my ears. Everything I see is muted. Everything I hear is 100 miles away. I've gone underwater. It's not desperate. It's not stifling. It's comforting. If I cannot hear something, if I cannot see something, it's not there. Right? The water felt like my covers when I was little, and I was afraid of the monster in my closet. My blankets were magic. And now as an adult, the water swims around me, keeping me safe, carrying me away from the other monster in my memory, like magic.

Underwater, I hear jovial noises in the distance, far away. There's laughter. I focus on the joy and ignore the rest of what's happening. It's how I lose chunks of time. I see Craig, the water rises, and I am adrift. Sometimes I pack up things and get on a Greyhound. Sometimes I walk for a few days. Sometimes, well, most of the time, I don't know where I've been or what I've done, but it's three hours later, or in really bad episodes, three days later. Sometimes I wake up at home; other times I wake up in hospitals. I can even wake up in different cities, like Columbus.

One of my shrinks called it dissociative identity disorder, like the old movie Sybil. Back then it was called multiple personality disorder. In the movie Psycho, it was just called batshit crazy. There's nothing as dramatic as that in my life. I don't smash my hands through windows like Sybil. I don't dress up like my mother and murder women in the shower like Norman Bates. I simply slip underwater, and the water carries me wherever it may, leaving my body behind to lash out, crumble in fear, or shrink as small as I am able.

•••

"Caleb?"

I shake my head. *"What? Wait, where am I? Oh, that's right, the shelter in...Columbus. How long have I been sitting here at the cafeteria table?"* I recognize Malik in front of me. He's on staff at the shelter. He wanted to meet with me.

That's right, I had an appointment.

I extend my hand, and he gives me a short handshake. I wonder if he realizes I was checked out. He doesn't say anything, so I guess I'm OK. Pointing over his shoulder, he says, "So, normally, I take clients back to my office. Will that be OK with you?" He places his hand on the side of my shoulder lightly. It's an unexpected gesture. I don't react to it except to keep my head down, looking at the cover of my book.

"Sure, however the process goes," I say.

"Great," he says, turning away from me, walking toward the door to the administration hallway. He waves to a few other clients in the cafeteria as he makes his way through the tables. He holds the security door open, and I walk through it. Malik is a nicely dressed man, probably about my age. He is very dark-skinned. It's such a difference from my pinkish, white skin that when we shook hands, it looked like a yin and yang symbol. He opens the door to his office, and there is one chair right next to the entrance which seems to be the only chair someone who doesn't work there could sit on, so I sit.

"We've got about thirty minutes worth of questions," he says. "Will that fit your schedule?"

"Yes, that's fine."

As he is sitting at the desk, I look at his profile. His hair is cut very short, and his hairline is exact. Absent-mindedly, I touch my own bald head and stubble of blond, graying hair, which I keep cut very short with clippers. I can't think of anything more dissimilar than his hair and mine. He shuffles paper and then starts asking questions: age, race, working history. It's all regular questions, much like a job interview.

Then we get to the psychiatric history. I hate these questions. It's like talking about a bad relative you're embarrassed to know. The questions poke at the thin façade of confidence I put up during social interactions. This is a tough question-and-answer period because it's not a real social setting. It's just him and me, and I don't know him. Malik is part of the machine called public health and welfare. I'm just a number to him even though he keeps the questioning conversational, with all the trappings of being social.

I remember my place in all of this and answer the questions unemotionally. I must keep reminding myself I'm not here to impress Malik or to be his friend. He's here to provide me with services as a part of his job. When I'm not psychotic, manic, or depressed, I'm a quiet, introverted, and intelligent person. Most vexing to me, though, is that after all that has transpired in my life, I still find myself trusting people easily. Too easily. Way too easily.

I must remind myself that social service people are just that, providing a service. I go into these interviews thinking I'm trying to impress someone with my wit and vocabulary. That leads me to fibs and flubbing answers to make myself seem more normal. There was a time in my life when I functioned like a normal person, but that time ended quite a while ago. Now, I just try to stay clear of everyone and keep myself safe. I try as hard as I can to keep my responses truthful, no matter how desperate it makes me sound.

Finally, he asks if I've ever received disability for my diagnosis. I answer in the affirmative, and he says, "Good." I wasn't really expecting that answer. He continues, "Well, it's not good that you have that diagnosis, but it's good that you have a recorded income. That makes you a more attractive applicant for housing."

"Ah, ok." The answer is good, not because it reflects well upon me; it's good because it makes his job easier. For the next twenty minutes, he asks questions, and I answer. I don't remember much of what he asks because, really, what does it matter? At the end of this interview, I'll be another number in the system, like the number I had when I called to get a bed. I can't remember when I stopped being a person and became the series of numbers that would dictate how my life would unfold.

"So, Caleb," he says after all the blanks are filled in. "What we do here at Crossroads is take your information and match it with one of our rental customers. They know they are getting a pre-screened applicant who, in your case, has income and is ready to be a successful tenant. Generally, the client will take one-third of your subsidy. Your income from Social Security Disability Insurance is automatically deposited into your bank account at Regents State Bank. I know your gross disability income is a bit higher because of the garnishment of your student loans, so I'm going to submit your net income as your true income. Your rental responsibility will be about $330 a month. Additionally, in Ohio, if you receive that much disability, it's likely you won't qualify for SNAP, the food stamp program. I can provide you with a list of nearby food pantries. The $330 will include all your basic utilities: gas, electricity, trash, and water. Your phone, internet, and cable, things like that, will still be your responsibility." He paused for a moment. "Does that make sense?"

"Yes, I think so," I say. "I remember applying for SNAP in San Diego. I got $16 per month."

"Yeah, if you have any income, that's usually what recipients receive. It's a very low amount, I agree with that," Malik says. "I can't count the income you make through your part-time work because it is through the temp agency, meaning it could change at any time. The powers that be would rather not count it than recalculate it every month based on your hours."

"OK."

"OK then," he says as he tamps the papers into order. "I need to get this information into the system to match you with an apartment. Do you have any questions for me?"

I think about all the amenities that go along with an apartment. "Yes, should I worry about saving up for a deposit, first and last months' rent, like you do when you're renting an apartment the normal way?"

"Great question," he said. "I forgot to tell you about that, so glad you asked. We have a voucher available at Crossroads for the deposit amount, up to one month's rent, for the security deposit. We also have funds to help with the first month's rent. But I really want to encourage you to save up whatever you can because things like furniture, kitchenware, and everything else that goes into the apartment are on you."

I figure between Goodwill, Craigslist, and everything else online these days, I can get into the apartment pretty cheaply. All I really need is a twin-sized mattress and an internet connection. And a French press! The thought of having fresh, dark-roasted coffee brings a smile to my face. Some sheets, some plates, and maybe a shelf for books are about all I can think of that I might want to buy.

"OK," I say.

"So, this is all cool, Caleb?"

"Yes, this is great. When will I hear from you next?" I ask because I've heard that housing navigators are busy and hard to get in touch with unless they want to reach out to you.

"Another good question," he says. "Give me a day to get this in the system and a week to circulate your info to our housing clients. Check back in with me next week. That should be enough time to get a preliminary answer."

"OK, that sounds good."

"Any more questions?"

"Nothing I can think of right now."

"Well, if anything comes up, just write it down and give it to the monitor. They'll get your question to me, and I'll come find you."

"OK, thank you, Malik."

"Just doing my job, my friend."

"Right."

CHAPTER EIGHT

Malik — Smitty

I've never really been out of the city. I went to university here. I work here. As a kid, I would pass by Cliff's Shop after school and buy Pop Rocks and soda. My grade school, where I spent hours reading on large bean bags at the library, is here. My friends and I knew all the shortcuts through abandoned lots to our houses. Some people keep scrapbooks for their memories; mine were all laid out for me in a ten-block radius, which I would never forget. Everything I'd ever accomplished, I accomplished because of this neighborhood.

I never felt the need to leave. The thought of leaving makes me feel very uncomfortable. Columbus is a good-sized town for being in the plains of the Midwest. My neighborhood on the west side is a small sliver of the greater metropolitan area. Growing up, I could see the taller buildings of downtown while playing in the streets. Seeing those buildings always made me feel like I lived in a big city. Moms and I rarely left the ten square blocks of my neighborhood. If we did, it was for things like the doctor, family court, or Walmart. I didn't like going to the doctor or the dentist. Family court was always a long wait surrounded by loud, noisy people. And Walmart always seemed to put Moms in a bad mood.

These ten blocks were my world. It wasn't until I entered

middle school and was bused about a mile away that I realized how little my neighborhood had to offer. My school didn't have many after-school activities, but it did have a basketball team. I tried out and made the team, and I loved it. Coach Carl, who was also the 8th-grade biology teacher, took us ragtag kids in and worked with us every day after school. We practiced for about a month before our first game. It was an away game against Grantside. When we pulled into their school parking lot, I think my mouth must have been hanging open. Their school was huge and immaculate, filled with primarily white students. Our school was in disrepair, the playground was small, and the school had a majority Black student body. Grantside was a bit intimidating.

The bus parked in the Grantside parking lot. Walking into that gym was like walking into a church. The floors were polished. The basketball nets were new. The bleachers were huge. There were vending machines and a snack bar. It was all so foreign to me. I nearly lost my nerve until I saw Moms sitting in the bleachers with two other mothers. I waved excitedly, and my friends teased me about being a mama's boy. I punched them both in their arms.

We began our pre-game practice. We were on the visitors' side of the court doing our fundamental warm-up routine. The other side was making intricate runs, passes, and shots. Coach Carl saw what was happening, blew a quick chirp on his whistle, and called us over to the side.

"Gather round, kids," he said in his slow, serious voice as we circled him. He squatted down so our bodies blocked him from view. "Now I know whachu seein', boys. They're a really pretty team, all shiny and sharp. Don't pay them no never mind. Ya wanna know why?" He let that question hang in the air.

"Why?" a few of us asked.

"Because you guys play good ball," he said. "I have been watchin' those guys too. And you want to know what?" He pointed at my teammate. "Ryan, you make free throws almost every time, and I ain't seen one of them balls that pretty team is throwin' go in the hoop. I have been watchin' these other boys run they drills, and I'm tellin' you, Malik, you can run circles around every one of them." I bounce the ball five times. Coach always knew how to make us all get focused. His favorite phrase was, "Play the game."

And we did.

We ran quick, offensive plays that put our guy near the hoop. We put up a good defense, sometimes even preventing them from reaching the half-court mark. We shot the ball, stole the ball, ran the ball, and passed the ball quickly and efficiently. The other team attempted to intimidate with fancy alley-oop plays that did not seem to consistently get the ball in the hoop. "Play the game," he kept saying. By halftime, we were twelve points ahead. We just kept meeting them where they were on the court. Methodically. We outplayed the pretty white team. No one in the bleachers could believe it. No one, except Coach, who had known all of us since we were kids, had watched us play basketball on our dinky courts and had a sense of how tight that would make us as a team, thanks to his guidance. That day at Grantside was a game-changer in my mind. We won the game. It was astonishing for us. Our moms in the stands went nuts. The Grantside team never saw it coming. There were high-fives, hoots, and whistles on the bus ride home. We were all on cloud nine. But thinking about all of that, for me, the best part of that day was seein' Moms up in the stands yellin' and cheerin' like she was a kid. I almost screwed up a few plays because I was lookin' up in the stands to watch her watch me.

That day against Grantside was probably the best day in my young life. But like so many things growing up poor, it seemed there was always a dark cloud around the good stuff. The after-effect of that day at Grantside came about by knowing my school and neighborhood weren't shiny. They weren't clean. And they sure weren't white. When we were doing the hand slap after the game, teams lined up and passed one another to give the "good game" chant to each player. There were a few players who muttered the N-word. Their coach seemed not to notice. Coach Carl did. He walked up to the other coach and told him what he overheard. The other coach just shrugged his shoulders and said, "Good game, coach," neglecting to shake hands before walking away.

The lesson learned that day was that pretty, shiny things can be ugly. It stuck with me, too. I think somewhere on the basketball court with my teammates, I developed a sense of pride in my neighborhood. I came to understand that people would underestimate me coming from a poor, Black neighborhood. My Mom always taught me to be proud of my accomplishments and of where I came from.

When it came time for high school, I had to leave our neighborhood and take the bus to a school a few miles away, Pierson High School. Now that I was older, Moms started working full-time again. I know that being on food stamps and receiving welfare bothered my mother. Her options were limited, though. Our neighborhood, no matter how much we both loved our house and friends, was a dangerous place. She worked part-time during the day at Speedway, a convenience store. She bused to work after seeing me off to school, worked six hours, then bused back. We had a car when I was little, but Pops sold it out from under Moms. My being in high school with basketball practice and other after-school activities gave Moms the time to work again. She was ready for it, too. She was only fifteen years older than me, still young. The freedom of having a child who could look after himself really helped bring some energy back into her life.

Moms found herself again.

When I graduated from high school, I had a 3.5 GPA and the potential for a basketball scholarship. Moms and I looked at every way possible to send me to college. Scholarships became larger if I traveled away from Columbus, but I didn't want to leave Moms and my hood. Living at home would save almost as much money as the scholarships gave. So, I decided to stay at home and attend Ohio State University, just a #6 and #2 bus ride away.

College changed my life. I had friends. I had *white* friends. I did well in classes. I played basketball too, but I was so much shorter than the rest of the starting team that I only played when we were ahead by a large margin or if we were in a point crunch. I'm pretty sure that's the reason I made the OSU team. I could run faster than most of the six-footers and sink three-pointers nearly all the time.

During my sophomore year, I took a class to fulfill a graduation requirement, having declared sociology as my major. The class was Social Engineering, and it came with a project requirement to help organize an event in a neighborhood in need. It would be done in conjunction with three to five other students, with the goal of teaching team dynamics, as stated in the syllabus. The project would be evaluated based on letters of fulfillment from individuals within the neighborhood. I decided I would create The Four Corners Neighborhood Initiative. I invited three friends in the class to help create the event.

I was the only one from the neighborhood; the other three were white guys with good intentions from outside the community. My friend Drake and I played a lot of basketball together, so we headed up a two-on-two basketball tournament. My two other friends, Adam and Keith, thought of organizing a speed chess tournament since they both were avid players.

Over the course of the semester, we networked with several

churches, schools, and the library to create the events. The churches were happy to volunteer their parking lots and offered to have their various committees make food for the event. The school was very interested in the affair. The PTA organized a book fair, and the senior class offered to organize relay races and other games for kids. The Four Corners Neighborhood Initiative really took off.

Surprisingly, the speed chess tournament turned out to be one of the most popular events. Right off the bat, a ragged old Black guy who everyone called Smitty kicked everyone's ass. Everyone in the neighborhood knew Smitty could play chess, but to see him soundly defeat two squeaky-clean white boys from OSU was the height of the tournament.

The Four Corners Neighborhood Initiative was a tremendous success. Drake, Adam, Keith, and I received glowing reports, and we aced the class. What we didn't expect was the reaction of the neighborhood to the event. The churches were enthused and devoted themselves to partnering with the library and schools to keep the event alive.

We participated in the event throughout college and continued to attend after graduation. Neither Adam nor Drake ever beat Smitty, yet they returned year after year to try their best to do so. The annual chess tournament turned the Four Corners Neighborhood Initiative into a weekend-long event each year. It was one of the most highly attended events in the neighborhood, ranking just behind high school graduations and the middle school fall carnival. It also sparked the interest of dozens of kids in chess. The middle and high schools both started chess clubs. It became the new standard for Four Corners kids to carry portable chess kits in their backpacks.

About six years into the tournament, Smitty was diagnosed with cancer. The neighborhood watched as he played chess against opponent after opponent. Even though he was sick, Smitty beat everyone who challenged him. The chess tournament quickly became known as Smitty's Tournament, and Smitty had his own table where he could sit throughout the day.

A few months after the sixth annual Four Corners Neighborhood Initiative weekend, Smitty passed away. He died quietly with no family nearby. There were a few people, though, who sat with him in the hospital. Moms did when she could. Moms' friend Clarice did too, along with some folks from the churches. But it was Adam, the dopey white kid from Akron, my friend from OSU, who sat with him most. They had bonded throughout the years. When Smitty passed, Adam took it hard.

Smitty was not a churchgoer, but the churches all vied to host a funeral service for him. How odd that a person so introverted had become a neighborhood icon. Kids mimicked the way he shuffled down the street, not out of disrespect, but as a sort of close-knit inside joke that came from their love of the old guy. Smitty always wore a jaunty cap, too. The high school kids were soon wearing them, turned to the side, of course. Nearly all the participants in the tournament wore them. When the churches finally decided to hold a joint service in the high school auditorium for Smitty, everyone showed up, many of them wearing their jaunty caps.

It just always felt odd without Smitty in the neighborhood. Moms and Clarice often talked about him when we visited Clarice's house, and I sat with Shonda, Clarice's daughter with Down Syndrome. Smitty was a frequent subject in the conversations of the kids and teachers at school who participated in the chess clubs. He had made an impression on the heart of the neighborhood.

Even after his death, it became clear that he was not done making an impression. Smitty, the humble little pauper who taught a neighborhood how to play chess, was Charles A. Smith, a former

English professor at Howard University, a highly esteemed Black college in Washington, DC. He was from the neighborhood and quietly moved back after his tenure had ended. Smitty had always lived in the same small, understated home, with no fanfare. The only significant expense the community could see was the team of gardeners who showed up weekly to keep his yard in immaculate order.

All this information about Smitty came during the following year's kickoff for the Four Corners Neighborhood Initiative. The master of ceremonies, with tears in her eyes, came to the podium after the high school choir sang the *Star-Spangled Banner*. It took her a few attempts, but finally, she announced with a trembling voice that Smitty's will left no less than one hundred thousand dollars to the event. She went on to tell the shocked audience that Smitty had also established a scholarship program for children participating in the chess tournament.

There was utter silence in the crowd. Good news is hard to come by and often met with suspicion. It took a few moments, but finally, one of the church ladies yelled, "Praise the Lord!" Her utterance was the catalyst for the raucous applause that arose from the stunned crowd. Smitty's gift held the promise of real change. One hundred thousand dollars was a lot for a small neighborhood program, especially in Four Corners. Thankfully, a school board member and a neighborhood resident who worked at the local credit union offered to help formalize plans for utilizing the money. Drake, Adam, Keith, and I were dumbstruck. Watching this program, which was nothing more than a few pages of brainstorming seven years ago, became a true-life game changer for the neighborhood, for *my* neighborhood. It was astounding.

That year, Smitty's Table became real. Six concrete tables topped with granite chessboards were constructed in the vacant lot beside what used to be Cliff's Shop. Funds from Smitty's endowment went to buy the property from the Columbus Land Bank. Exterior safety lighting and high-end security monitors were installed. A large plaque in his honor was mounted right by the sidewalk that read:

> *"These young guys are playing checkers.*
> *I'm out there playing chess."*
> \- Kobe Bryant

The money from Smitty's gift helped transform tragic memories going back two decades. The death of that little girl and the turn of events that led to a dark history between the CPD and the neighborhood could perhaps now all turn a corner. The following year, after everything was built, the chief of police for the city of Columbus came down personally to kick off the event. He even sat down and played the first game of chess. He was beaten within three minutes by an eleven-year-old Black kid from Four Corners named Davion.

It was a good day.

CHAPTER NINE

Caleb — We Meet Again

Often, I feel a little like Forrest Gump sitting on that park bench telling a tale, only instead of developmental delays like Forrest had, I have a mental illness. It depends on the day. It can also depend on the hour. My brain chemistry flows a bit like one of those Icelandic volcanoes that erupts regularly in an irregular pattern. I watched a documentary about them on the Discovery Channel at the library. The spine of underwater volcanoes, stretching north and south along the bottom of the Atlantic Ocean, splits North America from South America and separates them from Europe and Africa. At one point, it rises to the surface, essentially creating multiple volcanoes and the nation of Iceland. A volcano, when dormant, provides beautiful landscapes and pastoral scenes. And then it erupts. Many have what is called a high volcanic explosivity index, meaning that when it erupts, it does so with epic force, causing widespread disruption.

That's me: regularly irregular with a high explosivity index.

When my neurochemistry is stable, I'm a serene component of the landscape, like Forrest Gump telling a tale on a park bench. When neurotransmitters and physiology begin sparking and elevating the ground beneath my psyche, that park bench starts shaking. Only I don't feel it. I don't know why people move away from my mounting energy. That confuses and compounds my mindset until my mind creates these eruptions.

I'm sure I'm a sight to see when the mania peaks. I'm even more certain that I become quite frightening when that mania passes into psychosis. I'm a big guy with a shaved head. I may seem intimidating, but I'm harmless. However, without someone nearby to calm the storm, who's to know I'm harmless? So, I rage. I erupt. I happen. I destroy relationships. I create scenes. I burn bridges. I delete social media accounts. I burn through cash. I file for businesses online. I write scathing editorials. I go berserk spectacularly.

I wish I could remember passwords to past Facebook or Gmail accounts. I've been journaling for over a decade, but I never have more than a few months' worth of entries to read. I'd really love to read what I wrote in the past. I can't remember much of it unless it's an article or poem that I have managed to get published. I recall the storylines of novels I started writing. I remember themes in poetry I have created. But the journaling I do is different. I want to read the old entries, hoping to fill in the blanks in my memory. I can remember waking up in hospitals, but not the days, sometimes weeks, leading up to the hospitalizations. Each time I wake up in the hospital, I can almost guarantee the written record has perished along with it.

There are lightning strikes of memory. They stop me in my tracks. Images of scared faces react to me. Memories flash and draw breath out of me so severely that I gasp to replace them. Everything everyone has said to me in the past that has broken my crown ricochets through my head.

And the words drop into place...

> I exist in balance, forces in status
> burning, churning, ebbing, returning.
> An unseen force will alter course,

burning fast, lacking remorse.
Crippling mind, a man left yearning,
to exist in balance, not lost in the stratus.

...but the words get swept away by the woman next to me sneezing loudly. I put in my earbuds and play k.d. lang's Ingenue album. I'm on the #3 riding to catch the #11 so I can take up my regular seat at the Columbus Metropolitan Library's Main Branch on Grant Street. There is a light drizzle. I get off the bus on State Street in front of the hospital. I remembered to buy a weeklong bus pass, so I don't have to find change for the bus constantly. It's a great deal. It makes a significant difference to have access to the entire city. I can now easily get to the shelter, the library, social services, and any job interviews I may get in the next few days, now that I'm working with Malik.

The library is just across the street from the hospital. It's a stately building with a nice statuary and benches out front. The marble steps bring you up to the iron security glass doors. The foyer has beautiful, evocative sculptures hanging from the ceiling. I don't know if 'sculpture' is the right word for something hanging from a ceiling, but the large globes are woven art pieces with a bold, overhead presence.

The artwork and intimacy of the foyer sit in contrast to the large openness of the three-story lobby, intruded upon by escalators leading to the second and third floors. In comparison to the foyer, the lobby is white, clean, and open. Glass railings along the second and third floors make it appear more spacious. I really love it. The openness, to me, is like taking a large fresh breath. The simplicity of open space is calming after the tight quarters of the shelter.

Usually, I love entering this big, grand building. Today, for whatever reason, my chest is tight. I feel like I've had too much coffee, but the coffee they serve at the shelter is decaf. I take solace in the winter scene the library has set up: an elaborate train set winding around miniature snow-capped mountains, through multiple stone tunnels, tiny pine trees, and fancy castle-like buildings. It appears to be a pristine scene from a remote area in the Swiss Alps. It was done without any overt Christmas décor, yet still exudes a Christmas theme. Librarians are clever that way.

I cross the grand room toward the coffee venue and gift shop. I tried the coffee once and wasn't particularly fond of it, which is unfortunate because I'd much rather my money go toward the library than Starbucks. But I just can't abide bad coffee. I feel warm, so I take off my coat. I look around for an empty table on the first floor and don't find any. Turning around, I walk to the elevator and take it up to the third floor, where I find a table hidden behind the Ohio State Map section and the stacks of books. This spot in the library is my unofficial hiding place. I know the third-floor librarians already. There are a few tables apart from the rest of the library where I can usually sit and read or write in peace for long hours.

Man, my chest is uncomfortable.

I set my backpack down on the ground next to the chair and take a seat. I take out my computer and phone along with their corresponding cords and get plugged in. A piece of paper pops out, and I remember it's my list of books to grab for the long weekend before the library closes for Thanksgiving. I selected a collection of John Steinbeck stories, a new Michael Connelly novel, and the *Complete Collection of Shakespeare's Sonnets.* I'm always so enamored by the great poets. I admire their skill in communicating complex ideas with words that flow like rivers. I try to write with their aplomb, but I know I'm inept compared to the poets I try to read daily.

As I get settled into my spot, I check my phone to see if any texts or emails have come through. There is one phone call. I stare at the phone. I don't receive many calls. It's an Unknown Caller, too. It came in while I was on the bus. I put my palms flat on the table.

I don't like phone calls. I don't like messages. I usually have the phone icon hidden and the ringtone on silent. I set the phone aside and finish setting up my impromptu workstation. I use a small binder with paper to take notes while I have my computer screen filled up with the text of my novel. It's a good way to take notes without having to change screens.

On the table, my phone vibrates. *Weird*, it's shut off.

I put my palms back on the smooth, cool table to ground myself.

My breath quickens. I feel tired. I feel like I'm

... slipping.

Am I slipping?

Yes, I'm slipping. I feel the water.

My phone vibrates and vibrates and vibrates.

It's him.

It's hard for me to move my arm from the table.

to my backpack where I want to get

a napkin to wipe my forehead.

My mouth is dry.

I reach and turn off the phone, again.

It vibrates again. *Again.*

The water rises. My hearing becomes muted.

Why is this happening?

I look again at my phone: Unknown Caller

Chest. Is. Tight.

Who is calling?

How are they calling?

My phone is off now.

My eyelids close and open slowly.

With much concentration,

I move my hand to my phone.

It's darker in the library than I remember it being. I'm very thirsty.

I bring the phone to my ear. "Hello?"

...nothing...

"Hello!"

...nothing...

My breath quickens. My face is hot. My eyelids lower.

It's him. I know it's him.

I try to put the phone down, but I don't want to let go. I work to push my chair back, but it feels heavy. Everything moves in slow motion. I finally get to standing. I'm so hot. Sweating.

My breathing is erratic.

Is he here?

I look around me and try to see through the stacks.

With my head down, I walk toward the wall.

I make my way toward the drinking fountain.

I'm holding my phone so hard my hand is beginning to shake.

I'm underwater.

That's when it happens.

Correction.

That's when I happen.

I look for Craig and see glimpses of him disappearing behind walls, slipping onto elevators.

He's down there.

Someone yelling breaks the silence, and I gasp for air.

The yelling, loud and throaty, comes from nearby.

Looking down at the lobby, I see everyone looking up at me.

Several mothers, looking at the perfect winter scene, grab their kids.

"He's here!" someone yells.

...and I realize it's me yelling.

I'm yelling about Craig. *Again.*

Security is on the lobby floor.

They are looking up at me and talking on their radios.

"Help me," I scream. "Get him."

I listen to the voice and realize I must get away...

Four security guards meet on the lobby floor. Two guards start coming up the stairs, their eyes never leaving me.

The other two wait on the ground floor.

OK, I gotta get out of here.

I can't let Craig get to me.

Security downstairs is looking for him,

so I am going to take the elevator.

I back up to the elevators about twenty feet behind me and repeatedly press the down button. Third-floor librarians look at one another and then back at me. One of them is on the phone. My face is filled with tears, and I look at them frantically, pointing down. "He's down there."

They don't know how to respond. So, they stand there.

Looking back at me.

The elevator doors open.

I step in and press the down button aggressively.

The doors close, and I sink onto the floor.

I can feel Craig looking at me.

I see his reflection in the stainless-steel elevator door.

I can hear the voice screaming again.

Or is it me screaming?

I don't know.

As the doors close, I hear one of the librarians shout, "He's going down!" *How can Craig be going down; he was in the lobby... wasn't he?*

Beethoven's *Moonlight Sonata* is playing in the elevator.

I love *Moonlight Sonata.*

I can play that on the piano.

My eyes are closed, so I don't see Craig.

The doors open, and a flurry of activity happens. There is a wall of black uniforms. I see waist belts full of gear and security personnel with their hands on tasers.

I hear, "Sir, we need you to calm down!"

I open my eyes.

Craig is standing behind the security guards.

I try and stand up, but I'm too tired.

I hear myself moaning.

"Sir, we need you to calm down!" I hear.

I open my eyes momentarily, and his face fills my mind.

I get to my feet.

He's right behind them.

I stumble forward, trying to get out of the library.

Wrong move.

I always make the wrong move.

I am happening...

again.

The wind is knocked out of my chest. Pain erupts through my face as my chin connects with the marble floor. I'm thrown to the ground. I smell blood. I taste blood. My arms are pulled behind me. I hear the clanking of handcuffs.

I remember handcuffs. In the closet. As a kid.

They were cold. They hurt. That was the point.

I hear them shouting at each other. They are expecting me to struggle.

I do not.

If you struggle, he just does it more.

The best thing is to forget about it. Drift away.

My arms and legs are bound. Craig is in control. I don't know how he called me and got the guards to cooperate with him. But none of that matters now. My vision blurs. Not from injury. It's what happens when Craig is in control. My hearing is muted. I am underwater. I don't hear their voices, but I still hear the *Moonlight Sonata* clear in my head. My arms are stretched behind me, bound in cuffs. It hurts, but that doesn't register. Nothing registers. They shout at me to get to my feet.

"OK," I say meekly.

"Now walk."

"OK."

A baton slips between my cuffs and the small of my back. He pilots me out the back door away from the crowd, where one of the cops is already working with security to tell people that everything is OK.

Everything is OK.

I've heard that a lot. It rarely is OK.

I see Craig off to the left through my fuzzy vision. He's laughing. He's got his gun in his hand. He's petting the barrel of his pistol. I turn my head slowly toward one of the cops escorting me out, and he slaps my head straight forward again. Craig laughs.

I hear my name spoken by a familiar voice. "Caleb...what

happened?" It comes from a flustered librarian. I know her. We've had a few conversations about Billy Collins' poetry. His poem *An Afternoon with Irish Cows* drops into my mind…what was the last phrase of that poem?

"*…she regarded my head and shoulders above the wall with one wild, shocking eye.*"

"Don't talk to him," a cop shouts back.

That's the last thing I remember…her one wild, shocking eye, looking at me.

CHAPTER TEN

Malik — Bay Four

I'm sitting in the conference room searching the same old outlets for information on my father when my phone buzzes on the table. My screen reads: Franklin County Hospital. Hmmm...that's unexpected. *Why am I getting a call from the hospital?* I don't have any clients who recently transferred there.

"Hello?" I answer.

"Hello, is this Malik Arons?" a woman's voice asks, mispronouncing my name.

"Yes, is this Franklin County Hospital?"

"It is. Do you know a Caleb Taylor?"

...from this morning. "I do."

"Are you in service to Mr. Taylor as a social worker?"

"Why don't you tell me what's going on before I talk about Mr. Taylor?"

There is a slight huff on the other end of the line. "Actually, I can't until I understand the relationship between you and Mr. Taylor. HIPAA."

"Yes, I have Mr. Taylor as a client."

"OK, thank you. Mr. Taylor was admitted to the ER and is currently waiting to be transferred to the BHU. Paperwork from The Crossroads Men's Emergency Shelter was in his jeans pocket, and your business card was stapled to it."

"I see."

"His wallet has a Medicare and Medicaid card, so he's OK to be admitted, but we need to contact someone who can oversee his discharge and take him home when released."

"Gotcha."

"Can you be that person, Mister?"—she pauses to check her notes— "Arons?"

Can I be that person? I think to myself. *I'm not obligated to do anything. I should turn this over to Case Management.* Tap. Tap. Tap. Tap. Tap. *I should mind my own business. He's not even a client anymore.* But even as I'm thinking, I already know I will go down there. Problems. I like to solve them. Tap. Tap. Tap. Tap. Tap. So, I guess I'm going to try to solve Caleb. The woman and I continued to talk. There aren't many details, just that something happened while he was at the library. It sounds like a psychotic episode. I can't fathom how this calm and competent guy I just met could create such a problem. That is, however, the hallmark of mental illness—it is essentially an invisible illness, until it's not.

There are many ways to approach my goal of helping Caleb. The professional approach would be to advise the front desk monitor that a client has been hospitalized and, therefore, should be removed from their client list and their bed given to the next client on the list. That's what I *should* do.

Another option would be to speak to the program administrator about getting some exceptions for Caleb. A psych admission is a medical issue, so the shelter won't kick him out for being hospitalized. I chuckle at my naiveté. No, they absolutely will kick him out. I know that. It's the beginning of winter. Beds are needed. Someone who does not check in automatically forfeits their bunk. I see it done repeatedly. It happens so fast. They pull all the sheets off the bunk, spray it with cleanser, re-sheet the bed, and pass it on to the next guy. Anything in their locker is placed into a black Hefty bag, sealed with duct tape, and stored in cold storage, labeled with their name written on masking tape. They will have two weeks to retrieve it.

If he is kicked out of the shelter, he will also be removed from the housing program. *What else can be done?* I do have one option. I think about Drake and any openings he might have in one of his renovated houses, but that will have to come later. First things first. Caleb is lying in the hospital, strapped to a bed, according to the hospital personnel. It is four thirty in the afternoon. He's been there since two, after the arrest. I can leave now and go to the hospital and see how he is doing, and maybe discuss options about what will happen when he gets out of the hospital. I exhale. Tap. Tap. Tap. Tap. Tap.

My two officemates are discussing their client cases with one another. "Hey, guys, I'm taking the day off. I'm going to swing by the hospital and check on a client who got admitted."

"OK," they both say in unison.

La Rae asks, "Hey, did you get the email about the Crisis Intervention Team training? It got moved to the following Saturday."

"Yeah, I saw that," I answer. "Thanks." I gather up my backpack and begin to leave.

Dex adds, "Peace out, bro."

"My man, Dex," I reply. I fist-bump both on my way out of the office and schlep my backpack over my shoulder. It has my laptop, reusable grocery bags, a collapsible umbrella, and a few case files that I will review this evening.

I turn left to exit the building by the restricted access door. I do this most of the time to avoid running into client questions. I should make myself more available to clients, but it is a matter of completing the daily workload. It is relentless. I am already taking work home each evening to catch up, so slipping out the restricted-access door is okay.

I open the door to find that this escape is not without foil. A few guys are standing underneath the eaves, getting out of the wind as they smoke their home-rolled cigarettes filled with cheap tobacco. I don't recognize them, but I know they're clients.

"'Sup," I chirp.

There is a smattering of responses: "Fine," "Good," and a nod from underneath gray and black hoodies. It is such a forced exchange, but at least they participate in the societal custom of greeting each other. I learned that you never ask, "How are you?" Most guys are OK, but sometimes asking how someone is leads them to explode on you. How they are is not a good situation. Asking "How are you?" is, in all honesty, condescending. So, unless I'm meeting directly with a client, greetings are kept to "'Sup."

I slip past the clients and walk into the parking lot, reaching into my pocket for keys. I click the key fob, and the lock to my silver Kia Forte disengages. I bought the car a few years back. My first new car. It felt great to buy a new car, knowing I had the finances to put money down, afford the $279 monthly payment, and pay the $112 insurance premium. I have a pretty solid life.

I am still renting an apartment while saving to buy a home. It's such a huge expense; it always makes me nervous. I am not in a hurry, even though renting an apartment is considered a waste of money. I'm not ready to buy yet. I have gone with Keith to look at another fixer-upper Drake is going to buy. Perhaps that makes me wary, because any house I could afford would most likely need repairs. I am not handy that way, and anything I can afford now isn't in a neighborhood I want. Despite growing up in Four

Corners and loving my old neighborhood, if I have kids, I'd like them to have more opportunities and a yard where they can play safely.

I back out of the shelter parking lot and drive downtown.

What am I doing? Why am I doing it?

Tap. Tap. Tap. Tap. Tap. I keep asking myself, and I keep tapping. I'm driving to see someone who is no longer a client. I wouldn't have even known about it had that damned paperwork not been in his pocket. It's my superhero complex again. Without much assessment, I am responding to need. That's a phrase Moms used. She always taught me the importance of trying to understand people. "*Sometimes you need to step up and respond to need,*" she would say. My mom grew up going to church, but I don't think she would consider herself a Christian anymore. The church and its members, women we called the Thumpers, were tough on her when she got pregnant. The abuse she suffered from Pops also made her feel, perhaps, that if there was a God, he wasn't watching out for her. I'll be damned, though, if she didn't lead more of a Christian life than most who proclaimed to be people of faith. She lived the Gospel without having to preach it. When the Thumpers got on her case, Moms would raise a hand and say, "Hallelujah."

So, here I am, responding to need without knowing the outcome of doing so. *I don't have control over this, but I can get control of my life.* I repeat the phrase and consider if I want this to be a part of my life. *Will this somehow erode my way of life, even if only for the short term?*

Traffic is light. I make the trip downtown in about ten minutes. I turn into the gaping entrance to the parking lot next door to the hospital. I grab my ticket from the electronic dispenser, and the metal arm in front of me rises, allowing me to drive through.

I park on the third level and put the ticket on my dashboard as instructed. The first hour is free; let's hope I can get in and out of here without it costing anything. I walk into the skybridge hallway, which connects the parking lot to the hospital. I enter the hospital and look at the signs hanging from the ceiling: ER, Oncology, Neonatal, Lobby. I need the ER, and the arrow pointing down indicates taking the elevator to the first level.

I step into the elevator and press "L" for the lobby. Muzak is playing some classical version of an eighties pop tune. *Odd*, I think. *I wonder what the eighties celebrity singer would think about their tune ending up as some elevator arrangement.* You never know what the stuff you put into the world will end up looking like.

The elevator door opens. The third floor, where I enter the hospital, is nice and orderly. This changes dramatically as I enter the ER. The waiting room is filled with an assortment of characters akin to a carnival event. There is crying, coughing, moaning, and arguing. An enormous man with blood on his shirt and a hand wrapped in a bathroom towel, also soaked with blood, sits next to a mother and father clutching a colicky baby. A white trash family dressed in sweats and hard rock T-shirts stands around a young woman with the better part of her earlobe ripped away and a blossoming black eye. There is what looks like an extended Latino family sitting around an elderly woman who is red in the face and coughing a very congested cough. I identify another head wound, someone with a breathing mask hooked to an oxygen tank, and several others with varying degrees of injury.

ERs take admissions based on a triage routine. If Caleb had been strapped to a gurney upon entrance, he would have been admitted immediately. I approach the counter, where three women are intensely engaged with their keyboards. Behind the women are a few nurses looking at paperwork and trying to keep the circus in the front waiting room under control. To say this place is as busy as a beehive would be an understatement. I have some experience with the extensive paperwork that can be required for clients. It must be ten times worse in an emergency department setting. No one looks up at me as I wait for a few minutes. Tap. Tap. Tap. Tap. Tap. Finally, I venture to say, "How may I find a patient who was admitted here?"

Without looking up, the woman in the middle asks bluntly, "Name?"

"Caleb Taylor."

"Date of birth?"

"Um, I'm sorry, I don't have his file with me." Mentioning a file garners me a quick look from the woman still typing furiously at her keyboard.

"Relationship to Mr. Taylor?"

"I'm his caseworker," I lie. I know hospital staff are typically happy to have a case worker around with homeless or psychiatric patients. It allows answers to be given quickly and usually means an admission is shorter and less chaotic. For the moment, though, there is just more urgent typing.

"ID," she says, and I hand her my shelter badge. She looks briefly at the badge, types a few more things into the computer, and says, "Four B. Do you know your way through the admission bays?"

"Yes," I lie again, but I'm guessing they will be marked.

"OK, you can go back."

She hands me a visitor badge, which I clip to my shirt. I walk past the nurses and through the ER doors. Tap. Tap. Tap. Tap. Tap. The ER bays are more organized and subdued than the waiting room, which presented like a casting call for the next *Saw* movie. In the ER bays, patients lie on portable beds separated by curtains. Each bed has its own row of machinery, the uses of which are beyond my level of understanding. As I suspected, there is distinct signage for the bays. If I turn right, I will go to beds one to eight. If I turn left, I will go to beds nine to fifteen. The nine to fifteen bays must be for the more serious cases. There is moaning coming from one bay, crying from another. The bays where Caleb is seem quieter and less emergent. As I walk down the corridor, bed one contains an incredibly old and tiny woman lying face up, mouth open. In bed two, there are several quiet and sad people holding vigil around an older man who is barely noticeable beneath the blankets. Bed three contains a young kid of about ten years old, his parents at his side. His leg is in a splint, and his face is riddled with bruises.

I arrive at bed four, Caleb's bay, and pull back the curtain.

Empty.

Dammit.

CHAPTER ELEVEN

Caleb — Again

I'm in my bunk at the shelter. The overhead lights turn on. It's early. A rush of comfort runs through me as I turn over to put my palm against the wall. I want its reassuring coolness. I move my arm to feel the wall but am caught by a restraint on my forearm. I raise my other arm only to have it catch as well. A slight movement of my legs indicates that my ankles are also restrained. Once again, I woke up in a strange hospital with bruises, trophies from another altercation with the police.

My heart sinks like a prisoner who has dreams of freedom but wakes up to find the bars jutting up from the prison floor. The weight of my circumstance descends upon me like my foot in that icy puddle on my first day in Columbus.

And the words drop into place:

> Raising hand to cheek
> to confirm I am here,
> restraint on wrist and ankle,
> why can't I disappear?
> Tethered to a bed
> without an iota of control,
> poses the question
> is life worth the toll?

I realize my clothes are gone, and the words fall away. I'm in a hospital gown, which means at some point I was naked, and someone handled my body. I wonder who. I don't even like being naked when I'm alone. I spent my childhood not being in control of my body. I try to push away the feeling of despair, but it is pernicious. Looking through squinted eyes, I recognize the components of a standard ER room. The weight of my situation presses me into the hospital bed. I'm strapped down, which means, at some point, I became violent or was perceived as violent. Slivers of memory come back. Craig was there. He always is when I go underwater. I remember cursing at the police. I remember a struggle. I remember being tackled. I remember the taste of blood in my mouth.

When will life change?

I can feel the beast waiting in the shadows. I've been here so many times. The question I've asked myself time and time again floats to the surface. *Why does it happen?* Trying hard to ignore the thirst in my mouth, I endeavor to remember.

I remember the Cold Toast Buffet.

I remember being sluggish at the shelter.

I remember someone breaking through. *Malik talked to me this morning...then what?*

Someone told me I had to go. *Was I arrested?*

I realize that a sizable chunk of time is lost. That's not a good thing. I remember sitting in the cafeteria. I don't remember getting up from there. I remember being on the way to the library. *That's right...I was going to tally the pages and word count for my manuscript.*

For a few seconds, I feel like I'm getting somewhere, remembering something good. But that is swiftly replaced by remembering my chin smashing to the floor. I remember several pairs of black boots near my head as I lay there.

I remember wondering if the blood on the floor was mine.

I remember Craig's laughter and wishing I could move. I need to write these things down, or I'll forget them. And then, compounding my state of confusion and anxiety, I think about my computer, phone, backpack, and jacket. *Where are they?*

In the right side of my peripheral vision, something flutters. Someone has turned a page in a newspaper. It is a woman sitting near the door. She looks at me as I begin to rouse. She watches me for a minute. She picks up what appears to be a remote control and presses a button, turning the TV off. She looks like one of the ladies who would come to do crafts at the shelter. My mouth is desperately dry.

She looks over the pages of the newspaper she is reading. Our eyes meet. I can tell she has done this before, just as I have. She doesn't come out with a sugary greeting of hello as if a sweet persona is all a crazy person needs to regain their wits. Nope. This lady knows I could be schizophrenic and talk gibberish. She knows I could be a manic patient and talk nonsense at 1000 miles an hour, skipping over all forms of sanity. She also knows that I could be a sociopath, someone who doesn't care about anyone, and could punch her in the face to get to the glass of water on the tray in front of her. All she knows is that a guy is restrained after becoming a threat during a mental health crisis, and he is now waking up.

I ask what time it is as calmly as possible.

She considers the question, turns her arm to look at her watch, and replies, "Five thirty p.m."

"Thank you," I reply in a raspy voice. It's going to be curfew time at the shelter soon.

"You're welcome," she says noncommittally. She is a volunteer. Over time, I've found that most volunteers who sit on security watch for psych admissions in the ER do so because someone in their lives deals with mental illness. Volunteer monitors are free and more effective than paid staffers who have to take time out of their schedule to babysit.

I ask, "Have you been here long?"

"Since 2:30," she replies flatly. And then, a little softer, "Are you feeling better?"

I laugh softly, which sounds gritty through my dry throat. Her face relaxes a bit. "Well, isn't that the sixty-four-thousand-dollar question?" I get a smile.

"Yes," she replies after a few moments. "I suppose it is."

A brief pause. "Thanks for babysitting," I say, not knowing if she started before they sedated me or not. I'm sure, if history is any teacher, that I was sedated in the ambulance. The ambulance sedation is generally not as strong as the sedation they can give you once in the hospital, so I may still have come in screaming.

A few moments later, a nurse shows up with a stern face and hair pulled back tightly into a neat bun. Without looking at me, the nurse asks the volunteer, "How is he?"

"Just fine, Rita," she says softly. "He won't be a problem." And with that, the volunteer pats Rita on the arm, glances at me, folds her paper under her arm, and leaves.

"Can I take these restraints off you, or do you think you'll be a problem, Caleb?" Rita asks with one hand on her hip and the other holding a chart from which she is still reading. It's strange to have someone call you by name when you've never met. I see her name badge. It takes me a while to distinguish that teddy bears are clipped to it. That's when I discovered my glasses were gone.

"I won't be a problem," I say softly.

"Is that a promise I can believe?" she says, finally considering my eyes. Hers are deep brown, surrounded by crow's feet from too many hours doing what she's doing right now.

"Yes," I respond.

She sets out to undo the straps. I allow her to do so without protest. She does my legs first, and my only motion is to cross my legs at the ankle. When she moves up to my arms, I can see her face clearly for the first time. She's seen a lot of this. When she looks at me, she's not seeing me. She's evaluating whether this will get ugly or if I will react violently like so many soft-spoken people in my position no doubt have done before. To be honest, I'm surprised she doesn't have some security with her. Something in her mind has already answered the question of whether I will be a problem. When she unstraps my arms, I place my hands over my belly.

"Thirsty?" she asks, already reaching for the bed tray with a water pitcher next to where the volunteer had been sitting.

"Yes, I am." My words are still a bit soggy from whatever sedative they applied.

She moves the bed tray over to me, pushing the table part over my midsection. "Just take sips first," she says. "You're still coming down off the sedative, and you don't want to upset your stomach."

"Yes, ma'am," I answer.

While I am bringing a cup of water to my mouth, she walks around the bed and takes my blood pressure. It is then that I notice an oxygen meter is already on my finger. She takes it off after reading 99%.

"Your systolic number is higher than it should be, but I think you are out of danger," she says. She adds, "You had some bad numbers when you came in here."

Not knowing what to say in response, I simply say, "Thank you."

She steps back after putting the blood pressure cuff away. She has one hand on her hip again and one hand holding the chart. I imagine she often stands this way.

"I hope you get better, Caleb," she says with a touch of empathy in her voice. She knows the life many people with mental illness live. Her comment is a nicety. We both know it probably will not get better.

"Me too," I say.

She turns without another word and leaves the room.

So, here I am.

Again.

Now that Rita is gone, the heaviness comes back and presses into me. This is it: my life of unwanted psychotic episodes, shelter bunks, curfew violations, and lost beds. And always, like an unwanted reunion, life back on the streets. I'm sure dozens of Facebook feeds are featuring my meltdown right now. A life of scaring young kids and police intervention seems inevitable. Mine is a life of bloodied chins and limbs in restraints. People always talk about suicide never being an option. I would say to them, "Maybe it is, goddammit. A life must be worth living, not just a sentence to be served while living."

It feels like the words should drop in place, but the sedation and my exhaustion block them from landing. All I see are fragments:

Fists in restraints.

Craig recessed inside me.

The concrete sedation.

Volcanoes...

Staring up at the ceiling, I reflect upon my unwanted life. I've been in therapy most of my adult life. I've been on every medication known to all the psychiatrists who have interviewed me. I've been diagnosed with schizophrenia, PTSD, bipolar disorder, major depression, and dissociative identity disorder — one even went out on a limb and diagnosed me with psychogenic fugue states, a condition like dissociative disorder just on steroids.

I've been a willing participant in these psychiatric endeavors. At one point, we thought we had made a breakthrough when we discovered I was diabetic and that perhaps my high blood sugars were co-mingling with my psychiatric symptoms to exacerbate everything. I took medication for diabetes, lost a bunch of weight, and became an avid walker, which is a good thing for someone who experiences homelessness. I discovered the Appalachian Trail and the Pacific Crest Trail, both of which traverse the United States from north to south. The Pacific Crest Trail goes from the border of Mexico to the border of Canada. The Appalachian Trail starts in Georgia and goes all the way to the top of Maine. When I had money for the bus, I would ride to one of the trails and hike for days on end. Sometimes, I did it while I was in a manic state, but most of the time, I went because I truly loved it. We got hopeful when I went for eighteen months without an episode. I even found a job.

Then Craig showed up at work.

I destroyed the copy machine and basically took two co-workers hostage in a storage room with me before the cops came. I was out of a job and into police custody before the staff went back to work after lunch. And, just like that time, I realize now that I am most likely out of a job again. If you don't show up at the assembly line, they replace you with the next decrepit soul.

With all the therapy I've undergone, all the medications I have swallowed, and all the electricity that has coursed through my brain, I still have visions of Craig. He wasn't my dad, my brother, or a creepy uncle. Craig was part of my idyllic childhood. I don't say that in jest. Were it not for Craig, I really would have had a perfect childhood. My dad worked full-time at a great job. My mom was a full-time homemaker. My backyard fence backed up to the elementary school where my brother and I went to school.

We all attended church on Sunday mornings and youth group on Wednesday evenings. Our Protestant church culture made us less likely to make a fuss about things like neighborhood pets going missing or kids who cried when they went near Craig's house.

I cried once upon a time, but eventually I stopped. In my young child's vocabulary, I couldn't explain what was happening. When I did try, I was told to mind my manners. I was repeatedly escorted into the lion's den when our families would get together. The lovely Protestant world I grew up in could not comprehend anything like what my six-year-old words were trying to say. I was told to behave, so I did.

That's when I learned to leave.

To disassociate.

To lose time.

To swim under the water.

Meanwhile, I became an overly sensitive kid. As a youngster, my emotions were over the top for things that seemed trivial because the big emotions were being suppressed deep down inside.

When I was a bit older, Craig killed his parents in a fashion that baffled police. He shot them one morning over breakfast and then sat in the driveway waiting for the police to arrive. Our families were gutted. The water rose to my neck, not enough to send me away, but enough to make my entire world feel muted. He was sent to prison, but even though he was securely behind bars, I would see him. He would be coming to get me, to kill me. He'd told me if I told anyone what was happening, I'd be punished.

I went once with the older siblings to a parole hearing for Craig. I was an adult. I wanted to see him in prison, to give me some relief that he actually was in prison behind steel bars. When we arrived, there was only space for a limited number of visitors. The others went inside. I sat in the car outside in the parking lot, looking at the large prison facility with its razor wire.

Was he really in there?

I went to the prison seeking closure; instead, I was denied confirmation that he was in a prison cell. My older sibling said he didn't show up for the hearing and that he stayed in his cell. The game my mind plays on me now is that he isn't in prison at all, since no one saw him. He's out. And I'm on his mind. The conversations we had as kids played over and over; in the dark places I had shut out. Now I deal with Craig showing up whenever he wants. And the sick part about it is, when I'm not psychotic, I know damn well that Craig is not after me. This puts front and center in my mind how completely nuts I really am.

•••

Rita pulls on some of the tubing used to draw blood from above my wrist. It startles me. I've drifted off into memories. My babysitter is no longer here, but I guess I've been lying here for about an hour waiting for the discharge papers. I remain calm while Rita finishes preparing me for my journey to the BHU.

I know the drill, so I behave. When the doctor monitoring my admission to the ER finally comes to see me, he keeps his eyes on the clipboard. He asks a few perfunctory questions, scribbles his name at the bottom of the forms, and utters the words, "Good luck." He still has not looked at me. I don't blame him. *How many malcontents like me come through his room? How much sympathy can you hold onto?*

Rita comes in with another woman: shorter, rounder, and less pleasant.

"Caleb, this is Carol. She's going to take you over to the BHU. Do you have any questions?"

"No."

"Good," Carol answers for Rita. "I have a few."

"Go ahead," I answer, noting her strawberry-blond hair. The top part is pulled back into a clip, and the rest is cut bluntly just above her shoulders. Her face is freckled, and I mean 100% of it is freckled. Her face is non-descript otherwise. She wears a white turtleneck shirt under her blue teddy bear scrubs.

"Can you sit up on your own accord?"

"Yes."

"Good, please do so."

"OK." I put my legs over the bed and touch the floor with my feet.

"Please put these on," she says, handing over a pair of socks with grips on the bottom to prevent me from falling.

"OK."

"Do you have any physical disabilities that would warrant special accommodations?"

"No."

"Do you have a regular psychiatrist?"

"In Columbus? No."

"Anywhere?"

"Yes, San Diego," I answer. The mention of San Diego causes her to click the end of her pen several times.

"Name of the treating psychiatrist?"

"Ben Cohen."

"What facility?"

"San Diego County Homeless Outreach Project."

"San Diego," she repeats. A slight shake of her head. She clicks her pen a few more times, attaches it to her paperwork, and says, "Please have a seat." She motions toward the wheelchair against the wall. "Hospital policy," she says as though I asked a question. She pushes me out the door and down the white sanitary hallway toward the BHU.

Those are the initials for the Behavioral Health Unit. That's what loony bins are called now. I get the reason for the new terminology; a behavioral health unit implies that our mental illnesses are behaviors rather than organic problems with brain chemistry. The whole terminology is just a little too Brave New World for me, like Berard Marx sitting in a boardroom discussing the benefits of classical conditioning to enhance the overall functioning of society.

The term Behavioral Health, at least to me, gives the shrinks an out. They can't understand why one minute I'm lucid, and the next I'm shouting in libraries, crying in grocery stores, or running through malls. Since they can't explain what's happening in my brain, the term Behavioral Health puts the responsibility on my behavior, not the actual cause of my lunacy.

I take stock of the fact that I'm on my way to yet another BHU where counselors and psychiatrists will positively talk to me because I'm calm, have an interesting vocabulary, and can speak to them without drooling on the paperwork. Generally, when I get admitted after a psychotic event like the one I had, they will keep me for forty-eight to seventy-two hours until their liability is covered. They will take notes on how their magic concoction of medication meets their standard of treatment for the diagnosis upon which they have settled. It's usually the same thing the last doctor diagnosed, with a tweak to make it their own.

CHAPTER TWELVE

Malik — No, really, I can't.

I walk back to the beehive that is the ER registration area. More people have arrived to stand with the elderly Latina woman. The man with the bloodied hand seems to have nodded off despite the blood-soaked rag. There are now a few young women dressed in cheerleader uniforms standing with another young cheerleader, whose ankle is swollen to the size of a cantaloupe. There are more people with less obvious issues sitting nervously.

I stand again momentarily to see if any of the women at the admitting desk will raise their eyes to ask if they can help me. Nothing. I interrupt them with a question.

Tap. Tap. Tap. Tap. Tap. "I went to 4 B, and the bay was empty. Can you tell me where Caleb Taylor is?"

All I hear in response is the sound of three keyboards being manipulated at high speed.

"He's not in 4 B?" one of the keyboard jockeys asks.

Tap. Tap. Tap. Tap. Tap. "No."

"One moment."

I look back into the ER crowd. Past the waiting room is the driveway for the ambulances. One is pulling in outside the admission doors. The back of the ambulance opens, and two medics jump down to pull the gurney out. They wheel the patient into the ER. There is a woman on the gurney dressed in a business suit strapped to the bed with an implement of some sort, perhaps a letter opener, protruding from bandages wrapped around her neck. Her chest is also strapped down to the bed. There is a profuse amount of blood on the right side of her body. As she is wheeled by, I see her eyes blinking. She's awake. *Dear God.*

My attention is brought back to the registration desk when one of the women says, "Sir?"

"Yes."

"Mr. Taylor is no longer in 4 B."

"Yes, I'm aware of that. I just came from 4 B, which is empty, so that's why I asked where he was," I said with a touch of irritation creeping into my voice.

"I'm sorry, sir, I can't tell you more about Mr. Taylor."

Tap. Tap. Tap. Tap. Tap. "What do you mean?"

"I have no further information for you."

Tap. Tap. Tap. Tap. Tap. "Where is he?" I demand.

"No, really, I can't give you any more information." For the first time, the woman looks up at me and stops working her keyboard, her eyebrow arching up. "You are a social worker, right?"

"Yes." *I don't have control over this, but I have control of myself.*

"He's no longer in the ER."

"Yes, I know." Tap. Tap. Tap. Tap. Tap.

"Sir, he's no longer in the ER."

"Yeah, I get it. What now?" Tap. Tap. Tap. Tap. Tap.

"You are aware of what kind of admission he was?" She blinks at me.

"Yes, there was a disturbance at the library, and he was brought here."

"Yes, sir. A disturbance," she says. "You are aware of what kind of disturbance?"

"Yes, of course!"

More blinking at me.

Then, it dawns on me what she is doing. The hospital moved him into the psych ward, probably for a forty-eight-hour involuntary hold. These admissions are private, and due to HIPAA laws, the hospital cannot confirm or deny an emergency psych admission. The nurse has deftly told me where he is without saying a word.

"Gotcha," I said.

"Good luck." She turned her head to the monitor again and began typing. I think about taking my chances on the floor where the BHU is located. I could present my credentials and ask about a client. I could tell them I'm family. I decide to give it a try. I walk out of the ER and into the main lobby of the hospital, where I find the elevators. Stepping on, I push the button for the fifth floor. A few people in hospital attire share the ride with me. Two people are talking about surgical procedures. The third is dressed in scrubs and listening to music through her earbuds.

A chime rings, indicating the second floor. The two doctors in white coats, engrossed in conversation, leave. The next floor is where the surgical theaters are, and the doctor in scrubs exits. I ride up to the fifth floor by myself. When the doors open, it is immediately apparent that this floor is different. Instead of Muzak, colorful watercolor paintings, and historical hospital pictures, there are stark, white hallways that smell of disinfectant. The hallways are equipped with heavy mechanical doors. The fifth floor is a labyrinth. It was not a part of the remodel a few years ago, so the signs hanging from the ceiling are worn. It feels like it could be used as a location for a horror movie in the near future if there were blinking overhead lights and a bit more dirt.

Finally, I reach a large plate-glass window with the letters

BHU stenciled above it. A few people are in the office, talking and working on paperwork. A younger woman with freckles and kinky curly hair sees me and slides the window open.

“Good afternoon,” she says in a surprisingly chipper tone.

“Hello,” I say, taking out my shelter badge. “I work at the Crossroads Shelter across town. A client of mine had an admission here this morning.”

“Do you know if your client put you down as someone we can share information with?”

“To be honest, I don’t know.”

She tilts her head to the left and says, “I’m sure you know I can’t give any patient information out.”

Tap. Tap. Tap. Tap. Tap. “Yes, I do know that. May I leave a note for him?”

“Yes, you can, but like I said, I cannot confirm whether your client is here or not unless he has given permission.”

“It’s Caleb Taylor, tall white guy.”

“Like I said, you can leave a note, but I can’t tell you if he’s here or if he’s gotten the note.”

“I understand completely.”

She pushes a small pad of paper and a pen through the slot at the bottom of the window. I’m not sure what I want to communicate now that I have the chance. I think for a few moments and proceed with something simple.

Hello Caleb.

This is Malik from the shelter. I just dropped by to see how you are. Feel free to call me if you need anything. (614)223-2978.

Malik

As I slide the note back to the staff person, I say, "Can I ask you a hypothetical?"

"OK, sure."

"If someone were to come in shortly after having a mental health crisis, is there a certain amount of time that person would be here?"

"If police bring them in, it is usually a forty-eight-hour hold to properly observe the patient. If a therapist or psychiatrist admits them, it is up to the doctors, but it is usually longer because there are medication adjustments they want to oversee."

"So, the minimum is forty-eight hours?"

"Yes, that is safe to say."

"OK, thank you."

"No problem. Sorry for the bureaucracy."

"Yeah, I bet that's fun for you guys."

She laughs and goes back to her paperwork. As I maneuver my way through hallways and elevators, I'm thinking about how the system at the shelter creates cracks the size of the Grand Canyon for clients to fall through. Caleb had a severe episode and will get the boot. I know clients at the shelter have had medical intervention and were allowed to return. I feel a modicum of culpability because I'm part of the system. I don't create policy, but I do have a voice, albeit a small one. I remember a quote from one of my classes about the psychology involved in social work. Hale, I think was his name, and it was from back in the 1800s, I believe. He said,

> *"I am only one, but I am one.*
> *I cannot do everything, but I can do something.*
> *And I will not let what I cannot do interfere with*
> *what I can do."*

“What can I do?” This is the notion that keeps recurring in my mind. I think of Mom and how she always said, “Respond to need.” There is a real need to do things differently. I wonder if Caleb will get my note. *I wonder if the staff is even allowed to convey notes such as the one I slid under the window. I wonder if it is possible to effect change for a problem so big. I cannot do everything, but I can do something.*

I just have to figure out what that something is…

CHAPTER THIRTEEN

Caleb — Intake

My primary concern is my bunk. The housing placement awaiting me is contingent upon my being an actual client of the shelter. It's what Malik was working on. What the shelter lacked in hospitality, they made up for in a very progressive housing placement program. Checking into the BHU means I'm going to be out of a bed at the shelter. It's nearing the end of November, and I don't relish the idea of sleeping outside while I wait for my new number to enter the shelter.

As Carol wheels me through a labyrinth of hallways, elevators, and skywalks, I'm surprised at the length of the trip to the BHU. Normally, they are located right next to the ER for easy delivery. This walk feels like we are going to the other side of the world. After a reasonable amount of time, we come to two steel, electronic doors. She waves her badge over the digital door panel. There's some internal clicking, then the doors swing toward us, slowly and mechanically.

"Here we go," Carol says.

"Right," I say.

Inside the interior hallway of the BHU, the odor changes. It's not bad, just more antiseptic. At least it's not urine. I think to myself about the intake wing in Kansas City, MO. That was horrible. The actual BHU was quite nice once you made it past the 48-hour intake period, during which you were monitored in what they called the intake wing. It was depraved. People were lying on bath towels in the hallways because there were no beds available. Women without shirts, men without pants. And the ever-present smell of urine. But this is Columbus, not Kansas City. It's not San Francisco, Yuma, Shreveport, or Wilkes-Barre, all of which I have been through.

We take an immediate left to a counter with several nurses staring into computer monitors.

"This is Caleb from the ER," Carol says. "Dr. Santos admitted him for review."

Dr. Santos, I think to myself. *THAT was his name.*

I try to remember the names of doctors who have admitted me into various hospitals over the past decade. Wow, the past two decades. I dwell for a minute on how some doctors have punctuated my life: Dr. Shint, Dr. Crowley, Dr. Kapowski, and Dr. Lui...too many to remember. It's humiliating. No matter how far down this road I go, I always start back at the beginning, in yet another BHU. I hate this road. My thoughts are interrupted by a pleasant voice.

"Hello there." The greeting comes from a handsome nurse whose name badge reads Erik.

"Hello," I say. He has the classic good looks of a kid just out of college. Dark hair, brown eyes, good jawline, almost tall. Strong hands.

"Now, Caleb is it?" Erik asks, looking up from the computer at me.

"Yes."

"OK, then, here are some forms I need you to fill in if you can. If not, we can get a social worker to assist you. I've highlighted everywhere you need to answer. You can go ahead and get started, and feel free to ask me any questions as you go through them." Erik types for a few moments and then adds, "Do you have any insurance?"

"I have Medicare."

"He has insurance!" Erik says to the computer. Two nurses, one behind him looking at paperwork and another at the other computer, both reply, "He has insurance!"

Erik leans forward. "We don't get a lot of insurance carriers in here, so it's always great to get someone who has been able to maintain their insurance. Good job, Caleb." That's condescending; I mean, how hard is it to send in the renewal form each year? Even easier since they now allow you to do it online, but I get what he's saying. I have to remind myself that with all my moves and mania, it's a wonder I've kept up with the updates. *OK, Erik, I'll give you that.* I finish the forms and push the clipboard back to Erik. It's only then that I notice Carol has left. The nurse who was behind Erik comes around the desk and introduces herself.

"Hi, Caleb," she says in a lovely, slightly accented, Jamaican-influenced tone. "I'm Mariel. I will be your intake nurse, so we'll be spending a few moments together getting to know one another." And by one another, she means she's going to ask all the penetrating questions needed to figure out where I will be placed within the collection of nut jobs they monitor.

I'm riveted by her hair, which is a maze of tight braids. I remember watching the movie *Good Hair* about Black women and what goes on for them to have these long weaves or complicated braids. Her hair is truly a masterpiece.

Just then, my chin sends a reminder that it recently met with a marble floor. I reach up to touch it and feel the bandage, underneath which are five stitches from my introduction to the Columbus Police Department. I had pretty much forgotten about them, and I realize, quite pleasantly, I'm still a bit high from sedation. I imagine it is the residual effects of my shot of Haldol, or painkillers for the stitches on my chin, or something else given to me during the medical intervention.

I used to like getting high. I remember back to high school and my fondness for dropping acid on the weekends with my friend Ricky. We often ended up at *The Rocky Horror Picture Show* or Pink Floyd's *The Wall.* Back then, it was all about escape, and being high in the audience of those shows was sublime. Nothing felt better than that. It's a marvel I'm not addicted to anything today. Being high allowed me to avoid thinking about dreadful things, and it worked for me, until it didn't.

I was never attracted to speed drugs. I spent my life feeling anxiety, so I had no affinity for cocaine, crack, or the meth that would come later, after the late '90s. So many of my friends went on to have a relationship with meth. It never ended well. I lost a few friends along the way to overdose, and for someone who didn't have a lot of friends, it hit me hard. As an older adult, looking back on my high school years, I can understand what I was doing. I was trying to bury a past I loathed. Being high just felt better.

"Caleb, my dear, are you OK?" Mariel asks, looking at me with those beautiful dark eyes.

"Oh, yes...just thinking...I still might be a little high."

"OK, I just wanted to make sure you understood what we are doing," she says with a warm, soothing voice. She pats my hand and smiles at me. She is so lovely.

She finishes her interview. She turns on her stool and grabs a roll of linens. If experience has taught me anything, this roll of linens will contain sheets for my foam mattress, much akin to the shelter bed I slept on, a towel, and a pair of scrubs. I receive the bedroll with two hands and feel that something inside is...crunchy?

"Inside your bedroll is a very nice hygiene kit," she says, noting my curiosity.

"Great."

"Yes, it really is," she says and then continues in a hushed tone, "I use the lotion all the time." She winks. "You'll be in bed 43."

"Great," I respond, thinking, dear lord, are there really forty-two other maniacs here?

"I'll show you the way." And with that, the lovely Mariel invites me to walk with her. Both Erik and Mariel are very attractive. I wonder if the nurses here are all models, and then, remembering Carol, I realize they are not.

Mariel shows me to my room, providing instructions to shower with the soap provided, change into the scrubs, and place my clothes in a bag so the staff can put them through the washer and dryer. It's their way of keeping bed bugs and cockroaches to a minimum, like the shelter.

I reply in the affirmative and follow Mariel to the 12-by-12 sleeping room. I'm no longer a stranger to this intake process. She closes the door, and I set about removing my clothes and putting them in the brown paper bags . It's become familiar enough to know, basically, what's ahead of me for the next day or so. A few weeks ago, I lived in San Diego. A few days ago, I was living in a homeless shelter in Columbus. Today, I'm in a psychiatric unit with my clothing in a grocery bag.

And the words fall into place.

> Maya tells us she knows why
> the lonely, caged bird sings,
> and in this country of amber waves,
> our freedom loudly rings.
> But what if that caged bird
> never learned the song,
> and freedom is not ever found
> in a life devoid of renewing dawn.

CHAPTER FOURTEEN

Malik — God's Work

Having missed Caleb in the ER, I'm considering grabbing a coffee and figuring out a few things. There's a Starbucks on 3rd Avenue in the German Village neighborhood just south of downtown. Parking isn't the best in that neighborhood. It's largely residential with small streets. It's picturesque, with brick homes and cobblestones still in the roadways. I looked at a few places in this area before renting downtown. They were all out of my range. However, the Starbucks lounge made me feel like I could occasionally rent a few hours of the neighborhood.

I get an Americano and a slice of lemon pound cake, the kind with the white frosting: sheer decadence. I grab a seat in an overstuffed armchair. I notice a woman in the corner. She's ebony black, a lot like me. Her hair, mostly gray now, is wrapped in a large scarf gathering legions of ropey dreadlocks. She wears reading glasses, but they have no lenses. Her nose is broad and flat, with a rough, grayish appearance, despite the darkness of her skin. I've seen this with Black homeless people who have suffered frostbite.

She wears several layers of shirts, flannel over print over solid, which are held together at her neck in a tight fist. She wears cargo pants, every pocket loaded with things trailing out: pieces of paper, feathers, a plastic bag, a piece of fabric, straws, a banana. Black boots meet her pants, the laces in knots. A pull-behind suitcase stands tucked behind her chair. She has a small coffee cup in front of her, and she is quietly chatting with someone who is not there.

Every few moments, the hand not holding her shirt collar pulls at a rogue dreadlock, and then she coughs into her hand. I don't think she's clearing her throat; I think it's a nervous tic. Despite all her eccentricities, her posture is perfect. She holds her chin very high. If her clothing weren't weather beaten and rough looking, she'd appear matronly.

I'm in the opposite corner, pretending to be looking at my phone, even though I'm really taking in this woman's appearance. I frequently watch people like this with voyeuristic anonymity, whether it's out in public or at the shelter. I'm sure she's someone with disorganized schizophrenia. Someone with this illness can be asked, "Do you have a spare fifty cents?" They will answer with utter sincerity, "Grandma has a green octopus." But they'll reach into their pocket and give you fifty cents.

As the disease suggests, their brains are disorganized, but their minds still function at top speed. They hear voices, sometimes incessantly, demanding their attention. The voices come from within their own heads, but they register as if they are outside input. The voices can be harmless or conniving. In some cases, though it is a rarity, they can be extremely dangerous when they encourage their host to harm themselves or others.

It's a bizarre illness. I think of Caleb sitting somewhere over at the psych unit. I know if I go, I won't be able to see him. It would require written permission for anyone to see him. I know he had the shelter paperwork on him, but I don't think Caleb would think of putting me down as an emergency contact. Even if he did, the supervising psychiatrist would have to sign off on me seeing him, and I don't see that happening until Caleb has met with his intake doctor.

The woman coughs loudly into her hand again. I want to approach her, chatting to her invisible colleague, but I know that to do so is purely selfish on my part. I want to watch her disengage from the voices and focus on a real conversation. Imagine the stories she has to tell. I sit and observe. This feels predatory in a way. As I weigh whether to chat with the woman, she moves her arms, and I see a Bible.

I spent my life growing up with people speaking about God and how God is always good. Some of the older Black ladies in my neighborhood were downright militant about God, praying, and subjugation. My mom was never a churchgoer. What little part she did play in the church, mostly as a courtesy to her own parents, vanished after her relationship with my father ended so explosively. His parents were Pentecostal Christians, real Bible thumpers. Every once in a while, Pops would try to pull a verse from Timothy or 1st Peter about women being subservient or submissive. Moms just wouldn't have it.

When I was in middle school, we were at an assembly of some sort. Some of the Bible thumpers approached her about not seeing her in church. She smiled politely and said, "I try to live a Gospel life, ladies, and I'm far from perfect. I'll try better." The reference to the Gospel and her admission of imperfection seemed to placate the Thumpers. Looking back, I think that's all they really wanted, to see her subservience. I can't believe she would even tolerate it. But that's a whole different generation than mine. My mom never said, and perhaps she didn't really know herself, but I'm sure she was agnostic for all intents and purposes. She knew enough Scripture and church language to keep people at bay about faith issues, and if cornered, she would say an "Amen" or "Hallelujah" when needed.

Agnosticism in the Black community was about as popular as someone being gay. My mom taught me many lessons early on that seemed rooted in Christianity: do unto others, hospitality, and other principles that the Thumpers would attribute to God. She never said so, but Moms showed me by example how to be a good person. She didn't need a book to tell her how to be gracious. There were just certain things you knew, or you didn't. Moms made sure that I knew.

I thought about Moms a lot when I was around people with mental illness. Growing up, there was a young girl down the street who had Down Syndrome, named Shonda. Shonda's mother's name was Clarice. Moms made it a point to take her a casserole every so often. She also visited thrift stores and found inexpensive yet nice clothing for Shonda. Moms said she just loved shopping for girls' clothing. I wouldn't say that Clarice and my mom were the best of friends, but they were there for each other when needed. The life of a single mom didn't really leave much social time, and since Shonda went to special classrooms at the school, she and I never knew each other, even though we were just a year apart.

When she was getting ready to take something over to Clarice's house, Moms wouldn't ask me if I wanted to go, she would just say, "Grab your coat. We're heading over to Clarice's house." We never stayed long, but as soon as we were through the door, Moms would direct me to the living room where Shonda would be watching some show on television. Shonda and I never really said much more than "hi" to each other. I would sit and watch the television show with her while Moms and Clarice talked in the kitchen. We did that about once a month. It wasn't until I was in college that I realized what Moms had done, even though she herself didn't know it at the time either. When I came home from class one time, Moms was sitting at the dining room table. When I came in, she got up and wrapped her arms around me and said, "My baby boy."

She always said that when she was proud of me, no matter my age.

"What?" I asked, not understanding.

"Clarice came by today," she said.

"Is Shonda OK?" I asked immediately because some people with Down have health issues when they become adults, and I thought maybe Shonda was sick.

"Yes, baby, she's fine," she said. There was a yearbook on the table that wasn't mine. It was from my old high school, though.

"Look at Shonda's picture," she said, tears in her eyes.

I picked up the yearbook and opened it. I had to flip through the pages of cheerleaders, sports teams, and club pages before I could find the Special Ed department. I found the three seniors who graduated that year, and Shonda was in the middle. I looked at her picture. It was there on the page, her lovely, crooked smile and squinted eyes. Her hair must have been done the morning of the picture because it was pulled back beautifully, with a large silver bow.

"She looks great, Moms," I said, still not understanding.

"Just keep looking," she said.

So, I did. She was wearing a simple white dress. She had earrings, which I had never seen her wear. I was just about to give up looking for what Moms was talking about when I saw it. Underneath her picture was her senior quote, "Life is good when you have a best friend like Malik."

I read it again. A funny feeling got caught in my throat.

"You see, my baby," she said. "Look what you did. You gave that girl a best friend, without even knowing it."

She hugged me close. I did feel proud, but I also got a sad, hollow feeling. All I did was sit with her for an hour or so once a month. Truth be told, I could have done so much more. I let Moms hug me. After seeing Shonda's yearbook quote, I made it a point to keep up our monthly visits, more frequently if possible. Shonda could read at about a third-grade level, so when I visited, she and I would walk to the Four Corners library and pick out a few books. I thought at first I would read to her, but what happened is that she ended up reading her books to me, slowly and with a little stutter.

I don't know what was funnier, hearing storybooks read in Shonda's funny way of talking, or Moms and Clarice standing in the kitchen all teared up over the two of us interacting. Every so often, I would overhear Clarice talking about what an angel I was and the beauty of what she called God's work.

I think about Shonda as I sit here watching the schizophrenic woman at Starbucks. Their conditions have nothing to do with one another, but indeed, sitting in front of me is another real example of God's work.

CHAPTER FIFTEEN

Caleb — Anti-psychotics

After I finish my shower and change into a pair of pale blue hospital scrubs, I find that they are a bit too tight around my waist and a tad too short for my legs. The rest of my belongings are delivered to my room. Anything that could potentially be used for suicide is removed: the shoelaces from my boots, my belt, and the string from the neck of my hoodie.

Sitting down, I feel the plastic coating of the foam mattress through my thin scrubs. I stare down at my toes. My two big toenails are pale. The toenails are dead. The boots I bought from the thrift store were a tad too small, putting pressure on my toes. My last manic episode in San Diego put me on a walking binge before I took off on the bus. Walking without a break, jamming my toes into the front of my tight shoes, damaged my big toenails. I'll probably lose them again. I didn't break any toes this time, though. The pale souvenirs of that episode peek back at me before I slip on my hospital no-slip socks.

Atop the small table next to my bunk is a schedule. I pick up the spreadsheet, recognizing the Excel format. I imagine how I could have formatted it better. I always do that. I'm great at identifying errors. I could be an editor if I had any credentials. The notion is valid, but for me it's an impractical aspiration. No matter how smoothly life is running, eventually, Craig shows up to throw a gargantuan wrench into whatever successes I am stringing together. Sooner or later, Craig happens, and subsequently, I happen.

I'm impressed, though. Everything is in order for tomorrow; they even have my current medications, from Dr. Ben in San Diego:

Seroquel 1200 mg
Lamotrigine 300 mg
Clonidine 2 mg
Amlodipine 20 mg
Lisinopril 10 mg
Pravastatin Sodium 20 mg
Metformin 1000 mg
Glipizide 5 mg
Humalog 75 units
Levemir 50 units

Those are the big ten, helping manage my brain and diabetes. I take antidepressants and antipsychotics, but what I really need is an anti-Craig medication. I know I can't live without medication. I wish I enjoyed the life I lived while on medication. I wish the life I lived on medication instilled a sense of purpose. It doesn't. That's the conundrum for people like me: life is a daily toil without much reward.

I envy the lifestyles depicted on the covers of yoga magazines. I'm envious of the trim people exuding flexible, strong bodies. When I was younger, I had a very different lifestyle. When I did have those things, I was living a lie, though. Everything looked great from the outside as I struggled daily to project that image. It was all a fraud. I was always envious of people's timelines on Facebook. Everyone was happy and accomplishing things. I felt like a Martian, battling my own toxic mind.

Looking at the schedule on my desk, I see it is time for

medication. The previously empty hallway is now filled with a lineup of characters making the People of Walmart look like fashion models. I must actively remind myself that, indeed, these are my peers. Maybe not intellectually, but in life, these are the people with whom I share the most in common.

I'm suddenly aware that I am without my phone and earbuds. It hits me for the first time that I will be without music. Music is the one thing that prevents my mind from focusing on the depravity I feel my life has become. It will be a constant battle, especially when trying to go to sleep, to keep the gloom of my mind from infecting my outlook. What a strange war to wage, all within the confines of my own skull.

There are approximately seventeen people in line before me. I feel as though I'm in a Stanley Kubrick version of *The Canterbury Tales* by Chaucer, a string of jolly lunatics on our pilgrimage to the apothecary. Thankfully, this BHU enforces a hygiene schedule, so at least everyone here is washed, for the most part. Right away, you can recognize those with schizophrenia. They are perhaps the most adjusted to this environment because, no matter where they are, they are surrounded by familiar voices in their head. The voices pull them away from reality into a world of their own creation, much like the disturbing thoughts in my head keep me from a sound mind.

The worst ones, of which I am a part, are those with mania. When episodes hit, we are so over the top with everything that it's not worth a conversation. I've seen videos of me when I'm manic. It's unnerving. Plus, if you do engage people who are manic, they often seek you out as their buddy to keep their impossibly energetic, stream-of-consciousness, word-vomit conversations going. It's exhausting for me and exhausting to anyone around me.

Depressed people are usually quiet and tearful. Most aren't

hostile toward you personally unless they have a delusional doomsday scenario where life, no matter the reality, is soon to be extinguished. Religious people do that a lot—they are fearful of the End of Days, so on top of being depressed, they're trying to convert you even though their lives are a ruin. I guess in their depression, the only thing they have going for them is saving a few decrepit souls on the way out. I used to think to myself that these people could go straight to hell, but then I sadly realized they were already there.

The ones you want to avoid at all costs are sociopaths. They present as normal. Which I guess I should be cognizant of because I often present that way. As far as I know, and a bevy of shrinks corroborates this, I'm not a sociopath. I experience stress about how my actions affect others. I feel bad about what my behaviors have done to people in my past. Experiencing and feeling remorse or shame places me in the category of not being a sociopath. You can be having a perfectly normal conversation about politics or daily events with a sociopath, only to find out from someone else that they're in here because they just tried to kill someone or because they slaughtered a bunch of pets. It's scary.

There are a healthy number of folks in the psych ward who shouldn't be here; people who are mentally diminished with intellectual disability, traumatic brain injury, or severe learning disabilities. There is also a smattering of drunks and addicts coming off their benders who've been assigned a temporary hold until they can be assessed. It's ugly to be around addicts while they are detoxing. They're mean. They're mean because they're in pain, actual physical pain. It usually takes a whole week before they are tolerable. This is the solution our faulty healthcare system has created for the outcasts: One-stop shopping for real estate to park the defective models of society.

At one point in my life, while I was new to hospital admissions,

I tried to make friends. I don't do that anymore. Everyone here is on a different path. Some have been here for weeks and will be gone tomorrow. Others just got here and have hell to go through as they adjust medications, get sober, or get their first diagnosis. People get released at all different stages depending on what kind of homes they have to go to, what type of insurance they have, or what legal actions have placed them here. There are people here who remind me of my first admissions. They are trying to be perky and happy. They freely give out their phone numbers, hoping the person they gave them to will become a new friend. A few days go by and the new friend, who got released, never calls. The BHU is a desolate place to start relationships.

As I lean against the wall for my first scoop of pills from their dispensary, I remember once again about my computer. I'm sure someone, someone with ill intentions, picked it up and walked off with it. I'm lost without my laptop. I'm hoping this BHU encourages journaling. One hospital I was in years ago had a drawer full of those old-school black composition notebooks. I went through six or seven of them, writing down my thoughts. Electronic devices are generally confiscated. Outside forces can really inhibit progress. Outside influences are usually inextricably tied to a person's mental health. It was the Modesto BHU that had all the journals you could use. That would be terrific. I could use them to continue writing.

I am always interested to see if I write more poetry than prose. There are many moments in a psychiatric ward that translate perfectly into poetry. It's so detached from what people see in the real world. The deranged vignettes I record are more about the emotion of what is happening rather than an actual event, and that, at least to me, is the essence of poetry: the emotion of words.

A poem I wrote and memorized from a few years back about a

woman in Eugene, OR reads like this:

> Today I die a bit inside, no more than yesterday,
> a slowly moving sequence, transpiring in the fray.
> I know not peace, I know not love, in my life of
>   pitch and roil,
> those tenets of my psyche do not grow in spoiled
>   soil.
> Today I die a bit inside, just like the day before,
> a slowly moving sequence, becoming slower
>   evermore.

Everyone here is a work of poetry. Every BHU is an anthology of sorrow, confusion, and anxiety. As I'm considering the people ahead of me, a woman about six places in front of me with maroon, mussed-up hair, starts a gentle sob. The man in front of her, with a trim body and crew cut, turns around with a glower. He has no teeth. An enormous man, almost near the front, leans to one side and allows a preposterously loud fart to issue from somewhere beneath the folds of his sweatpants. Some protest, some laugh, and most don't pay any attention.

Their antics, however, settle down as they notice Nurse Carol coming down the hallway. She provokes a hush from everyone. I think to myself, *Nurse Ratched?* The people before me certainly don't exude happiness at the sight of her walking by. Employees at these facilities have the real power to make our lives miserable, much like the underpaid monitors at the shelter.

I had been the last in line until a woman emanating the telltale thwap-thwap of flip-flops walked up behind me. She sports a coiffed, blonde, blunt haircut reaching her chin. She's smiling a million-dollar smile. A well-manicured hand full of perfect French-tipped fingernails holds her gown closed. Her eyes are intense. It looks like her lip has been stitched. I think to myself, *coke addict.*

"Hello," she says.

"Hello," I say. "How are you?"

She doesn't say a word but allows her bathrobe to fall open, showing off small, perky breasts, and then replies, "I don't know, you tell me."

From down the hall, a thunderous command issues forth from Carol, "KATE, WRAP IT UP!"

Kate responds to the verbal command and closes her bathrobe, feigning astonishment that it has opened.

"Hi," I answer. "Nice to meet.... all of you."

Kate pauses, then adds, "Are you queer?"

I chuckle a bit and say, "Who wants to know?"

"Well, me. I know how to do it in the laundry room without getting caught."

"Well, tell me how that works out for you."

"OK," she says, wrapping herself tighter. "Well, anyway. I need a companion in here. You're not drooling, so that's a good sign."

"Thanks, I guess," I say, knowing I'm trapped here with her for the duration of the Med Line, so it's either sever the communication now or open myself up to this possible train wreck of a woman. It's not a decision I want to make, but here I am making it. I decide to roll the dice.

"Oh, c'mon, what could it hurt you?" she says, slapping me on the shoulder.

Ignoring her advances, I say, "The nurse said you were Kate. Is that accurate?"

"Accurate?" She laughs out loud. "OK, Mr. Thesaurus, yes, it's accurate. I'm Katherine. Katherine Clansman."

"Clansman?"

"Yes, I know, idiotic name. But there ya go."

"What's in a name?" I ask, quoting Shakespeare in a British

accent.

"OK, Nancy," she quips. "You gotta stop with that. What's your name?"

"Caleb," I reply.

"Caleb. Caleb what?"

"We'll just go with Caleb if that's OK by you."

"Well, you're no fun," she responds. "So, what're ya in for?"

"I'm nuts like the rest of us."

"Well, I'm not nuts like the rest of you," she says. "They released me from the drunk tank to here. I may have mentioned a time or two that I wanted to kill myself."

"Do you want to kill yourself?"

"Well, shit," she says. "Of course I do. Doesn't everyone?"

Kate gossips with me as she gives me the skinny on the people in line. Margaret, an overweight white woman with salt and pepper hair, is the secret daughter of Donald Trump and is insisting that she be transferred to Palm Beach, Florida so she can be near him. Kevin, a small Black guy with tattoos and a shaved head, is here from jail after a suicide attempt. Kate said he admits it was just an act so he could get out of the county jail and hang out in the BHU. Miriam, a pleasant and primly dressed Jewish girl, sits in a chair by the phone, waiting for the call from her parents that never comes. Grace, a frightfully thin woman with hollowed-out cheeks, paces the hallways like a meth addict coming down. Ricky and Tate, two young boys who could be brothers, sit sullenly by one another for hours without uttering a word to anyone. Peach, a lovely, older woman who wears only scrubs and has a tangle of gray hair, sings her thoughts aloud. Kate never heard her speak.

And then, of course, there's my new companion. She carries a Vogue magazine with bookmarks made of scraps of paper. When she's not talking to me, she flits from one person to the next, giving them style tips whether they want them or not. With Kate, it's like she's perpetually at attention. She answers questions in other people's conversations. She will go into people's rooms and organize their belongings. Staff talks to her constantly about her behavior, but it's like trying to convince a penguin to fly. Some things just won't happen.

A couple of days ago, Kate told me that Grace found her in her room organizing paperwork, and she went ballistic. The screaming was loud and enduring. Kate couldn't understand why Grace didn't want the help, and Grace couldn't stop screeching once triggered. Grace landed two blows to Kate's face, and Kate fell to the ground with a bloody lip. The staff subdued both of them. Grace was confined to her room, and Kate went to the ER downstairs, accompanied by a staff member, for evaluation. Kate returned with a puffy, stitched lip.

I have a lot of sympathy for Kate. I recognize in her the phenomenon that happens to me. The mania sneaks up on you. If you have milder mood swings, like Kate, it can go on for weeks, sometimes months as it slowly builds. Mine is a more rapid increase in behavioral antics. I tend to skyrocket, but I still collect the bloody lips or busted chins like Kate did. I usually end up hurting myself, like riding a bike erratically through traffic, bouncing off the hood of a car, before tumbling to the ground.

•••

Thanksgiving is tomorrow. It's an odd way to celebrate Thanksgiving, but such is life for those of us whose minds like to steer them into mayhem. In BHUs, there's usually some homage to a traditional Thanksgiving meal. There's a turkey loaf of some sort, canned carrots, instant mashed potatoes, and gravy from a powdered mix. Most of us have grown accustomed to celebrating holidays in isolation. William Wordsworth has a poem about solitude. I can't remember anything except the first line, "I wandered lonely as a cloud..." It's an apt metaphor because here we are, all strangers, yet having more in common with one another than we do with our own families. We don't have to explain ourselves. We recognize in each other a version of ourselves. We are a tribe lost in the wilderness, trying to find our way to that most elusive of things for the mentally ill: stability.

CHAPTER SIXTEEN

Malik — Bourbon or Xanax

I spend most of Thanksgiving serving food at the shelter. Thanksgiving is a mixed bag for me. I hate it because Moms isn't here to share it with me. Most of my friends have plans with their families. I use the day to volunteer some hours at the food line. I make a plate of food for myself to take home and put it in the office fridge. I catch up on paperwork in my office in the absence of my rotund co-workers. I let the day lead me where it wants to go as I try to be Zen about having the holiday to myself. What I find, though, is I'm already thinking about how to end my evening: Bourbon or Xanax.

I crave both when someone yells in my face because I'm not doing enough for them. *I don't have control over this, but I have control of myself.* In this case, it is how I react to hostility. It doesn't matter that they have skipped out on three consecutive meetings and have managed to save nothing while they are in the shelter, even though their check is over one thousand dollars a month. Xanax, waiting at home for me, is a mental salve. I can handle dealing with homelessness, addiction, and mental illness. I can deal with all of that, but I come close to losing my damned mind when I've got to deal with stupid. Or on days like today when I try to pretend I'm not lonely.

Some people enjoy solitude more than company. I don't know where I exist on the spectrum. When I'm with people, I often wish to be alone; when I am alone, I yearn to be with others. I always carry some element of awkwardness when it comes to my interpersonal relationships. I wonder what it's like being in a shelter, surrounded by people all day and night, endlessly. It must be hell on those who are more introverted. I think about Caleb. He seems to be someone infinitely more comfortable with solitude than most.

After getting home, I sit at my dining room table with my microwaved leftovers. I'm in my cozy apartment contemplating my two options for relaxing tonight: Bourbon or Xanax. If I have bourbon, it means it isn't serious, and I'm just whining. If I take Xanax, it means I'm really going through anxiety, and I can't calm down on my own to get a good night's sleep. It means the anxiety will start screwing with my functioning at work, or at least that is what I told my doctor to get the Xanax. If I am honest with myself, Xanax feels awesome. A little trip through the Valley of the Dolls every now and again never hurt anyone.

At least, I don't think it does.

I feel better having them, like a security blanket. The high is perfect. It feels like my brain is just a little bit puffy, filled with laughing gas or something, putting me on the edge of a giggle. Problems in my life are pushed out onto the periphery. The only thing that matters is what delicious thing I'm eating, what fantastic magazine I'm reading, or the plush comforter on my bed. All of that happens, but I'm totally coherent. I can answer phone calls, pay bills, or read a book. I wouldn't go to work or anything like that, and I certainly wouldn't drive or do anything stupid. I can't abide stupid.

That's the name of the game. How stupid can some of the guys at the shelter be? I know half of them are high when they come to see me. I know the reason they don't have any money isn't because they are out renewing their annual contributions to NPR. No way, man. They are out smoking crack, or snorting it, or going for the big dragon trip and smoking heroin right off the foil. I see the damned pieces of foil in the garbage can out in front of the shelter when I leave at night. Addiction is insidious. I have sympathy for those who are addicted, but honestly, it really pisses me off too.

I chuckle a bit at the irony of me sitting here at the table, thinking whether I should take Xanax or drink a nice big tumbler full of bourbon with some ice, as opposed to the crutches the guys at the shelter use. Six degrees of separation, I guess. When I talk to my doctor, I just talk about general anxiety. I don't tell him about my panic attacks. He gives me a nice little suburban prescription for 1 mg tablets that I can take twice a day. I get sixty tablets each month, and I probably use ten of them. Two of them, I probably actually need. Today is not one of them. It's going to be a bourbon kind of night.

I kick my shoes off under the table and push my chair back. I have felt pads on the bottom of the chair legs, so they slide back smoothly across my oak floorboards. I walk over to the antique buffet, bend down, and take out the bottle of Maker's Mark. I love the bottle and the red wax collar. I broke it open a few weeks ago when Keith and Drake came over to celebrate the house's siding being complete before the snow started to fly for this season. I grab one of the glasses on top of the buffet and turn it over. It clinks against another glass. I love that sound. I imagine well-dressed people at a cocktail party raising a toast to some ridiculous A-list thing. A heavy tumbler makes me feel like I'm in a scene from *The Great Gatsby*, that is if *The Great Gatsby* had any Black people in it.

I turn the bottle over and pour in a good three fingers' worth of whiskey. Walking over to the kitchen, I place my glass against the tab and tumble ice into it. More clinking. I swirl the ice around the glass to bring a frost to my whiskey. I hold up my glass slightly, like I'm making a toast, and say, "Happy Thanksgiving." I take a sip. It warms my mouth and feels great going down. I keep the glass to my nose, smelling it. There is just nothing I don't like about bourbon.

I walk over to my sofa and let myself sink down into it. I love my sofa. It is my kingdom. The taupe color of the plush. The dark brown beaded throw pillow glistening in the low light. The sofa table behind it with its stack of high-end magazines and two huge pillar candles. I pick the lighter up from between them and bring the candles alive.

Another sip from my tumbler.

And another.

Tap. Tap. Tap. Tap. Tap.

I feel warm and push my back into the cushions. I pull the cream-colored chenille throw blanket onto my legs. I rest my hands and my drink on top of the blanket. I allow myself to warm up inside and out. My mind drifts toward Caleb.

"Dammit, Caleb," I say aloud, not really meaning to do so.

Missing bunk check, even if it is by admission to the hospital, may be a deal breaker at the shelter. I'm not totally up on the rules, but I think missing roll call without permission, and without it being for work, means you get "put out."

I should call Tarisha.

I have her number. Ha, she made sure of that. Tarisha is on the prowl. I know we can hook up if I call. That would be just too much damned trouble, though, regardless of how fine she is. No way I'm tappin' anything at work. I try to redirect her advances to Deshawn, but she is all about finding someone who can make her life better. Deshawn makes less money than she does, and that is a deal breaker. I finish my drink. I fix another. I'm feelin' good. I get back into my sweet spot on the couch and decide to give the girl a call.

"Heeey," is the answer after barely one ring.

"'Sup, T," I say. "Happy Thanksgiving. How's your evening?"

"It just got a whole lot better. Thanksgiving is always a pain in the ass at my mom's. She insists on doing everything, so by the time the meal rolls around, she's in a bad mood and cussin' everyone out," she answers. "Anyway, to what do I owe the pleasure of your phone call?"

"Well, I wanted to say hi first," I say and am cut off.

"Every day of the week goes by without you sayin' hi to me at the shelter, so wassup negro?" Tarisha quips. "What do you need... or do you just need a little bit of T?"

I know I will be getting the hard-up treatment from her because she is right. I never call her except for work stuff.

"I gotta client at the shelter who wigged out and got admitted to the psych ward."

"OK."

"I don't know how many days he's gonna be in there."

"Mmmm-hmmmm," comes the reply.

"Is he gonna lose his bed?"

"Does staff like him?"

"Yeah, I think so. It's Caleb Taylor."

"White guy?"

"Yeah."

"Big white guy?"

"Yeah," I say.

"Yeah, I know who you're talkin' about...most of the staff likes him. He's quiet as hell, so I'm assumin' everyone likes him."

"He got a mandatory forty-eight, but I don't know if it will be longer than that," I say.

"Well, Malik, you gotta ask yourself one question."

"What's that, T?"

"It ain't whether staff likes him..."

"No?"

"No, baby," she replied. "It's whether Tarisha likes you."

"You trippin'," I say, and then add, not so surely, "Right?"

"I ain't trippin'," she says. "Everybody knows clients can't be gone unless someone on staff vouches for 'em."

"Would you do that?"

"Well, that's why I asked the question," she says. "How much do you like Tarisha?" Her words are slow and staccato.

"Well, I..." I'm not sure what she is proposing, but suddenly I am thinking this is getting a bit out of hand.

"Oh, shut up, boy!" Her laughter erupts on the phone. "I'm just playin' with you." More laughter. "Let me look tomorrow at the waiting list and what kinda record Mr. Big White Guy has, and I'll let you know."

"Oh, man, you got me, girl." She laughs aloud. "That'd be tight."

"Oh, honey, ain't nobody sayin' anything gonna be 'tight' anymore."

"Girl," I say. "Shut up."

"Did you just shush me!"

"Guess I did." I laugh.

"And here I thought you liked me."

"You know it isn't about liking you, it's about I can't date anyone at work."

"Oh, hush," she says. "I ain't gonna tell no one."

"Girl, it ain't about that...but I tell you. If I ever decide to break my rule, I'll call you."

"Ooooh, Mr. Bad Boy Breaking the Rules," Tarisha teases over the phone. "You know I like them bad boys." More laughter.

"You my girl, T," I say. "I really appreciate it."

"Mmmm-hmmm." The connection ends.

Just as I am hanging up, a text comes through. It's from Tarisha. It's a selfie of her and her four-year-old daughter. They are smiling and working on a Kumon math book. I recognize the book because she was talking about the new thing white parents were doing for their white kids. I texted back a thumbs up. Tarisha is a lot more than what she puts out into the world. She reminds me of Moms a lot, which I know would be the absolute wrong thing to say to her. But as I sit and look at the picture of her and her daughter, I see the bookshelf in back full of selections to read. I see an orderly apartment. A simple, cozy life. Her daughter is named Cecilia. Cecelia is smiling and hugging a red Clifford dog. The two of them are happy, and it's beautiful.

I remember talking to her about her daughter's name once. She kinda leaned over to me and said in a whisper, "I ain't namin' her no ghetto name like mine, hell no. When she goes to college, I don't want anybody judging her before she gets into class or when she's takin' a test. Nope, my girl got a quiet little white girl name."

Tarisha is like that. She is all about living her best Black self, Black Lives Matter, racial equity, and everything a young Black woman is supposed to be. But she takes it further and doesn't let being Black define her. Maybe I will break my rule someday. Lord knows she is good-looking enough to get whomever she puts her sights on. I sit and allow my thoughts to roam over what an evening with Tarisha might entail. It feels good. The bourbon feels good. The couch feels good. Life is good.

CHAPTER SEVENTEEN

Caleb — Baby It's Cold Outside

Two days after Thanksgiving, I'm assessed as someone who has recovered from a psychotic break triggered by an acute PTSD episode. I've had quick trips to the BHU wing as well as extended stays. This time, I got the "treat 'em and street 'em" approach. They forgot to cut the telltale white plastic bracelet off my left arm when I left the BHU. It's hidden under my coat sleeve and glove for now, but I can feel it beneath my clothing. A silent reminder of how quickly life can detonate.

Dr. Rob, along with the social worker, strongly advised therapy. I nodded yes. The hospital's social worker helped me qualify for Medicaid in Ohio so I could continue with medications and also get into therapy. Therapy is great, but the thought of starting over with another therapist feels overwhelming to me. I realize I need it, but I also realize slogging through all the trauma and loss to bring a therapist up to speed sounds excruciating. I leave with the name of a therapist and a first appointment scheduled.

We'll see.

It has been five days since I was admitted. In that time, I've not been outside, per the psych ward rules. Even though it's cold at the bus stop, I breathe in the fresh air with appreciation. The intense cold snap that rolled through has moved on to the east. I'm thankful for the change in the weather. It won't be comfortable sleeping outside, but at least it won't be deadly.

My thoughts about the past days in the hospital are all over the place. The adjustment of medication has left me a bit fuzzy. I have a new medication to replace the one they took me off. Or did they just add one? I'll have to look through the big bag of pills when I get to wherever I'm going to call home after the shelter. I've been fed my meds by the person behind the plate glass window, so I'm not certain what I'm taking and when. I have instructions typed out in the bag. I'll sort it out later when I get "home".

Home... I muse. The term is relative, I suppose. You do not grow up thinking home will be a room full of men in varying stages of midlife crises. It hits me again that the room full of men would be a step up from what I will be heading into after I pick up my bags and leave the shelter. The entire world will be my home, and by world, I mean the world outdoors: concrete floors and brick walls.

I think back on the past forty-eight hours. A lot happened.

I think about Kate. She joked about suicide. We talked about suicide. I did not realize how close to the edge she was. Neither did the staff who found her. Nobody thought Robin Williams was depressed. Ellen DeGeneres's sidekick, tWitch, was perpetually cheerful. Anthony Bourdain had the world at his feet. They all died by suicide, too. Most of the time, you cannot recognize in someone's face if they are suicidal. Years ago, decades really, one of my first therapists diagnosed me with major depression. I thought it was a ludicrous notion. I went to work. I laughed. I was productive. There was no way she could have known about how I spent hours just trying to get out of bed. I did not tell her I was asking friends if they owned guns and if I could borrow them. I did not tell her any of those things, so how could she know I was depressed? Did the crushing anxiety and the endless self-loathing show through?

And the words fall into place:

A smile before the knife cuts,
a grin before the noose,
a laugh before the gun shot,
I'm a man without use.
A smirk before the drowning,
a giggle before the pills,
a snort before the car crash,
curing all my worldly ills.

On the psych ward, patients received a well-check every fifteen minutes, regardless of where they were. They'll come right into the bathroom. The staff member poked her head into Kate's room, "Hey, Kate, you OK?"

"Yes, of course, just taking a shower," she responded from the bathroom.

Kate heard the door close.

•••

Go time.

She had fifteen minutes. She'd been planning. She was quick like a cat. Smart as a fox. Earlier in the day, during a time in the schedule called Grooming, staff brought out combs, brushes, and other things to keep people from getting too far gone. There was a small dish with plastic, disposable razors. She waited until the orderly looked away, and she casually put a razor in the palm of her hand, holding it with her thumb so it was out of sight. After grooming, she took it back to her room where she placed it on the door jamb, letting the heavy door close, smashing the plastic head and allowing the razor within to fall to the ground. She was ready. She had fifteen minutes.

She plunged the small razorblade into the fleshy part on the bottom of her wrists, guided by the scars of previous attempts. One minute passed.

She gouged deep. The pain was shocking. The blood was immediate. She stifled her scream with a towel held between her teeth. She repeated the effort on her other wrist. Two minutes passed.

She bit down harder and screamed into the towel between her teeth as the shower muffled the noise. Three minutes passed.

She dug deeper into each wound. Her wrists pumped blood out to the rhythm of her heart. Rivulets of deep red mixed in with the water. Four minutes passed.

She kept her wrists in the stream of water to slow coagulation. The water caused more pain, but she could feel herself getting lightheaded. There was so much blood. Five minutes passed.

Her dizziness became strong. She slumped to one side. Six minutes passed.

Numbness crept in. Seven minutes passed.

Organs, deprived of blood and oxygen, began to fail. Eight minutes passed.

Her eyelids fluttered. Nine minutes passed.

The pain was severe, but she had no energy to react. Ten minutes passed.

The pain was severe, but she didn't have the energy to scream anymore. She closed her eyes, unable to keep them open as the towel dropped from her mouth to the bottom of the shower. Eleven minutes passed.

Eyelids shut. Twelve minutes passed.

Finally, the pain started to subside. Thirteen minutes passed.

Life left her body. Fourteen minutes passed.

Fifteen minutes passed.

•••

I heard the knock at Kate's door that night. "Hey, Kate, are you about done with your shower?"

No answer.

"Kate?"

No answer.

The staff member entered the room. "Kate?"

I heard the gasp, then the yelling, "Code Red! Code Red!" We stood in our doorways. Others ventured into the hallway and congregated. I could hear it from my room. More staff members ran into Kate's room. Shortly afterward, administrators in ties showed up, talking in hushed tones in the hallway. A nurse ran from Kate's room up to the office next to the Med Line. More doctors converged around Kate's room. Finally, after about forty-five minutes, somber staff members rolled the gurney down the hallway with the body zipped into a black cadaver pouch. Orderlies with mops and buckets entered Kate's room.

We saw everything; we were told nothing. We all just folded it into our collective experience of life with mental illness. Some cried. Some were angry. Some were unaffected. Most of us have sat with the idea of ending our lives. If you live a life of constant pain, the thought of suicide can be a comfort. It's a selfish option, not considering those you may leave behind, but how can you abide a lifetime of agony for someone else?

I wish everyone could find their way back from wanting death upon themselves. Edgar Allan Poe wrote, "I became insane, with long intervals of horrible sanity." Escaping it seems reasonable when life becomes a constant replay of horrible sanity. I looked at the ground as things on the ward returned to whatever normal might be in such a place. *Are they really not going to say anything to us?* I imagined some lawyer was sitting in the admin office telling everyone what to do. The door to Kate's room was ajar. After things settled down, I walked over and looked in. It was sparkling clean.

Kate's bed was filled with another client the following morning.

•••

I notice the leaves shimmering in the wind. The reds and golds of the deciduous trees are sparse. It must have been windy the past few days. Baseball caps have been replaced over the past few weeks with stocking caps. Sandals have given way to boots. Winter in Columbus is a far cry from winter in San Diego. Being on the streets in San Diego is tough, but the elements won't kill you. The icy foot I got upon arrival in the Greyhound depot a few weeks back could be dangerous. In San Diego, even in winter, you can hang a wet sock out to dry. In Columbus, you'll get a frozen sock.

I'm on my way to get my things at the shelter. They'll be put into black plastic garbage bags like a thrift store version of Santa's bag of presents. Like a camel across concrete dunes, I'll take them away with me to wherever I go. I have a few hours before I will have to figure out exactly where "home" will be tonight, but for now, I'm happy to be out of the hospital, in the fresh air, and waiting for the bus. A few buses pull into the stop, none of which are the ones I am waiting for, so I have a good amount of time to breathe the cold, refreshing air. I can feel my inner world adjusting. Tonight, I know I'm going to be outside. I know the rhythm of finding a suitable place to sleep, making sure my belongings are safely tethered to me, and waking up before heavy foot traffic brings unwelcome eyes. You never see a well-rested homeless person. It's probably the main reason the homeless are so gruff. They're sleep-deprived and in pain from their slumber on the ground.

The collection of souls around the bus stop is the normal crowd. Poor folks going to work. A few millennials trying to reduce their carbon footprint. There are a few young mothers with strollers filled with a collection of kids. The bus stops have simple shelters, so there are a few guys getting out of the wind. The nearby garbage can is full. One of the mothers, despite her proximity to the garbage can, tosses an empty Newport cigarette box onto the ground. Her little girl picks up the box and starts to walk to the garbage can. *What a nice little girl,* I think to myself, just as her mom swats her hand, sending the cigarette box back to the ground.

"Don't touch trash on the ground, dammit!" she yells at her daughter, whose eyes well up with tears that dare not fall.

I'm just starting to get chilled when my bus pulls into the stop. The door breaks open. Several people get off, some dressed in hospital scrubs, most dressed in dark, baggy clothing. One overweight man, eating Cheetos and carrying a two-liter bottle of Pepsi, huffs his way past people trying to enter. The hand-slapping mom enters the bus before me as the lone cigarette box still lies on the ground. I step up onto the bus.

I swipe my pass through the turnstile and move down the aisle crowded with strollers, shopping carriages, and people who don't give a damn about their feet jutting into the aisle. I maneuver myself midway back in the bus and find a seat by an older Black woman. She is primly dressed, her coat collar pulled up over her mouth. When I take the seat, the woman turns toward the window, I'm guessing to keep my germs away from her. And with that, I'm back in society.

The bus is full of its regular passengers, mostly people going to and from work. But it always seems like there are more reprobates than normal folks because the hoodlums are so loud. Young men with their pants slung low under their butts with headphones slapped over their ears reciting filthy rap lyrics out loud so the prim little lady next to me is forced to hear about how "fat that ass I slappin' be."

And the words fall into place:

> Black thing, white thing,
> ain't but a thing
> sittin' on busses;
> all jesters, no king.
> Lookin' into phones,
> buds to the ear
> textin 'bout nothin,'
> makin' image a career.

It's just the way things are now. At the shelters, I used to get a kick out of the guys my age, in their early 50s, trying to pull off the low-slung pants and the tough rap aesthetic. It's not tough, it's silly. Maybe social media and the vapid nature of entertainment make an aging man think he can look like the kids of the day. I don't know. I have the lesson of balding to tell me I am not a kid anymore. I also realized later in life that who I am is an internal process rather than an external one. But who the hell knows? I'm a few hours out of a psych ward and a few hours from being homeless, so I guess I shouldn't offer my intellectual ideology as one to emulate either.

A few minutes into the ride, I realize I've been sitting on a small pamphlet. It's a simple trifold piece of advertising. There is an image of a wrapped present on the cover. It reminds me of the silly boxes I assemble at the warehouse. I should say I *used* to assemble. The title of the pamphlet is Eternal Life is a Free Gift. Staring at the cover, I shudder at the thought of eternal life, as if dealing with a normal life span is not bad enough. I cannot fathom living like this for eternity.

I open it to find the interior full of single-spaced Bible quotations. My eyes fall on the section entitled If You Do Not Get Saved. It reads Revelations 14:11, “And the smoke of their torment ascendeth up forever and ever: and they have no rest day or night.” That passage pretty much describes being homeless. It goes on to quote Romans 6:23, “For the wages of sin is death.” I chuckle. Shouldn’t it read, “For the wages of sin *are* death.” I think to myself, *didn’t God have an editor?* I fold the pamphlet back up and leave it on the seat. After a few moments, I think again about the pamphlet. I pick it up and walk up to the front of the bus, and drop it in the small waste basket.

After a half hour meandering through downtown Columbus, the bus pulls up to my stop. Thanksgiving has passed. Christmas is a few weeks away. It’s what most people would call the height of the holiday season. When you’ve been homeless and away from your family long enough, holidays are just like any other day. It’s not depressing, as some may think. At least it isn’t for me. It’s somewhat freeing. There’s no shopping list lowering my bank account. There’s nothing to decorate. There’s nothing to plan. No relatives are waiting to make a gathering awkward. Instead, I am concerned about where I will eat. Where will I sleep? And where will I go to the bathroom? In other words, everything’s normal, at least normal for me.

Embracing the cold winter air, I walk the few blocks to the shelter. It’s a slow walk because I know what’s coming. I’d love to be able to shower every few days, but I can make do with gas station bathrooms if I have enough wet wipes and deodorant. I like to keep my head shaved. It’s a sign I haven’t given up, and it always helps to blend in when you’re clean-shaven. Even though beards and facial hair are "in" right now, facial hair on the homeless is different. It's hard to trim a beard every day. The cheap disposable razors get damned near dangerous after a few trims. They leave your face bloody, so you let it grow out. A few days is fine, but after that, it gets scraggly unless you have clippers, which I do.

I pause for a moment before turning down the driveway to the shelter. There is a telltale trail of discarded cigarette butts. Several of the guys are out smoking. I nod because that's about as communicative as it gets around the shelter. They nod back as the smoke from their cigarettes eddies about their heads. I walk up to the security door and ring the bell. I hear the internal lock turn over and the short buzz signaling me to turn the knob and enter. I pull the door back and am greeted by the rush of warm air and the scent of sanitizer. I had become cold, so I am now grateful for the warmth. I know warmth will be elusive after I leave the shelter this time. I hope they'll probably let me put on my winter clothes before I leave.

Deshawn, a huge, friendly guy with a shaved head, is sporting his perpetual OSU stocking cap at the desk. He looks up as I come into the reception office where he is seated. Everyone comes through the office. Personnel from the shelter reserve the right to search anyone coming in. When I first arrived, they patted me down every time I came through. Once they got to know me, the frequency of pat-downs lessened.

"Hey, bro," he says calmly. "Good to see ya."

"Thanks," I say. "I think I've got some bags of stuff to pick up."

"Right. Hang on, Mr. Taylor." He picks up the phone and presses a few buttons. Being called Mr. Taylor is a strange formality, but most staff will address you as such. The bunks are assigned by last name, so it's easier to remember the last name than the first; at least, that's my assumption about the usage of last names.

"Hey, Angela, Mr. Taylor is here to pick up his stuff." He puts the receiver back down. There's a chair next to the small desk in the office. He motions for me to have a seat, so I do. My bags are already in the office, which answers my question about the slim chance of being able to stay despite my absence for the last few days.

Every time I've been in a shelter, it's been after some rough times on the street. I'm always thankful, even if the monitors are discourteous. I have dispensed with enough of my ego to know that I must go along to get along; after all, they're just doing a job. Getting put out of a shelter means I won't be allowed to return, or if I can return, I cannot come back for thirty days. Those thirty days can be lethal. I never want to burn a bridge with a shelter. I never know when I'll need them. I never know when the next episode will happen. I never know when I will happen.

I start thinking about where I'm going next. I have a good pair of gloves, so my hands won't freeze. I look at my two trash bags of clothing, shoes, paperwork, medication, and whatever else I collected at the shelter. I start taking stock of what I will need once I leave. Thankfully, because of the shifts I worked at the warehouse, I have a few hundred dollars to my name until my disability comes. I can buy a coffee and sit in a warm cafe when the library is closed. Sleeping in the Greyhound Station, especially when I have baggage, is usually good for a night or two until the agents realize I'm not going anywhere. They usually give me three or four nights if I look normal and am not disruptive. If you look like a bum, they usually give you just one night. It all depends on who's behind the ticket counter. Sometimes, I can catch a nap for a few hours overnight in a hospital if I can suitably hide my bags behind a chair or a planter. The hospital is used to patients' loved ones sleeping on chairs or couches. If I can find a safe place to stash my bags, a bathroom stall in a luxury hotel is a great place to nap. If I can get past the bellhops, the bathrooms are scented, and I can sit in a stall for several hours before they inquire if I am OK.

I snap out of my thoughts when Deshawn shuffles some paper. He is going through the sign-out sheet for the residents when Angela's many fingernails do their tappity-tap on the window of the door to where Deshawn and I are sitting.

"Hello there, Mr. Taylor!" Angela says in her never-ending happy retort to the world. She is the singular person in the shelter with a positive outlook, no matter the circumstance. I think if the world were to implode and the final destruction of man were to take place, Angela would find the silver lining. It is a pretty admirable trait, considering what she is surrounded by every day. She is the eternal light in an otherwise sullen world at the shelter.

"Hi, Angela," I say in response to seeing her. Since Deshawn and I are in the room, her presence takes up the last of the small office's space. She leans against the wall, looking at both Deshawn and me. With her clipboard pressed into her bosom, her chubby-cheeked, lively face gives a radiant smile.

"I'm so happy you are able to be with us today, Mr. Taylor," she says. "I know the BHU can be tough. I talk to those people more than I care to, but like the shelter, I'm glad they are there to do what they do."

"Yes, ma'am, I agree."

"Do you feel like you are all sorted out now?" she asks. I wonder if she's talking about my mental health, but I believe she is referring to the bags containing my belongings.

"Yes, ma'am." I have much to say about what happened in the BHU and getting kicked out of the shelter, but now is not the time. It won't change the inevitability of me leaving here in a few moments. Her hands are tied. So, I decide to go along, you know, to get along.

"Oh good, Mr. Taylor." She looks down at her clipboard, not really reading anything. I imagine she's just choosing her words about how to tell someone that, even though they've been excellent residents, they were gone from the facility longer than allowed. Now they are back out in the cold. The decision was not hers, but "them's the rules."

"Well, I guess you know what I've got to do here."

"Yes, ma'am."

"Today is your discharge day." She must say the words even though we both know what's happening. "You were gone from the facility longer than our leave allows; therefore, you surrendered your bed."

"Yes, ma'am."

She pauses for a moment and then continues, "Now, Caleb, I understand the circumstances of your leaving and why you violated the policy of the shelter. You really didn't have a choice."

"No, ma'am," I say, dropping my head. I hope she can finish this and let me start puzzling about which underpass or tent city is in my future.

"I talked to the shelter board about your situation. Everyone agrees that instead of barring you from applying for a bed for thirty days, you will be eligible for one if you start the process over." The process she's talking about is the 800 number. "I took the liberty of putting you on the list when the board reached its decision yesterday when we learned you were released from the hospital."

"Is there any chance to come in under the emergency shelter?"

"I'm sorry, no. The temperature has risen into the 40s, so we are not providing that type of shelter at this time unless the weather drops below freezing again."

"Well, thank you very much." I look up at her and see that she has a comfortable smile on her face, and Deshawn is nodding.

He utters under his breath, "Right on."

"I'm happy to say that your number is 17."

Seventeen is a good number. When I started the process at the beginning of November, I was much higher on the list.

"Man, Angela, seriously?" I'm somewhat shocked and genuinely appreciative. No one is required to step up to the plate for me. I am clearly outside the parameters that allow them to extend a bed to a resident.

"Oh, honey, it just didn't seem right to penalize you for something, well, for something like what you just went through. You are a good resident, and we are happy to help where we can," she says warmly.

"I'm just...thankful." I look down because I can feel my eyes tearing.

"Yes, Mr. Taylor," she says. "I wish I didn't have to put you out tonight, but aside from that, it seems we will still be able to help you despite this little hiccup."

"Ma'am, I completely understand."

"OK, baby," she says, and her clipboard emerges. "I need you to sign a couple of forms acknowledging you are being put out, that we got you back on the list, and the phone number you want on file for the shelter to call when the bed becomes available." She shows me the areas I need to sign and initial.

"I, uh, lost my phone with all the trouble at the library."

"OK, then it will be up to you to call the hotline to hear where you are on the list. Can you do that?"

"Thank you, ma'am, I can do that," I answer, handing the paperwork back.

"And the last bit of news I have is that on December first, we go into Mandatory Emergency Shelter status for the winter,"

Angela said. "That means everyone who needs an interior shelter will receive one. It gets crowded in here, but, at the very least, you'll be inside at night."

"Just a few days?"

"Yes, Mr. Taylor. Can you make it out there for a few days?"

"Sure."

"OK, just to be clear, you won't be getting a permanent bunk during emergency days. You will retain your current placement on the list while you receive an emergency mat. At 17, though, you should be back in a bunk fairly soon. Until then, you know the drill. You've got to be up and out of the cafeteria by 6:00 a.m. so breakfast can be served, but at least you're not outside overnight."

"I can manage a few days. I found a good coat and good gloves."

"I'm glad you're blessed with those," she says.

I cringe a bit inside at the word "blessed." I'm not sure buying items at a thrift store is a blessing, but I get what she's saying. I have more than a lot of homeless people have. And for the time being, I have my wits about me. That'll work in my favor for sure. I'll be cold, but I won't die from it. I'm almost sure of that.

CHAPTER EIGHTEEN

Malik — No Mo'

I miss Caleb by about an hour when I get back to the shelter. Angela updates me about his status.

"He indicated a few days out would be manageable," she says. I realize I would be beside myself if I were in that position. I can barely stand camping; I can't imagine being out on the streets. I recognize it is an experience that cannot be understood by people who have not been in that position.

I thank Angela and head down to my office. "Hey guys, what's good?"

Without looking up, La Rae asks, "What's up with your guy?"

"He got put out," I say quietly.

"Damn."

"I know." This type of thing happens frequently at the shelter. Guys miss their check-in, and they get put out for it. Usually, it's because they are drunk or high or whatever act of stupidity they committed. We are a first come, first served emergency shelter. The rules need to be cut and dry; otherwise, too many of the guys would come stumbling home drunk and cause havoc.

Tarisha tried everything she could think of this morning to save his bunk, but after forty-eight hours, everyone's hands are tied. Angela told me he is already back on the list to gain a bunk.

It was going to be a crap shoot because as the weather turns cold, the list grows longer and moves more slowly. I hope he gets a good number.

Caleb isn't answering his phone. I don't even know if he has his phone after the incident at the library. I have no way of reaching him. Caleb isn't a stranger to homelessness, so I know he'll figure something out. The library and hospitals have phones he could use. Hopefully, whatever money he has will help him along as he waits to get back into the shelter.

It's almost lunchtime. I tell Dex and La Rae I am going to take lunch and run a few errands. They both nod without saying anything. I make my way down the corridor thinking momentarily that I'd do a few searches for Pops, but decide against it. I let myself out the front. The usual smattering of clients is there again, smoking.

"'Sup?" I say, walking past them.

A muttering of responses comes back to me. I stop and turn to the guys.

"Any of you guys know Caleb Taylor? He's a tall white guy, real quiet."

"Ya mean No Mo'?" one of the guys responds.

"No Mo'?" I ask.

"Yeah, that big guy who doesn't talk to anyone. He just says 'no' when anyone tries to talk to him."

"That's No Mo'," the red-nosed, puffy-eyed client says.

"Could be," I respond, realizing I barely know anything about him and am not sure if this is the guy I'm trying to contact.

"Always got a book?" the client asks as a huge plume of smoke streams from below a yellowed, bushy mustache.

"Yeah," I say, remembering that indeed Caleb always carried a book with him. "That's the guy I'm talking about."

"He took off," the client said.

"Yeah, I know that," I say. "Do you know where he went?"

The client points over his shoulder, meaning 'out there somewhere.'

"Shit," I say. "Well, if you hear anything about him, let me know."

"Sure," the client says.

I knew this would be a dead end. Like the guys said, he didn't talk to people. Why would any of them keep tabs on him? I get into my car and sit. *How do you find a homeless guy in Columbus*? I sit in my car, looking through my windshield, not really knowing what to do next. I think about calling the homeless hotline to see if there is any way to reach someone on the list. I guess that privacy laws of some kind will stand as a barrier to reaching Caleb, so I don't even try.

I think about what the guy said about Caleb, or "No Mo,'" as they call him. Then I remember the book. Caleb always carries a book. I think about the library. Maybe someone at the library knows something about him. It couldn't hurt to check it out. I pull out of the shelter parking lot and head downtown to the Main Branch of the Metropolitan Columbus Library.

I wrestle my phone out of my pants pocket. I click the microphone symbol and say, "Phone number for Columbus Metropolitan Library." My screen displays the numbers for all the branches. I tap on the Main Branch. The phone number comes up, and I tap the phone icon.

The recording provides me with several options, none of which seem to directly connect me to someone in administration. I choose "Customer Service" and wait for a human. No such human comes. Instead, another recording asks how the library can best help, giving me six more options. I choose "Contact a Librarian."

This finally puts me in touch with a human.

"Hello, I'm a social worker with the Crossroads Men's Shelter," I state. "I'm hoping to contact someone there about an incident three or four days ago. A client of mine had a psychotic break and was ejected from the library. Does that ring a bell?"

"Yes," comes the male voice on the other line. "I remember that day. What exactly do you need?"

"I hope to gain some information about the incident, if possible. I'm trying to get him help, and knowing the details of the incident would assist me in getting him that help."

"Can you hold?"

"Of course."

The line mutes. I keep my eyes on the traffic as I drive. I really don't know what I am doing. I don't know if they can talk to me about Caleb's event. I don't even know what I will do with the information should they be able to give it to me.

"Hello, sir?"

"Yes."

"I'm going to put you on hold for just a minute, and I will transfer you to the Security personnel. Is that OK?"

"Sure," I say. "Anything would be great."

"OK, what is your name, sir?"

"Malik Arons with the Crossroads Men's Shelter."

"One moment."

Muzak fills my ears as I wait for the security personnel to pick up. It sounds like they are playing some melodic version of *Hungry Like the Wolf* by Duran Duran. For a moment, I forget about Caleb and laugh to myself, imagining what the band would think about this rendition of their song.

"Mr. Arons?"

"Yes, sir," I say.

"My name is Jarvis McCann. I'm head of security here at the Main Branch. You were calling about the incident from three days ago?"

"Yes, Mr. McCann. The man involved was a client here at the Crossroads Men's Shelter. I'm trying to figure out what happened so I can assist Mr. Taylor. Caleb Taylor was the name of the man arrested the other day."

"Well, to be clear, no one at the library arrested Mr. Taylor. Our security merely subdued your client until the CPD arrived."

"OK, thank you," I say. "Do you know if any charges are going to be pressed by the library?"

"Charges?" he says. "No, no charges. It was obviously an event for the Crisis Intervention Team to handle. It's just too bad that the responding officers weren't CIT."

Right, I think to myself. CIT would have officers trained in handling people with mental health issues. "OK, gotcha, that helps me a lot," I say, not knowing how it helps me. I hate winging things like this.

Tap. Tap. Tap. Tap. Tap.

"I have information on where he was admitted, and I'm following up on that." I pause, thinking of what to say next. "Is there any other information now?"

"No. The whole incident only lasted about twenty minutes."

"OK, I really appreciate your time."

"Sure. No worries."

"Thanks." I'm feeling like I'm hitting kind of a dead end.

"Do you want his stuff?"

"His stuff?"

"Yeah, he was working at a table up on the third floor. I've got a computer, a phone, and a bunch of paperwork of some sort."

Score!

"Yes, I'd absolutely love to gather his belongings and get them to him. He'll be very appreciative."

"Sure thing," McCann answers. "I'd be going crazy if I didn't have my phone with me, so if you can get these to him, that would be great. I'm here 'til five o'clock."

CHAPTER NINETEEN

Caleb — Frosty Wind Made Moan

I could try a hospital waiting room. There is the Greyhound depot. Sometimes, industrial buildings will have back doors left unlocked by workers who smoke. All of these options are made harder because I'm carrying two large black plastic bags, which are not exactly subtle. I should have asked if the shelter could stow my bags while I'm outside, but that's wishful thinking. Rules are rules at the shelter, and I'm sure there's a rule against keeping bags for people who aren't there.

When you're downtown, the wind can get caught between tall buildings, creating a whirring sound. Any moisture in the cracks of sidewalks and streets turns hard. I look at my surroundings with the gray sky and chilly wind and think about a song I used to hear when I was a kid in church. It's a Christmas carol of sorts. I've never really thought much about the song, but it rings true this afternoon in the grim weather.

In the bleak midwinter,
frosty wind made moan.
Earth stood hard as iron,
water like a stone.

Hard as iron, water like a stone...*what a beautiful use of words.*

It seems like an impossibility that I should be who I am. My belongings are shoved into plastic bags. I was recently discharged from a psych ward. Disability is my only income; aside from sporadic temp jobs, I usually leave or lose. The gauge of how successful my day will be is dependent on the pills shaking like maracas in my bag. Sleeping often means a concrete mattress.

I can't shake the feeling of defeat. I should stop right here and change what I am thinking. I know I'm supposed to take charge of my emotions and stay in the present. The past, though, knows how to creep in. I remember my elementary school days. The other kids called me Caleb the Creep. I don't know when it started, but it stuck. Like so much in my life, I didn't understand why I attracted such negative attention. Some of it had to do with my size. I was tall for my age, so my parents thought it would be a good idea to start me in school early, so I didn't stand out because of my height. My parents wanted me to fit in. So, even though I was as tall or taller than my classmates, I was actually a year younger than they were. I looked like an older kid, but I was emotionally and socially behind everyone.

Besides Caleb the Creep, I also got called Timber. The kids used to get on their hands and knees behind me while someone in the front pushed me so I would topple over and hit the ground on my back. They would all yell, "Timber!" as I fell. The laughter that followed was deafening. I became the favorite trick on the playground. I would lie there until the laughing stopped or they got tired of seeing me on the ground. Even at that early age I would be waiting on the ground for the water to recede.

I was so scared of going out to recess that I begged teachers to let me stay and help them in the classroom. I became a teacher's pet. It fit my personality. I was so relieved each day when the teacher said I could stay in and help. My whole spirit shrank to nothing when I couldn't stay in for recess. My mom raised a little boy who was caring. She believed that God would take care of me. She thought that if you treated people nicely, they would treat you nicely in return. I never learned how to be assertive or stand up for myself. If I couldn't stay inside during recess, I would take to walking the perimeter of the schoolyard, away from the other kids. I enjoyed walking alone. It was peaceful. The only drawback to my little walks was when I saw a group of boys marching across the lawn directly toward me. It meant I would soon be on the ground with them laughing at me. I never fought back. The water wouldn't let me. I just lay there with a dull expression on my face until I heard the bell ring. Sometimes, I wouldn't hear the bell, and a teacher would have to come and find me.

I shake my head hard to dispel the thoughts of my wasted life. "Stop it!" I yell at myself to the surprise of passers-by. I silently admonish myself for not keeping my emotions in check. I think about a Serbian guy in the shelter. He'd been in Columbus for two years. His English wasn't the best. It was one of the reasons he got fired from the construction jobs he came here to take. He used a phrase that was funny to me, a phrase much like "someone is crazy as a loon." In Serbia, someone who is nuts is "laughing like a madman at flour." The notion of laughing at flour is absurd, which makes the phrase all the more humorous. I imagine, when it happens, that I yell into the air like that, I am that madman laughing at flour. Words are so funny that way, both absurd and fantastic.

Pedestrians make a wide berth around me. I begin the walk toward the more impoverished area of the city. It's more dangerous where I am headed, but Homelessness 101 teaches you that the poor parts of town are patrolled less by cops, so the chance of spending a night uninterrupted is greater. There are usually soup kitchens and food pantries available in these neighborhoods as well. The threat of getting mugged for my few possessions is higher, but I'm pretty good at finding spots that are hidden. The sun is setting earlier and rising later, so the chance of sleeping is better.

Walking to the southern side of town, I see fellow shelter mates. The staff at the shelter has a designated area for storing their belongings, so if they are dressed reasonably well, they blend in with the crowd. I see one such guy. I can't remember his name, just that he is #10 at the shelter. He's inside a diner. He's reading a newspaper and sipping something from a large white mug. The window is decorated with frosted edges and a painted Christmas tree. It almost looks like a Norman Rockwell painting. As I walk by, our eyes meet. He raises his mug toward me, and I nod in return. I think about joining him but am quickly reminded that my bags and appearance aren't exactly right for blending in. I don't want to embarrass #10 or myself, so I keep walking.

It's approaching the end of the month, and I still have some money left because the shelter and the hospital provided a bunk and food. I have a couple hundred left in my account. I take a deep breath of crisp air. The cold won't kill me tonight, but maybe I can find a crappy motel. I heard some of the meth heads talking about a motel on the outskirts of town. They liked it because they rent by the hour, letting them do deals behind closed doors where the cops can't see. I wonder if that's something into which I want to insert myself. It amuses me that I am picky about the surroundings. I look exactly like someone who would be in such a place. As I walk, I try to remember the name of the motel. It'll come to me...

Today is the last day my bus pass will work, so I decide to hop on the #6 that goes up and down the main avenue, bisecting the unkempt neighborhood where I am headed. For the most part, everyone on the bus is quiet. It's nearly dark out now. People are going to work for the night shift, coming home from the day shift, and a few ride the bus to keep warm. It's the Americana many people never see. Those on the margins exist daily with little hope for change.

The bus driver doesn't look at me as I swipe my card. I get a ticket telling me I have six hours left on the card. I think about buying another one, but if I wait until morning, I will get one more day out of it, so I wait. These decisions punctuate my day. Finding a quarter lodged in a crack in the sidewalk is a small triumph. An apple costs more than a box of mac-n-cheese, so diabetes or not, my food intake is a decision driven by poverty. I don't have a stove, milk, or butter, so even the mac-n-cheese is out of reach. When they discharged me, I let them know I had nowhere to go. She gave me an insulin pen but said if it freezes, it won't be any good. She said I could use this vial, and hopefully, I'd have someplace to keep the medicine.

As the dinner hour approaches, I think about the guys back at the shelter lining up for dinner in a warm cafeteria. Envy creeps into my thoughts.

And the words fall into place:

> Envy looms large in my mind
> when life erodes my sense of self.
> I'm alive and locked into
> failings of my cursed mental health.
> Things grow green on the other side,
> where all my attention has gone.
> Leaving me wanting and fearful,
> more and more withdrawn.

I gaze out the window at the environment where I most comfortably exist. How different it is from where I used to reside. I used to blend into suburbia. I lived in a neighborhood full of children in a large, well-appointed home. My mania at that point fueled my ability to run a business, be active in my community, and be a good partner in my relationships. Mania, however, has its way of breaking down a life, dismantling it into pieces. I wonder if that is where the phrase "falling to pieces" came from, because that's spot on.

My past family grew accustomed to life in my absence. I became resigned to a solitude brought about by symptoms too egregious to manage. Things like accidentally discovering a girlfriend was unfaithful fueled anger, fed by a lifetime of trying to be a caring person, pushed me further into depression and anxiety. Every sordid act of my life drummed into my head that I was of no use in this world. It's enough to drive someone to an irrational rhythm of thinking. It's enough to keep you awake at night. While life around me continues forward, I become mired in melancholy, deeper and deeper each passing day. Days turn into months, and months into years, until who I am becomes a distant memory. I broke under the mélange of people's condemnations. I shake my head with near violence. I don't yell this time, but I need to change tonight, or I may be heading down a dangerous path again.

I will not surrender myself tonight to concrete and discomfort.

I can't.

I will be back in a shelter soon. I will slowly save money. I will begin therapy again. I will take my medications. I will eat in a fashion to stave off symptoms of diabetes. I can do a thousand other little things to improve my life. And I will. As long as Craig stays away, and the medications quell the mood swings. I miss my room in San Diego. I miss the ragtag, grubby family I collected at the shelter there. I miss many things. I shake my head again, this time drawing attention from the few riders on the bus. *What do I care?* If they think I'm crazy, then bully for them for figuring out the truth about their fellow rider. I am mad and laughing at flour.

The bus rambles down the avenue, now pitched in the darkness of late fall. Neon signs blink. Reflections of the bus in large storefront windows echo back at me. Pedestrians with hoods pulled tightly around their faces walk down the sidewalks, their hands plunged deep into their pockets for warmth. Smoke from their cigarettes wafts around their heads like ghostly apparitions. In this neighborhood, there are no banks, just check-cashing businesses. There are no supermarkets, just convenience stores. There are no playgrounds, just abandoned lots. And it all feels comfortable to me. People from my past would never frequent such neighborhoods; ironically, my peers of today are its inhabitants.

A car alarm blares nearby. A few laughs, thick with liquor and cigarettes, arise from people. A few women walk aimlessly down the street. They are not scantily clad like in the movies. They wear normal clothes, but their roving footsteps and watchful eyes communicate what is available to opportunistic men driving slowly around the neighborhood. The women walk and wait for cars to slow down, to be assessed by their potential customers, and to participate in their carnal commerce.

CHAPTER TWENTY

Malik — DWB

There's gotta be a different way of doing things for guys at the shelter.

This thought is at the front of my mind as I sit down at home after getting Caleb's things. I look at my phone and tap the weather app. It will be 34° tonight, still above freezing, so there won't be an emergency shelter placement. Caleb would've left the shelter with his clothing and whatnot, but I'm pretty sure he didn't have a sleeping bag, or at least that's what Angela surmised by the amount of things Caleb had when he left.

It makes me feel uncomfortable for a moment, sitting on my plush couch with my thermostat set to 70°F.

Tap. Tap. Tap. Tap. Tap.

A phrase used often at the shelter when patience runs thin is, "No one grows up wanting to be a junkie." It's a simple reminder that although lots of the guys have made bad decisions, many of those decisions are being influenced by addiction, mental illness, or extreme financial hardship. That would apply to Caleb, I imagine. He's a bright guy, always reading and courteous to others. I fear that he gets caught up in a Law of Attraction loop, where he is drawn into a world of negative reinforcement that he doesn't deserve.

My phone rings. It's Drake. "Hello?"

"Hey man, are you busy tonight?"

"Not really. Why, what's up?

"Would you be willing to run to Home Depot with me and help me load some lumber?"

I don't really want to, but it's Drake. Despite being a tight-ass conservative, he's a generous guy. He's helped me time and time again. I put aside my reluctance and answer, "Sure, no problem."

"Right on. I'll swing by your place in about thirty minutes."

"OK, just honk when you're here, and I'll come down."

I have learned a lot working on houses with Drake. He ran a tight ship. A friend of his was a contractor and donated time to Drake's projects. Neither the contractor nor Drake would abide slacking on the job, but in return, Drake would usually drop by the site with food or drinks a few times a week. He was also good at giving small bonuses to workers who went above and beyond what the contractor was asking.

Tonight, though, it was just a run for supplies, so the guys have the materials they need to continue with the renovation tomorrow. Drake's business model is pretty simple. He'll find houses owned by the local Land Bank, a repository for foreclosed homes. He selects a house in a marginal neighborhood, renovates it so it's sound, and then rents it out room by room for about $300-$400 a month per room. He'll give a little break to anyone in the house who shows rooms to prospective tenants when a room becomes available. For the most part, he has very few vacancies. He's not a slumlord; his homes are well-maintained. He sees to that.

Lumber from tonight is going toward building a closet inside one of the bedrooms that does not have one. It was supposed to be an office, but Drake could use the room for another tenant, which, in the long run, would be more beneficial to him. Drake attracts a lot of men who have recently been divorced and need a place to regroup. He also gets a lot of recovering alcoholics after hitting rock bottom and then turning themselves around. He rents to men only. His thinking is he doesn't want mixed-gender buildings, mostly for the safety of the women, but also because he doesn't want to deal with relationships gone bad and losing a tenant after love falls on hard times. There are enough "female-only" ads on Craigslist that he doesn't feel too bad about the gender restriction.

Even though Drake was an administrator for social service outreach with the city, he's never lost his "social worker" frame of mind. His model is designed to make him money, but it's also because he knows that, with rising housing prices, some guys need a break from the responsibility of owning or renting an entire home.

I hear the car horn from below. I grab my coat to go downstairs to meet Drake in his Dodge Ram 1500. My buzzer rings. Odd. I buzz Drake through. He's at my door in a few seconds, saying he really needs to use my bathroom. He puts his satchel down on the table and rushes to the bathroom. I hear him talking, and I laugh to myself about how the age of cell phones makes anywhere you are a meeting place. Anywhere, including the bathroom, even while using it.

Drake finishes up both types of business, and the faucet turns on as he washes his hands. He asks if I can drive because he has some phone calls to make to his contractor about the accuracy of the materials list. I agree, and we head downstairs. We pull away from my apartment and wind our way to the interstate. We're cruising along when lights flash in my rear-view mirror. *Shit,* I think. I'm not speeding. I didn't change lanes incorrectly.

Shit.

Drake looks up and says, "Aw, crap, man, I'm sorry." I drive to where there is room to pull over, and Drake continues, "I swear I will pay for the ticket if you get one."

I hear Drake, but I'm focused on the flashing lights in the mirror and the cop who is lumbering toward my window. The darkness makes the swirling red and blue lights seem larger than they really are. I think about being a kid and the swirling lights at night. My chest tightens.

I don't have control over this, but I can get control of myself.

I don't have control over this, but I can get control of myself.

I don't have control over this, but I can get control of myself.

I don't have control over this, but I can get control of myself.

I don't have control over this, but I can get control of myself.

The silhouette of the police officer walking closer fills me with dread. I dig my wallet out and put my ID on the dashboard. I roll down my window. I put my hands on the wheel at ten and two, fingers spread wide.

"What are you doing?" Drake asks, his profile changing from blue to red from the squad car lights.

"Trying not to get killed."

"What do you mean?"

The officer arrives at my window. He's wearing his cop hat pulled down just above his eyes. I see his stern face and a mustache with a thin white patch on the left side.

"Driver's license and registration," he demands.

"Officer, I'm going to reach for the registration. My license is on the dashboard."

The officer doesn't say anything, but he moves his right hand over his holster. I hand him my documents. The officer looks at them. "This license does not match the registration."

"The truck belongs to my friend here. I'm driving him to the store."

The officer leans down to look at Drake.

Drake asks, "Do you need my license?"

"Yes," the officer says.

Drake goes to withdraw his ID and realizes he left his satchel with his wallet on my dining room table. "Shit."

"Problem?" the officer asks.

"I left my wallet at home."

Tap. Tap. Tap. Tap. Tap

Tap. Tap. Tap. Tap. Tap.

"I see." The officer looks at my ID. "Mr. Arons, is it?"

"Yes."

"Step out of the car."

I do so without hesitation, making sure I move slowly, with my hands in plain sight.

"Seems you're driving a car that doesn't belong to you."

"I'm just taking him to Home Depot."

"I see. Well, let's just figure out what's happening here. Turn around and put your hands on the car."

I follow his instructions.

I don't have control over this, but I can get control of myself.

I don't have control over this, but I can get control of myself.

I don't have control over this, but I can get control of myself.

I don't have control over this, but I can get control of myself.

I don't have control over this, but I can get control of myself.

The passenger door opens, and Drake says, "Officer, is this really necessary? It's my truck. There's nothing wrong with allowing my friend, my licensed friend, to drive it."

Shut up! I think to myself.

The officer barks, "Stay in the truck!" He returns his right hand to his holster.

The officer taps the inside of my foot, indicating he wants my legs spread farther apart. He pats my shoulders and arms. He reaches under my coat to pat down my lower back and abdomen. He runs his hands down the outside and inside of my legs. He lifts up the bottom of my pants to check for any weapons that may be strapped to my ankles. Without a word, he leaves me leaning against the truck and returns to his patrol car. He sits there for what seems like an eternity. I don't dare move.

"What the hell?" Drake says, opening his door again.

"Get back in the god-damned car, Drake," I say through clenched teeth. My hand is tapping the top of the car. 10 times. 20 times. 30 times.

"This is bullshit. You're licensed. You weren't speeding. And the car is registered."

"I swear to God, Drake, if you do not get back in the truck, I will hurt you."

Drake is taken aback at my seriousness. He keeps looking at me. I don't have the ability to tell him this isn't about speeding. It's not about registration. It's not about a valid license. It's about being pulled over because I am Black.

"Right." He gets back into his seat.

The cop, taking his sweet time, walks back to the truck.

"All right," he says. "You're free to go." He hands me back my documents. He leans down to talk to Drake. "Son, you should never leave the house without an ID. Your friend could have been in big trouble. Who's to say he didn't steal this vehicle?"

My heart is racing, but I manage to say, "Thank you, officer." *But what I'm thinking is, thank you for what? For not shooting me?*

I don't have control over this, but I can get control of myself.

I don't have control over this, but I can get control of myself.

I don't have control over this, but I can get control of myself.

I don't have control over this, but I can get control of myself.

I don't have control over this, but I can get control of myself.

I get back into the truck. I'm shaking.

"Are you OK?" Drake asks.

"Yeah, I just need a minute."

"You weren't even speeding," Drake says.

I'm not sure he understands that I don't have to be doing anything illegal to be pulled over. This is the third time this year it's happened.

"It doesn't matter, man."

"I guess not."

We both sit there. I'm composing myself, and Drake is getting madder by the second. The oscillating lights of the squad car cease their display. I tell him, "Just be thankful you don't have to deal with this crap."

"It's ridiculous," Drake says.

"No, it isn't. It's deadly serious. I'm just glad you were in the truck."

"Like that makes a difference."

"It could have. That's the messed-up thing about this. You just never know. Every time I drive somewhere, there's a chance it may happen." I pause for a moment. "Let's go to Home Depot. Do you mind driving now?"

"I don't have my license."

"Shit, that's right."

"Sorry, man." I can see Drake's face as he tries to think of something to do. "Did you get that asshole's name?"

"Why?"

"Because that was bullshit."

My temper flares. "God dammit, Drake, just drop it. It's just the way it is. There are bad cops out there. But they know what they're doing. You can't stop a cop from making an arrest, even if nothing's been done wrong. It's just the way it is, dammit."

"But that's just wrong."

"No shit! Tell it to Sandra Bland, or Daunte Wright, or Philando Castile. They died!" Rage takes over my mind. "Body cams are a joke. Eric Garner and George Floyd were killed before everyone's eyes, some of them right on TikTok and Facebook. I'll bet you anything that dude had his body cam turned off."

"I get it, man."

I look at him. "Do you?"

"Hey, man, It's over. You're OK."

"I just hate it. They don't know me. I'm a Black guy driving a truck that's not registered to me. I can't just be the guy driving to the store, I gotta be the Black guy who's stealing a car." I don't know if it is even possible for him to understand. I'm glad he's upset about it, but he's trying to tell me to act like a white person. I don't have that choice. "Look, will you drive now?"

"Yeah, OK. Sure. Of course."

I tap the entire way to Home Depot and repeat my mantra under my breath.

This will be a Xanax night for sure.

CHAPTER TWENTY-ONE

Caleb — Room 9

I step off the bus with my Hefty bag luggage. I'm a block down from The Cheap Nite Inn, the place where some of the guys from the shelter go when they get their checks. It is supposed to be inexpensive and relatively clean. I used to think spending money on a motel room seemed extravagant for someone who is homeless, but after being homeless more than a few times, I understand completely the use of motel rooms. It keeps you human. It gives you access to a bed, a bathroom, and a window to look out at the cold while you are warm inside. And the solitude. It can literally be a lifesaver. You are purchasing the façade of security, twenty-four hours at a time.

I'm on the opposite side of the street from the motel. I look for a break in traffic to cross. It's dark now. The neon signs from pawn shops and convenience stores illuminate the street. Cigarette butts litter the sidewalk in good company with flattened beer cans still in their paper bags. There are a few characters hanging out on the street below despite the low temperature and time of day. There's a Wings shop across the street, the open sign blinking on and off, advertising an array of fried, inexpensive food.

Stores along the street are open for business. They exist between vacant buildings with plywood covering their windows and graffiti covering the plywood. Bags and wrappers flicker down the sidewalk when the wind blows. I walk by a man cloaked by his hoodie while leaning against a defunct payphone, the sweet scent of marijuana filling the air. The whole neighborhood looks like Sesame Street after Gordon and Susan were foreclosed on and Oscar the Grouch started dealing meth.

These are the types of neighborhoods that have been my home for the past several years, or is it decades now? I'm not conspicuous here with my plastic bags. I don't stand out for being homeless. Homelessness is common in this neighborhood. So are drugs. So are crazy people. I've already counted three needles on the sidewalk. Ironically, these neighborhoods provide a lot of comfort, although comfort is the wrong word. They provide cover. No one's judging anyone in this neighborhood. Judgment is for people who have achieved a certain station in life. If any of us on the streets here have achieved something in our lives, we lost it on the way back down to this neighborhood.

A blinking light illuminates the sign for the Cheap Nite Inn. It draws me in like a beacon. As I think about my choice to rent a room at the motel, I'm more confident that it is the right thing to do. Normally, if you know a few people, someone who has a motel room might let you crash on the floor. They might charge you. If you're a woman, you can always put out. If a woman has the room, sometimes I've brought food and beer to exchange for a piece of floor. Most times, though, they want stronger stuff to put up their nose or into a vein. I just don't have those kinds of contacts.

In my long history of psych admissions and homelessness, I've never had to deal with the destructive nature of addiction. I think this has saved me from dying on the streets. Being high in these neighborhoods is dangerous. No one judges you for it, but they will take your wallet, your shoes, your clothes, and anything else they can peel away as you flop down on a heroin high, unable to fend for yourself.

My personal nature makes me wary of creating any acquaintances. The motel room will be just for me. It's a gamble. If Angela was mistaken, or something else happens, I won't have any more backup money. I will truly be on the streets again. I decide that if I can't trust the word of Angela, I can't trust the word of anyone. If I get the motel room, I will have enough left over to feed myself for a few days, too. I know about the Lutheran place that serves meals and the Sandwich Line, so I think I'll be set for food.

Convenience stores do well in these poor neighborhoods. They charge high prices, but they take food stamps or EBT cards: the poor man's credit card. You can buy soda with food stamps. A lot of people buy a large fountain drink, dump some out, and fill it back up with a three-dollar bottle of bottom shelf Vodka. I've done that a lot on cold nights—the buzz keeps part of the chill away. To be honest, I think that theory is complete bullshit: booze taking the chill away. The chill is still there. The buzz is enough of a mood changer to make freezing overnight a little more tolerable.

I cross the street when a break in traffic comes. The Cheap Nite Inn is a two-story stucco building with faded beige paint, weather-worn doors, and cheap tin numbers on each room. The office faces the street. A small garden bed contains red rock and two very sickly-looking juniper bushes. A garbage can overflows near the glass door leading to the front office. Inside, a neon sign flashes VACANCY every few seconds. Taped to the inside of the window below the neon sign is a hand-written one stating, HOURLY RATES AVAILABEL.

The typo makes me smirk.

The rooms extend out behind the office in a two-story, crumbling, concrete U-shaped structure. There seems to be about twenty rooms, and a quick observation indicates most are available. A woman leans against the iron railing at the end of the second level, watching me as I enter the front office. The rooms all overlook the parking lot where two cars are parked haphazardly. Remnants of white lines painted on the parking lot suggest what used to be parking spaces. The cars have ignored the suggestions.

Pushing against the heavy glass door to the motel office, a sharp scraping sound grates in my ears. The wood paneled office is cut in two by a white Formica countertop that is well past its prime. The office smells heavily of smoke despite there being a NO SMOKING sign on the counter. A white guy with unkempt brown hair, reading glasses, and a beer gut held in by a red and black OSU sweatshirt sits behind the counter.

"Hi," I say, setting my plastic bags down on the orange and brown checkered linoleum.

"Need a room?" says the man whose name badge reads Gravy.

"Yeah," I say. "Got any deals for three days?"

"Three days?" he asks, apparently unaccustomed to having guests pay for an entire day, let alone three days. "Thirty-nine bucks a night."

"OK," I say, thinking I might be able to haggle a better deal, but I decide against the thought of arguing. I reach into my pocket to retrieve my debit card from my wallet.

"Ya don't have cash?" Gravy asks.

"Uh, no," I say. "Just my debit card."

Gravy sighs loudly and slides his girth off the chair and walks the three feet to the computer. He starts banging with two fingers at the keyboard like he's trying to chop wood. After several minutes, he takes the card I have in my hand, swipes it through his machine, and waits for a receipt to be issued. When the card reader spits out a thin white strip of paper, he hands it to me.

"Sign here."

There's a ballpoint pen duct taped to a small chain that is screwed into the Formica. I take the pen and sign the receipt. "Room 9," he says, pulling a key off the wall for me. "If you are selling drugs or turning tricks in there, I don't want to know about it. Sleep tight."

"Ok, thanks." I pick up my two bags and exit the office, triggering the loud scraping sound once again. I walk to Room 9, passing a soda and snack vending machine at the bottom of the staircase. The iron railing is sturdy, albeit rusted. My bags bounce against my legs as I ascend the stairs. I'm almost there. This will be home for the next three days or so. I don't even know what home feels like anymore. I guess that's why I look at Room 9 at the Cheap Nite Inn thinking *I may be put out of the shelter, but at least this time, I'm not outside.*

And the words drop into place:

> Homeward I go, forestalling cold,
> four walls providing cover.
> My bones feel weary as I grow old,
> as limits I discover.
> My hand searches out the wooden door,
> with a key to turn the lock.
> Dismissing nights upon a concrete floor,
> deaf to Grim Reaper's knock.

CHAPTER TWENTY-TWO

Malik — Yo Mama

The next evening, I sit and look at Caleb's computer, papers, and bag sitting on my dining room table. I stand there with my hands on my hips, staring at the components of Caleb's life. *Where is Caleb?* The question is vexing me. McCann from the library copied the Incident Report and included it with Caleb's things. I pick it up and reread it. It doesn't detail much that I hadn't surmised. The names of the officers involved are included, which may be of use down the road. There isn't much more I can do, which works out well because Drake and the other guys are coming over with takeout.

I am looking at the Incident Report when the buzzer sounds. I walk to the door and press the button, unlatching the street-level door. I unlock my door and leave it ajar so the guys can enter. I hear their voices as they ascend the stairway. Keith pushes open the front door with his foot, hands full of Chinese take-out and a six-pack of Crazy Dick's lager. The lager is his favorite and no one else's, which means he has the whole six pack to himself, the cheeky bastard.

Drake is behind Keith, flipping his curly, brown hair out of his face as usual. He holds up the signature bottle of Scotch he brings to all our get-togethers. Adam, always the slowest, holds up more bags of takeout from the Chinese restaurant down the street.

The order is always the same: Kung Pao for Drake, General Tso's for Keith, Almond Chicken for Adam, and Shrimp Lo Mein for me. You can feed a fifth person with the extra fried rice, complimentary egg rolls, and fortune cookies. The free egg roll is genius marketing on behalf of the restaurant owners. It lured us in once, and we have been going back ever since.

Everyone knows the drill. Shoes by the door to save my floor. Coats on the rack by the front door to keep rain, snow, and whatever other elements from hijacking rides into my home. After the shoes are discarded, they all sit around my elevated restaurant table between the kitchen and the living area. I love this damned table, dark wood like the rest of my apartment with low-back chairs. Everyone's feet are hanging in the air once seated, all but Adam, who is nearly NBA height, yet never played a day of sports in his life.

I gather up Caleb's things and set them on the end table by the sofa. Food is on the table. The white boxes are handed out. The fried rice and egg rolls are put in the middle of the table. Everyone knows to put beer in the fridge, grab one if they want it, or get glasses of water from the spigot in the fridge door. We all eat with chopsticks, so there won't be anything to wash. As the boxes are opened, the aromas blend together, and there's a few moments of silence as our palates are whet.

"So, what's new with you, dude?" Drake chimes in. "Any more run-ins with Officer Friendly?"

"No," I say, not quite sure if I'm ready to joke about it.

"What happened?" Adam asks.

"I had a front row seat to racial profiling yesterday," Drake says.

"Say what?" Keith says.

"Just another day in paradise, man," I answer.

"What? What happened?" Adam asks.

"Just another DWB." Tap. Tap. Tap. Tap. Tap.

"It happened again?" Keith asks.

"Yes, yesterday."

"Goddammit," he replies.

Adam walks over to the television and puts on ESPN. OSU is playing. He sits down on the couch as the game appears on the screen.

"I'm sorry, Malik. I don't even know what to say." He pauses a moment and then says to Drake, "Dude, grab me a beer."

"OK," he responds. He grabs one for himself, also.

"Malik," Adam calls out. "Can I eat over here?"

"Hell no," I say. "Get your ass over to the table."

"God, you're worse than my mother," Adam replies as he walks to the table.

Beer caps are popped. Glasses are brought over to the table for the Scotch. I have seltzer water from the fridge. By the time I sit down, chopsticks are clicking away as we dive into our entrees.

"Who paid this week?" I ask, knowing my week is coming up soon.

"I did," Adam says, which means next week is my turn.

"Thanks, man," I say as I pull an egg roll out of the box.

"Where's the duck sauce?" Everyone looks through the bags in front of them.

"Here it is," Drake answers as he puts the little plastic cup in the middle, taking care to peel the lid back. I dunk my egg roll in the sauce and bite off the end. Keith raises his arm and snaps a beer cap across the room into the sink.

"Hey, asshole," I say. "Get off your fat ass and put it in the trash. That'll end up in my garbage disposal."

"OK, Mom," he says. "Keep your panties on."

"Yeah, that's what I told her when she stopped by last night,"

I quip.

And it's on! The four of us could sit around the table trading "yo mama" jokes for hours.

"Yo mamma so fat I took a picture of her last Christmas, and it's still printing," Adam says to me.

Drake says to Adam, "Man, yo mama's so fat, she got arrested at the airport for ten pounds of crack. And that was just her ass sticking out of her pants."

Adam was ready with, "Yo mama is so fat when she goes swimming the whales start singing, 'We are family!'"

We are all laughing and trying to eat at the same time.

Drake adds, "Your mama is so fat she doesn't need the internet; she's already worldwide."

I add, "Yo momma's so fat, she makes Free Willy look like a tic tac."

I love our banter. It could start at any given minute whenever we are together. It is silly and juvenile, but it's fun. It takes us all away from our lives for a few minutes. I forget about Officer Friendly for the time being.

As the Chinese food starts to run thin, one by one, we all push back from the table, patting bellies and tossing chopsticks in the garbage. We gravitate toward the living area to sit down to watch the game.

"Hey, Malik," Keith says. "Whatever happened to your nut case?"

"Which one?"

"That guy who went ballistic at the library," Drake asks.

"Man, he got screwed. That's his stuff over there on the coffee table."

"You found him?" Adam asks.

"No, I didn't, but I got his stuff back from the library."

"What are you going to do with it?" Drake says, taking a long pull off his beer and settling into the couch.

"Hell if I know."

"He's not back at the shelter?" Adam asks.

"Nah, man," I say. "He got put into the psych ward, so he lost his bunk because he didn't check in for a few days."

"Why would he lose a bunk?" Keith asks.

"Because he's not technically homeless anymore if he goes to the hospital," I answer, knowing full well how ridiculous it is. There is a pause in the conversation.

"Damn," Drake says. "That's cold."

"Don't even get me started."

"So, where is he now?" Adam asks.

"I don't know, man." I'm getting frustrated thinking about Caleb's predicament and the nonsense rule about putting guys out when they are hospitalized.

"Man, there should be an app for finding homeless people. Chip 'em like a dog," Keith offers.

"That's messed up," I say, but then I consider my present situation. "But it sure would help."

"Aren't there about a million unused pagers now?" Adam asks. "We should write a grant to give homeless people pagers."

"Right," Drake says sarcastically. "More money for people who don't know how to use it."

And that's how a lot of our conversations unfold. Drake is a rarity in the social work field—he is a conservative Republican. Adam, Keith, and I are garden variety liberal social workers.

"You just sit and wait, Drake," I say. "The current Republican administration will take care of any money getting to people who really need it."

"Oh, whatever. Even you complain about how stupid your

clients are for not taking advantage of work and education programs."

"Hey, man, I'm not saying that a lot of my clients aren't lazy and messed up," I answer. "I'm just not ready to give up on programs that benefit them because there are some despicable dudes in the mix."

"I hate it when Mom and Dad fight," Keith mocks us from the couch, throwing a balled-up chopstick wrapper at us.

Drake and I both laugh. Like the "Yo Mama" jokes, we could go on and on about politics too. Our unspoken rule is only one of us can spar with Drake at a time, otherwise it just becomes three on one. It's all good though. Drake keeps us all on our toes, and deep down, I know he isn't as conservative as he lets on. He just loves being the devil's advocate. Truth is, he is a hugely generous guy.

We settle down for a while. OSU starts on offense and pulls away from Indiana. The court is a flurry of action. Passes are getting picked off every few minutes, and OSU is running them back for easy layups. The guys are into it, but I find my thoughts returning to Caleb. His stuff stares back at me. I'd be freaked out if I didn't have my laptop. That's when I realize I screwed up.

"Shit," I say.

"What?" Adam says. "OSU's up!"

"Nah, man," I say. "Not that. I think I screwed up taking Caleb's stuff from the library."

Tap. Tap. Tap. Tap. Tap.

"Who?" Keith says.

"My lunatic from the library," I answer.

"Oh," Drake says. "What did you do wrong now?"

"I took his stuff from the library," I say. "I should have left it. He's going to go back and try to get it, and it will be gone."

Tap. Tap. Tap. Tap. Tap.

"Oh," Adam says. "Yeah, you kinda did screw him."

"What're you gonna do about it?" Keith asks.

"Guess I'll be spending tomorrow at the library."

There it is, the tightness in my chest. It seems like an eternity between when I realize I have to go to the library tomorrow and when the guys will leave. Usually, after the game, we sit around and shoot the shit. Adam tells us how much his girlfriend annoys him. Keith tells us which guy, in the very long series of guys, he's seeing. Drake asks us all again if we want to partner in buying and renovating a home.

Tonight, though, I bring the evening to a close early. There is a feeling in my chest and a knot in my stomach. I offer an "early morning at work tomorrow" excuse. They, of course, accept the reason while simultaneously wondering if it is the truth, not in a nosey way, but in concern for my state of mind. It's no secret that I get moody and that I tap. I just generally don't involve others in my trials. It doesn't really matter; we all know each other well enough to respect each other's word for things.

"Ya sure?" Adam asks.

"Yeah," I reply. "Sorry to break it up early."

"OK," says Drake. "Ya want me to take the garbage down on my way out?" Drake is being kind, but I just need everyone gone.

"I'm good," I say. "Thanks, though."

Taking their cues, the guys get up, find their shoes and coats, and begin to head out. A series of fist bumps and well-wishes are exchanged, and then they are gone. I close the door behind them and lean against it. My forehead is sweaty. I pull my sweater off and stand there in my T-shirt.

Xanax or bourbon?

Tap. Tap. Tap. Tap. Tap.

My heart rate accelerates. The panic sets in. It's a Xanax night.

In the bathroom, I open the medicine cabinet, take the bottle, open it, and pop two into my mouth. I lean forward, sucking water from the faucet. Now, the wait. I'm hoping I got the pills in time.

The panic attack began the minute I realized I overstepped with Caleb by taking his belongings. I tap in increments of five. I tap 10, 15, 20 times. I needed everyone to go, but something in me said to ride it out until they left. That was a bad decision. It's a bad decision I make too often. The social worker/problem solver in me doesn't want the panic to affect me. It is pure pride. Hubris. I don't want to be like my clients. I have always put off seeking real professional help. I know enough about anxiety disorders to manage it, but sometimes it is unpredictable. And like tonight, the waves of anxiety just keep coming.

Tap. Tap. Tap. Tap. Tap.

Tap. Tap. Tap. Tap. Tap.

The truth is I am playing God with Caleb, and I shouldn't be. It's a thing we social workers do when we get involved without being invited. Social work is supposed to be methodical, not intrusive. But I have a need to solve problems. I need to control things. The need I feel often compels me to intrude on situations.

I have been intrusive with Caleb. Now he is out of the hospital without the one thing he needs to stay organized and grounded. It would be like me without Xanax. In my need to solve Caleb's problem, I have become Caleb's problem. The problem-solver has become the problem-creator. I wasn't asked to be involved. I substituted my solution for the reality of the client's life. And hell, he isn't even a client. He's been put out, so he isn't a member of the shelter. I just jacked the guy's electronics. Caleb could probably file charges against me. I am guilty of overreach, of arrogance, of playing God. Sweat returns to my forehead. My breathing quickens.

•••

I remember Pops standing in the kitchen. I was about nine years old. There was yelling. Pops needed money. Moms had money stashed in the house. Pops knew it, but Moms wouldn't budge. She was protecting me and protecting her funds. Funds she needed since Pops never helped financially. Pops charged at Moms, charged at us, because I was behind her. She backed up to the wall, pinning me behind her. Pops slammed his palms on each side of Moms' head. I remember being terrified. I remember moisture in my pants as fear took over. Moms screamed. Pops screamed. I stood silent, frozen.

"Imma kill you, woman, if you don't give me what's mine!" Pops shouted.

"Do your worst," Moms said steadily, in a low voice. The silence that followed was deafening. I closed my eyes. I didn't want Moms to die. I didn't want Pops to kill her. I wanted to be gone. The next thing I remember, Moms had my face in both of her hands, gently caressing my forehead.

"Baby," she said. "It's over now. You can open your eyes. He's gone."

Gone? I remember thinking. "Where did he go?"

"I don't know, baby. Let's get you changed and into bed." I remember looking down at my urine-soaked pajamas and wondering how that happened.

"OK," I remember saying. I also remember thinking, *If you don't know where he is, how do you know he is gone?*

At thirty-three years old, I still tap into those emotions. I feel nine years old. Triggers bring me back to those insecure days when a night with Pops could end traumatically. I just never knew when things would erupt. I was constantly tiptoeing on thin ice, not sure when the cracks would open and swallow me. My nine-year-old mind, once safe in bed, would sit and think about what I had done, about how I could have done something differently, about why when Moms protected me it ended with Pops hurting Moms and then Pops leaving. We never knew where Pops went. That was the scariest part for me. The monsters under my bed weren't goblins or ghosts...my monster was Pops. I would be in bed after Moms turned the night light on and left the room with the door slightly open. I lay in bed feeling like I was responsible for fixing what was wrong. I had no idea how to fix it, but I knew it was up to me. I needed to solve the problem.

•••

I open my eyes after going down the path of my sordid family history and into a convoluted dream. I must've fallen asleep quickly because the full effect of the Xanax is still kicking in. My T-shirt is soaked through. I walk into the bathroom. I sit on the toilet, one hand on the bathtub basin. My breathing is slowing down as the Xanax creeps through my body methodically, slithering over axons, calming nerves. Sleep will take over soon, so I walk into my bedroom. Moose is on the bed after hiding from the guys. I unbuckle my pants and allow them to fall to the ground. I step out of them and sit on the bed. I pull my comforter back and sink into the mattress. Maybe in the morning I can solve Caleb's problems.

But tonight, I'm letting Xanax solve mine.

Tap. Tap. Tap. Tap. Tap.

CHAPTER TWENTY-THREE

Caleb — Taking Stock

I stand in the doorway of Room 9. Light from the yellow lamps filters through the curtains. The antiquated clock radio on the bedside table tells me it's nearly eight o'clock at night. I drop my bags on the floor, close the door behind me, and sit on the bed. Surprisingly, the bed holds my weight without feeling uncomfortable. It is large enough that I can stretch out. The first night of sleep without twelve other men in the room or fifteen-minute bed checks will be superb.

The bedspread is rough to the touch, so I pull back the cover and feel the sheet. It is soft after many washings, not terrible. I assess how my body feels. I'm so used to feeling exhausted from carrying my bags that I'm unused to what I'm feeling now: The feeling of being comfortable. The room is warm, quiet, and houses just one person. I take it in. It's everything you'd think a dive motel would be. A room large enough for one queen bed, a side table with a lamp screwed down tightly, a nook in the wall to hang clothes, a three-drawer dresser, and a table with a chair next to the window looking over the parking lot. The bedspread, curtains, and carpet appear designed to clash. The carpet shows a worn pathway leading to the bathroom. It is small, but on the bright side, there are no bloodstains.

The side table, with etchings from past inhabitants, is heavy and sturdy. The nook for clothing contains no hangers, just an ancient fire evacuation map. The dresser, whose drawers sit askew, has about half the working pulls. The table next to the window, along with the chair pushed under it, seems to be the most stable of furnishings. I sit in the darkness for a few minutes, allowing my eyes to adjust to the atmosphere. As I sit, my memory strays to a place I haven't thought about in years. After one of my fraught moves, I ended up near Albany, Georgia, after reading about an opportunity to help an old guy out with his property in exchange for a free room. With cosmic irony, the ad was posted by someone whose mania was worse than mine. Despite the bedlam that took place inside the house, it backed up to a large pond that was secluded and peaceful. I sat on the dock, mesmerized by the surprising refuge...

•••

A dragonfly landed on my knee. Several more flew by, landing near, seemingly uninhibited by the large two-legged mammal sitting on their dock. I was captivated by the iridescent shimmer of the dragonfly's wings. I'd learned the names of the different dragonflies. The one on my knee was an azure bluet. Mosaic darners and eastern pond hawk dragonflies whooshed around as well. They landed deftly on nearby stalks of grass. Mechanical black legs brushed over their compound eyes while their wings settled into rest. The matrix of glassy threads glistened under the humid afternoon sun, with reds, blues, and purples tracing intricate networks across their crystalline wings. I remember my grandmother telling me one afternoon, when I was young, that the Native Americans, who were there before she tended to her gardens and cattle on the South Dakota plains, saw the magical insects as friends of witches, like an aerial familiar. And since, according to my grandmother, witches are the devil's creatures, the dragonfly must also be from the underworld.

I couldn't imagine such an angelic looking creature, with wings as thin as a poppy petal, being an agent of evil, but folklore runs deep, and opinions were hardened long ago. And almost as if the dragonfly had eavesdropped on my memory, it buzzed its wings and headed out across the pond, away from my admiring eyes. Fish jumped, breaking the tension of the water's surface, as the dragonfly made its way to safer ground. It wasn't too long before the dragonfly who was so offended by my memory was replaced by two, three, and then four more. They seemed to attach to stems of grass and splay their wings out to catch the sunshine.

They rocketed around my head as predators from below began crawling up the stems of grass toward their gleaming bodies. Praying mantises took one step after another, their barbed legs finding hold on the stems. I sat back to watch the scenario play out, one of nature's most repeated performances of the hunter and the hunted. It was primal. Neither the mantis nor the dragonfly held ill will toward one another. It was a simple life of eat or be eaten.

The low buzz of a bald-faced hornet sounded above me as it passed overhead on its way back to its paper-like, egg-shaped nest across the pond. A giant egret with wings outstretched glided over the pond. One sharp flap to its wings, and its legs reached down to grab the bark of a recently fallen pecan tree. It folded its wings up and stared with its prehistoric eye at the water below, waiting to pluck up small fish or turtles, the pattern of eat or be eaten repeating itself. For humans, the lazy and serene nature of the pond seemed pastoral and kind, yet to those insects and birds who made it their home, it was a daily adventure in survival.

My feet were hanging over the edge of the rickety dock. Tadpoles swam about furtively just below the water's surface. The cattails and sweet flag grass emerging from below the water line made a home for the little black amphibian larva, a place of refuge against the catfish and gizzard shads who sought them. I dropped a pebble in the water. Tadpoles scattered as the small fish gasped at the water, trying to eat whatever had broken the surface. I had an affinity toward the tadpoles, swimming away from ominous shadows cast by unseen assailants. Ants crawled across my leg, and I decided to move back into the screened area before the mosquitoes finished their harvest of my arms and legs. The dock creaked as I stood. I steadied myself, should it break apart beneath my feet. I made it back to the bank. Ripples of water extended away from the posts supporting the dock.

•••

The memory slips away as a car horn blares in the parking lot. The warmth of the Georgia sun is gone, and no dragonflies whir about my head. I find myself missing the wall from the shelter. The walls here are made from some type of dark paneling from the 70s. They have perfunctory paintings of seascapes with sailboats. They are bound to the walls with screws through the picture frames. *Who would steal such things?* I remind myself about the junkie frame of mind and how everything is a step toward their next fix. I consider all the people whose lives have brought them to this room. I wonder if anyone has died in here or what crimes this room may have borne witness.

And the words drop into place:

In my room, I embrace,
the company of my sordid peers.
Her legs spread to receive within herself,
a currency imbued with tears.
A tourniquet pulled tight, around an arm,

of someone ready to die.
Housewife in the bathroom, tending broken nose,
silently beseeching 'why'?
Kids of privilege on a street corner with smack,
distracted parents unaware.
Runaway youths, freed through emancipation,
now lonely in despair.
These are the companions
of my circumambulating mind.

I feel the impulse to open my computer to write the words down. It hits me again, as it has several times in the past few days. The absence of my electronic refuge punches me in the gut. I fall back onto the bed.

"Fuck!" I yell at an empty room. I really need my laptop back. It's my security blanket. I drag it everywhere I go. It's in rough shape, but I love it. I know I have to press extra hard on the "y" key. I know that the battery only lasts about four hours, so I have to bring my charging cable everywhere. I enjoy being able to open it up and click through the poems and short stories I've written, at least the ones I didn't erase during my bouts with insanity.

The library is open until nine in the evening. I have the number memorized, but I don't have my phone. I wonder if Gravy would let me use the office phone. I head down to the office. The scraping sound acts as a sort of alert for the staff. As I enter, I hear the sound of cheesy background music and some moaning. *Great, am I interrupting his evening porn binge? Gross.*

A red-cheeked Gravy comes out from the interior office and curtly asks, "What?"

I point to the phone on the counter and ask if I can use it.

"Knock yourself out," Gravy says and returns to whatever vice he's exploring in the back. "Press nine to get out." And he's gone.

Why would I want to knock myself out?

I dial the number.

"Columbus Metropolitan Library, Main Branch," a mechanical voice answers. The robot tells me to listen because options have changed and then goes through a list of numbers to push. The last is Customer Service, press eight. "Hello, Columbus Main Branch Library, how can I help?"

"Hello, I'm wondering if anyone has turned in a laptop and charger in the past few days."

"Oh, let me check real quick with our lost and found locations. Please hold."

I wait with bated breath for her response.

"Thank you for holding. I'm sorry, sir, but no one has turned in a laptop recently, but there are perhaps a half dozen laptop and phone chargers here if you'd like to stop at our first-floor check-out area and ask."

"OK," I say with a defeated tone. "Thank you for checking." I consider for a moment telling them I'm the guy who flipped out at the end of last week. I reconsider that impulse, though I'm not sure if I'm even allowed back into the library.

"You're more than welcome."

The line disconnects. I make my way back to my room and flop back onto my bed, staring at a crack in the ceiling that resembles the one across my laptop screen.

CHAPTER TWENTY-FOUR

Malik — Commonality

I slept like crap last night, and I'm not in the best of moods for this Monday morning. I wake up as I usually do before my alarm rings. I go about my business getting ready for work, feeding Moose, listening to the news for a bit, and doing the few dishes I left in the sink from yesterday's dinner. I head down to the street where my car is parked and set out for work. Construction in midtown creates bumper-to-bumper traffic as the entire city tries to navigate its way to work and school. Columbus isn't that big of a city, so it's annoying how renovating one of the buildings downtown can create such a backlog of traffic.

I catch myself becoming indignant.

Tap. Tap. Tap. Tap. Tap.

I remind myself that I'm sitting in a relatively new car with the heat cranked, on my way to work, where it is also heated. Caleb would probably be grateful for the circumstances for which I am complaining. That thought should placate me, but now I'm getting annoyed that every time I complain about something, I have this person flying around in my conscience telling me I'm a snowflake for complaining about the little things in life.

I take a sip of coffee from my travel mug just as the car ahead of me flashes their brake lights. I push on the brake, and coffee sloshes out of my mug and onto my khaki pants. *Perfect.* I want to pound on my steering wheel or curse the driver ahead of me, but I close my eyes as I sit stopped in traffic and try to let the anger go.

Tap. Tap. Tap. Tap. Tap.

My mantra floats through my mind. I haven't even made it to work, and the day is already a crap fest. My phone, sitting in its dashboard cradle, chimes a notification. It's Drake asking if I'm available.

I push the speaker icon and say, "Call Drake." The line connects and starts ringing.

"Hey, Drake. What's up?"

"Hey, how are you this morning?"

"Don't ask. It's been a shitty day already."

"Oh, sorry, man. I was calling to see if you'd be interested in working a few hours with me some evening on the house in Four Corners."

"Pounding nails sounds great to me right now. Sure, I can do that. What are you working on?"

"I've got to get the bathroom and kitchen tiled, but I've got people for that. I was hoping you could help me put in replacement boards on the front and back porches. Pretty easy, just crowbar up anything that looks like it's decaying and replace with the new boards."

"Right on, I can do that."

"Will tonight work for you?"

"Yep, that should work."

"Great, man, you're a lifesaver."

The line disconnects. I envy the part in Drake that allows him to save money and do these investment properties. Drake is very disciplined. He was talking about investing in houses while we were in college. It seemed so far off, thinking about buying a home while we were eating ramen noodles. I have to admit, even though I am saving money, I like comfort. I'm guilty of having Champagne taste on a Budweiser budget. I should have already saved enough for a down payment on a house, but I can't quite seem to stop buying all the little things in life.

I pay for streaming channels. There's the gym membership at a place I might go once a month. I have my car payment, insurance, and maintenance. The apartment is my biggest expense. I should have rented something more affordable, but I saw it and had to have it. I couldn't pass up the hardwood floors, fireplace, and great view of downtown. These things all contribute to my lack of savings, but my biggest weakness is food. I love to eat out. I love having friends come with me, and I often pick up the tab. Maybe I'll just rent from Drake one day. I wonder if he'd ever do a rent-to-own thing. I admire Drake. He's made sound investments. He has a contractor friend who finds good, efficient workers who can get a house ready for the market within a couple of months. He sells one every two years or so and spends that money investing in more rental properties.

My phone chimes again. It's La Rae from work. I press the phone icon on my dashboard, and it answers the call.

"Hey, Malik, what's good?"

"Good morning, La Rae. What are you doing up so early?"

I like to get in the office before Dex and La Rae come in, so I have some free time to get caught up. "I'm coming in early today to get ahead on paperwork because of the training scheduled."

"Shit, is that today?"

La Rae laughs. "Yes, didn't you get any of the memos? I told you about it, but I guess you had more important things on your mind." I know she is joking. She has kept me on track more than once. I tend to put these events in my phone without any notifications, so I don't remember them until I get the chime about ten minutes before the training starts.

"You're a lifesaver, La Rae."

"Yeah, ya know, someday I'm going to forget too, and then we'll both be in trouble."

"It's the CIT thing, right?"

"Yep."

"Is Dex coming in, or are we all just heading over to the training separately?"

"As far as I know, Dex is heading in from home."

"OK, I'll just head over there too. Hey, I'm going to stop and get a breakfast sandwich. Do you want anything?"

"That'd be great. My kids were being dorks this morning, and I didn't get a chance to stop for anything before I got here."

"I got you covered, girl."

"Thanks. See you in about half an hour."

The line disconnects.

The CIT training, the Critical Intervention Team, is a new program with the city police. Certain officers have gone through training in how to respond to calls involving someone experiencing a mental health crisis. It's a vital program, and the staff at Crossroads are invested in helping out the police because too many of our clients are getting arrested and put in jail rather than getting help for their mental health crises.

If CIT had been involved with Caleb's incident at the library, who knows how differently that may have gone. Perhaps he wouldn't have been wrestled to the floor and his chin split open had someone been there to de-escalate the situation. The training today is for social services personnel to meet and discuss procedures with trainees in the CIT program. Often, the two demographics are at odds with each other. Cops think we enable people, and we think cops are out for blood. There is truth to both of those sentiments, so training like today is meant to bridge the gap and figure out how to work with one another.

When I arrive, Dex is there, along with La Rae. They wave to me, and I walk over to them.

"Hey, Malik," Dex says.

"'Sup." I look around the room and see a lot of the same people as our last training. Several uniformed police officers are present. I wish I had a different reaction to cops. I know most do their jobs above and beyond reproach, but I'm always wary of them.

La Rae hands me a packet of information about today's training, and I hand her the small bag with her breakfast. Dex looks at me like I've just wiped my nose on his sleeve.

"Where's my damned sandwich?"

"Whatever, Dex, there's nobody here thinkin' you need another sandwich," I say jokingly as I pat his big belly. "Besides, tell me you didn't already have breakfast."

"Of course I had breakfast, I just wanted another breakfast."

We all laugh and settle into our chairs as the meeting is about to start.

The door to the back opens, and two officers enter and seat themselves at the table. I get a sick feeling when I look at one of the officers, the one who has that distinctive white patch in his mustache.

Tap. Tap. Tap. Tap. Tap.

Tap. Tap. Tap. Tap. Tap.

Tap. Tap. Tap. Tap. Tap.

"Shit, Dex," I say, hitting his leg. "That's the guy who pulled me over last week."

"Seriously?" he answers as he takes in the man with the spotted mustache.

La Rae overheard the conversation. "Are you sure?" she asks.

"Yes, I'm serious. There's no hiding that white part in his mustache."

I sit there, trying to convince my stomach to undo the knots stemming from seeing this guy. Thankfully, he isn't the one doing most of the training that day. In fact, he leaves after about twenty minutes when the pager on his utility belt alerts him to something and he has a hushed conversation with the presenter and then leaves by the back door where he entered.

"Thank God," I whisper to La Rae. I breathe out fully for the first time since I saw him.

The morning session of the training goes on for two hours. Good information. Good anecdotes from officers where the CIT worked, balanced against bad incidents where CIT wasn't involved when things went south. It's a hard subject for everyone in the room. During the break in the morning session, we all grab coffee from the cart in the hallway.

I hear a voice behind me and turn to see the officer with the telltale mustache. I'm almost face-to-face with the guy. Dex and La Rae look on with caution.

He reaches out his hand to shake mine. I do so before I even know I'm doing it.

"Hello, what agency are you with?"

"Crossroads Men's Shelter."

"Hey, I hear good things about that place. I'm Officer Gentry with CPD."

I search his eyes for some sign that he recognizes me. He doesn't. "We try to do our best. This is Dex and La Rae; we make up the housing placement team."

Gentry reaches out to shake both of their hands, which they do with some trepidation.

"It's important that we make these relationships stronger. I'm glad to have met you."

"Yeah, likewise," I say slowly. *We've already met.*

Gentry walks away to shake hands with another group of social workers.

"Boy, he sure knows how to work a room," La Rae says, stirring her coffee. All three of us look intently at the cop with the mustache. The looks on our faces must be nearly comical as we stare at the guy.

Dex leans over to me and whispers, "You think he even recognized you?"

"Well, if he did, he sure hid it well."

The next session takes place, and then we break for lunch. There are sandwiches, apples, and bags of potato chips in the hallway. We only have half an hour off, so we don't go anywhere. We stretch our legs and eat some of the offerings from the cart.

When we are called back into training, Officer Gentry takes the podium.

"Oh shit, here we go," Dex says.

Tap. Tap. Tap. Tap. Tap.

I just look ahead at Gentry. He begins talking about his role in the department. "Hello, folks, I'm Jason Gentry. I work mostly with robberies. I know that may not seem like a natural fit for the CIT, but I wanted to share a few stories with you about how all departments should have some type of CIT training." He goes on to share stories about how some people in crisis unintentionally break the law by "borrowing" things they think belong to them. "We've had people in crisis take appliances, clothing, even cars sometimes. In their minds, they are fleeing an invisible enemy or mistake things as being their own. Psychotic breaks aren't times when people are thinking rationally.

"I had an incident last week where someone, thinking they were being followed by the FBI, stole a truck belonging to their neighbor. He knew where the keys were and took them. All I knew was that this guy had stolen a black Dodge Ram 1500. The guy who reported seeing his neighbor drive off in his truck knew that the person had a firearm and often talked about shooting people to defend himself. It was a terrible day. I had to be a grade-A asshole to several drivers who fit the description. But time was of the essence. We didn't want him escalating things further. When we found the vehicle parked at the end of an industrial road, the guy was sitting by the truck with his head between his knees. The training I received for this situation had me acting very differently from how I would have acted before I received the training. I stopped about a half block away from him and called CIT. I sat with surveillance on him for about half an hour to make sure he didn't get back in the truck and leave. When CIT arrived, they were in plain clothes, had some food, and used a skilled, relaxed approach to get him talking. They were able to get him into custody safely, contact the owner about the truck, and resolve the situation without anyone getting hurt. That is exactly why CIT training needs to be brought to as many officers as possible."

I look over to Dex and La Rae. None of us expected to hear what we just heard. The training aside, Gentry's account of his collaboration with CIT gave me pause. But now, here he is with a plausible story about why he pulled me over the other night. *Was the way he approached me due to the call he was on?* Neither Dex nor La Rae has any words of wisdom. I am aware that incidents of police overstepping their roles as peace officers are reported in the news every day. We are definitely getting harassed. Hell, some of us die due to their behavior during routine traffic stops. I guess it goes to show that the situation between the Black community and the police might need their own kind of CIT training. The fear I had during the stop was real, brought on by a really bad relationship between cops and communities. I wonder what Gentry would say if I asked him about the incident involving that stop.

I decide to approach Gentry on the next break. I introduce myself again. My heart is pounding. I tell him about the stop. He puts his head down, looking at the floor as I tell him about it. When I finish, he simply says, "I'm sorry." He pauses for a minute. "I hate this part of my job. We've been conditioned to always be more cautious than is often warranted. Cops get shot during routine traffic stops. The guy I was pursuing was possibly armed. I reacted the way I did because that's what the protocol calls for. With each stop, I am potentially putting my life on the line."

"But do you understand that I was just going to the store with my friend, my white friend? I was driving as a favor. I understand that you're trained to do what you do. That doesn't make it any easier to be a casualty of that training."

"Yeah, I get it. I really do. Look, all I can say is that I'm sorry the stop left you unnerved. I know I was very short with people that day. It was only because I was trying to get that guy into custody safely. I promise it wasn't personal."

Wasn't personal? "Well, it felt personal."

"I'm glad you came up to me. Hopefully, this conversation can keep going. I don't target Black people, I swear. But I know there are probably cops who do." He pauses for a minute. "Let me rephrase that. I know that there are cops who target Black people." Another pause. "Look, I would like the opportunity to come to your shelter and work with your staff, if you think that would help. I'm hoping you can see that I'm not the bad guy, even though sometimes I have to act like the bad guy."

I manage to say, "Let me think about that."

There is a pause, during which we both simply look at one another. I have a bit more of an understanding of why he acted the way he did, but I can't help feeling the anger of someone who does their best each day to be a good force in the world, only to be thought of as just a Black guy stealing a car. I'm hoping he has a bit of understanding about how his behavior can cause unnecessary fear. Fear was the common factor that day. Both of us feared for our lives for very different reasons.

He reaches into his wallet and retrieves a card. "Here, take this. Let me know if I can come to your agency and help. And… thanks for listening." He extends his hand, which I shake in earnest. "Thanks for letting me know how that day affected you."

"Sure. I'll reach out. Maybe we can collaborate on something in the future."

"That's a good plan."

CHAPTER TWENTY-FIVE

Caleb — Judgement Call

This decrepit room is everything I need right now. Staying on top of sleep is primary to my health. Mania likes to slip in through a back door when my rest is interrupted. Working night shifts, standing shoulder to shoulder with ten other people on the assembly line, and generating a source of income was not ideal for my mental health. Being constantly surrounded by people in the shelter was also problematic, but it's to be expected.

The solitude of the motel room, using my own bathroom, and having a boundary between myself and the outside world will help immensely. I enjoy solitude, but similar to being without sleep, being without contact is a good way to take that first step toward reviving the beast. I shake my head at the totality of my circumstances. I've just spent most of my money on this hotel, hoping to leave here and return to the shelter again. If not, I will find the softest piece of concrete to call my bed.

I implore myself to make use of these hours. I walk to the table by the window and pull the curtains back. The parking lot, surrounded by the motel's doors and windows, extends before me like a dilapidated, depressive Ansel Adams photograph, if he had done urban landscapes. Looking toward the street, I see the edge of the Wings shop. Directly across from the motel is a liquor store. It's been a long time since I've been in a liquor store. I think about the luxury of a drink. I don't desire to be drunk, but the calming effect of a strong alcoholic beverage does indeed feel inviting. I pick up the pad of paper next to the lamp that's been nailed down.

And the words fall into place:

> The perfect companion to solitude
> is spirits at your lips;
> warming tongue, shaping mind,
> while you slip into eclipse.

I should be holding onto my funds, but I imagine the tableau of a lifetime now gone: a simple drink after work. It sounds lovely. And just like that, the decision to buy some booze is made, bolstering the façade in my mind that life will be ok. I stuff my room key into my pocket and leave. The same woman is leaning against the same iron railing. I wonder if she's a fixture here. Guys at the shelter stay here from time to time. I wonder if she is from a women's shelter standing outside for a smoke. Or is she perched as she is to attract the business from roving men?

I walk down the stairs. The woman by the rail is watching me. I approach the street, wait for a space in the traffic, and cross the four lanes to the liquor store. Although the storefront is all glass, the windows are nearly entirely covered in posters advertising different malt liquors and new flavors of margarita in a can. There's a sign letting passers-by know the ATM inside costs only $1. Several posters of thin women smoking long brown cigarettes occupy one section of the windows. The last glass panel has a large floor-to-ceiling crack that has been duct-taped and then reinforced with plywood. It appears to be an old crack because the duct tape is worn and the plywood is weathered.

The door sets off a chime as I enter. It's cleaner than I expected it would be. A kind-eyed gentleman stands behind the counter. He wears a turban and has a wispy beard. *Sikh maybe?* There is not much in the liquor world that appeals to me except a good, iced whiskey. As I walk, I spot a bottle of Jameson. It surprises me. Jameson is not cheap. It's a delicious Irish whiskey, and here it is front and center. There's a handwritten tag advertising thirty-one dollars for the large bottle. From what I remember, that is a pretty good deal.

I have thirty-one dollars. I grab the bottle by the neck and head to the counter. There are two people in line ahead of me. The first guy is standing, or more accurately, teetering at the counter. He is fishing through pockets to find money to pay for his two-dollar can of malt liquor. His old, Black face is weathered and tired. His hat sits atop an unkempt, nappy head. He has several coats layered over shirts and jeans. He is ready for the cold.

"C'mon, Stuart," the cashier prods. "These nice people are waiting." His tone is compassionate but stern.

"Oh, I got it, Rashid," Stuart answers in a surprisingly deep voice. His words sound heavy with intoxication. Thinking about what he is saying takes the place of searching for his money. He seems unable to do both at the same time.

Done talking now, Stuart keeps adding coins to his pile on the counter until Rashid tells him to stop. "That is two dollars. Have a good evening, Stuart."

"You bet, boss," Stuart says, putting the paper-wrapped can into his front coat pocket. He ambles out through the doorway, the chime sounding.

The woman in front of me, who watched Rashid and Stuart do their little ritual, asks for a pint of Scotch from behind the counter. She mutters a name brand that I cannot hear and places a twenty-dollar bill on the counter. Rashid hands her the bottle without a paper sack, and the woman quickly slips it into her patent leather bag. It's a transaction that has taken place many times in the past.

"Thanks, Rashid," the woman says in a low, sultry voice, which I imagine is steeped in a long history of smoking and Scotch. Her thick brown hair, containing a thousand strands of perfect high and low-lighted accents, is luxurious. It shimmers as it falls straight back onto her form-fitting black sweater. Expensive sweater. Her jeans are well formed to her legs which tuck into smart low-rise black boots. She is put together very well. *Maybe a realtor?* She's someone who looks professional and casual at the same time. The juxtaposition between Stuart and this woman strikes me as emblematic of the broad pull alcohol puts on the human species.

The realtor exits.

"Hello," I say as I put the Jameson on the counter.

"Hello, my friend," Rashid says, looking me directly in the eyes. "I don't believe I've seen you in here before. Are you from the neighborhood?"

"For a few days, I am," I respond. "I'm staying across the street at the Cheap Nite Inn."

"Oh, I see, sir," Rashid says. He's a charming man, polite and courteous. I'm sure he knows the class of clientele that frequents the motel.

"This is a good price on Jameson," I remark as I place two twenty-dollar bills on the counter. I have a ten and a five-dollar bill left in my wallet, the extent of my fortune.

"Indeed, it is," Rashid says. "I purchased a few cases of it during a promotion. But I fear it's a brand that is a bit out of reach for most of my customers."

I enjoy his sing-song accent. "Well, I'm certainly glad I found it."

"As am I, sir," he says, placing the slender green bottle into a paper bag fitted for it. "I don't know how you like your whiskey, sir, but should you need ice, I do have travel bags available. The hotel you are at does have ice, but I worry that it might have more than water in it."

"What do you mean?" I ask.

"Well, more than a few motel customers have come over asking for ice when they have found sundry things in the ice machine other than ice."

"Oh," I say, trying to hold back an expression of disgust. "Well, thanks for the tip."

"Of course, sir. Will there be anything else?"

"How about a bag of that ice?" I say. He nods his head, turns to a freezer behind him, and pulls out a bag of cubed ice. I grab the bottle and ask, "How much is it?"

"Since you buy the big bottle of whiskey, the ice is free, my friend," Rashid says with a warm smile.

"You're very kind."

"I am open until 2:00 a.m., sir. I hope to see you again."

I walk to the door. I can see the motel through the glass despite the numerous stickers and decals for credit cards and a sign displaying the store hours. The door chimes again as I exit. I stand on the sidewalk outside the liquor store in a quiet reverie. I have been at this place before, the feeling of being right on the edge of stability regarding money and housing and everything else. I don't know if I'll have a bed in three days, but that's in three days. For right now, I have the prospect of a few days inside, a nice bottle of liquor, and no one to bother me. Three days of vacation from being homeless or in a shelter. Three days of escape. Three days to grapple in the, what was the name of that song by Queensryche, *Silent Lucidity*?

Yes, that's it—the silent lucidity of my circumstance.

CHAPTER TWENTY-SIX

Malik — Superman

The training from earlier in the day was draining. It went on for what seemed like an eternity. Additionally, I was not expecting to run into Officer Friendly. I was also not ready to hear about him pulling me over from his perspective. It was confusing, to say the least. It didn't affect me to the extent that I could feel a panic attack coming. My feelings are rooted more in anger than in fear. I find some comfort in that. Panic attacks usually come from a place of insecurity. Despite his version of events, I know the fear of being stopped for DWB is real. DWB stops can result in injury or death for otherwise innocent people.

When I get home, I grab a drink, find Moose, and lie down on the bed with him. He's happy for the immediate attention, and his purring acts as a soothing balm over my nerves. I didn't realize how tired I had become. The few sips of bourbon, Moose purring on top of me, and the comfort of my bed allow my mind to settle down and wander. I think about Moms. She used to sleep with me when there were thunderstorms in our neighborhood. She would lie next to me, her hand on my head, softly patting my hair and singing softly. When I asked her why the thunder had colors, she would softly say, "Thunderstorms are beautiful, and they're nothin' to worry about." I never did worry about those thunderstorms. I drew thunderstorms a lot because the red and blue lights I saw in my room during thunderstorms were beautiful to me.

A long time ago, Moms and I saw Venus one night high in the dark sky. It sparkled. Moms said the red lights were from Venus, and the blue lights were the flashlights the stars used to help Venus find her way home. Thunderstorms in my neighborhood sometimes did not rain. Instead of rain, Moms said that the sirens that came around were not sirens from the police; they were Venus herself crying because she had lost her way home.

Moms taught me to let Venus cry on her way home because she always found her way no matter how lost she became. Moms was right too. No matter how loud Venus cried during the night, her crying ended, and she found her way home. Her lights would stop flashing, and the stars would put away their flashlights.

I always wondered why Venus would lose her way around Earth. Moms said Earth was the prettiest planet in the solar system, and Venus was the God of Beauty. It was easy for Venus to find her way to Earth because the moon shone a spotlight on Earth. She often left her orbit to gaze upon Earth, but she would not know her way back when she was done. Venus had no moons to show her the way back. That was why the stars and planets helped.

Everything felt safe during the thunderstorms that hit our neighborhood because Moms knew how thunderstorms worked. Everything felt safe until the thunderstorms came right into our house. On the nights when thunderstorms came into the house, Venus's red flashing lights and the blue flashing lights from Mars were pouring out of police cars. The sirens of Venus losing her way stopped quickly outside on my front lawn. Not understanding why Venus and the stars were flashing on my house, I crept outside my door, peeking slowly around corners. Down the hallway, I heard voices. I could hear Moms. She was... crying?

My heartbeat quickened in my chest.

I walked into the kitchen.

Moms was in a chair.

Another woman in a police uniform sat next to her.

"Moms?" I asked quietly. She looked at me quickly, too quickly. She forgot to cover the bloodied cheekbone, swollen eye, and broken nose.

"Oh, baby boy," she said, opening her arms. I walked into her arms, but I did not feel comfortable. I did not feel anything.

"Ma'am," the woman in the cop outfit said, "you need to come down tomorrow and file a restraining order."

Moms replied, but I didn't really hear her. I just held her. A guy in a different uniform wiped Mom's face and applied a bandage that smelled like medicine. I didn't want him touching her, but I didn't move. I just held Moms. She held me back, too. I had my Superman pajamas on. Superman could fix this even if I had to fly to Venus herself to fix it. I would. I will fix it. I think this thought over and over and over.

•••

I wake up suddenly. I'm in bed. It's one in the morning. I reach for the water on my bedstand and realize it's bourbon. I didn't bring water to bed. Hell, I didn't even eat dinner. I can feel the thumping of my heart. I breathe to calm myself. I hate these interruptions. They happen too often. During the work week, they really diminish my energy. I roll over and look at Moose's face. He is bathed in the soft light coming through my windows from the streetlight below. He is blinking slowly at me. His tail flips back and forth. He stretches out his front legs and yawns, exposing his fangs. He flops onto his back again and closes his eyes now that I'm sorted out.

Eventually, my thoughts return to Caleb. I'm finding that my thoughts go to him almost incessantly. It's so odd to know that a person you want to connect with is roaming the city. His phone is not receiving calls. With all the technology available today, it seems impossible that there isn't a way to find somebody living in the same city. I consider all the guys at the shelter. I think about Pops. *Is he out there somewhere inside a grubby sleeping bag? Or maybe he got his act together and decided not to interrupt Moms and me again. Perhaps he has a job and is living in a home, renting a room.* The thought feels pacifying to me. I drift off to sleep...

•••

He walks through the door. The dreads he had when I was a kid are long and pulled behind his head. He is carrying groceries. He fills the fridge. He takes a Mountain Dew and sips at the bottle. He does not drink or drug anymore. His face has filled back in from the hollowed out look he had when I last saw him. His clothes are clean. He has done it. He has changed.

He walks into a bedroom. It is tidy. A bookshelf is filled with novels and nonfiction books. He has a simple twin-sized bed. His dresser has a few trinkets on top: his 30-day, 90-day, one-year, and five-year chips from Alcoholics and Narcotics Anonymous lie in a small stack. There's a calendar on his dresser with his counseling and doctor appointments. There are two small windows overlooking a portion of the city with which I am not familiar. He lies down on his bed and folds his hands over his belly. He falls asleep and begins to dream.

I am in his dream. I see myself coming to shake his hand. He tells me how sorry he is for all that he did to Moms and me. He sounds sincere. I feel comforted. He confides that he does not remember a lot, but what he does remember, he apologizes for over and over again. He tells me that he has always loved me. From his pocket, he pulls out a cobalt-blue box. He gives it to me. It is small, like a ring box. What could possibly be in such a small box that would make such an enormous difference in my life?

He tells me that I already know what the box has in it.

Suddenly, I'm aware that I am no longer in my father's dream and that I do not know what the box contains. I think about opening it, but I am afraid to. What if it's some kind of trick? What if the content of the box drags me further down into my confusion about my father?

My grandmother used to sing a song called Alabaster Box. *It's a song about finding your way to Jesus. This box is not alabaster. My hand becomes hot where the box is touching my hand. I pull my hand away so as not to get burned. It drops to the floor with glowing embers, floating away. All that remains are ashes and the question of what was in the box. I sift through the ashes with my fingers, searching for some remnant. There is nothing but ash. A wind blows the ash away and the room turns black. I feel myself falling into the darkness.*

•••

I grab the bed to stop myself from falling as I startle awake at three in the morning. I'm thoroughly flustered by my dream. The vision of my father being alive and being healthy fills me with hope that somewhere out in the world, Pops got his life together. I allow the good feeling to sink in, but soon my thoughts turn to why he left. *Is he afraid to contact me?* I close my eyes and rationalize with myself that it was only a dream. It is not real. I can't shake the feeling, the desperate yearning, to know where he is and what could have been in that box.

CHAPTER TWENTY-SEVEN

Caleb — The Other Half

In the bathroom at The Cheap Night Inn, there are three glasses on the sink. Not the hermetically sealed glasses in a normal hotel. These are three sturdy plastic cups from different convenience stores left here in the hotel. I inspect the cups. They seem to be clean. I use a little bar soap and hot water to wash the one with the Bud Light emblem on it. I don't see an ice bucket, and I laugh a bit at myself for expecting one. The wastebasket in the bathroom is lined with a plastic bag. Should I use that?

Gross. No.

I end up just placing the bag of ice in the sink. I have this gorgeous bottle of Irish whiskey, but I don't want to get drunk. I should eat something before I start sipping my way into the night. I have no food with me. I remember the vending machines. What the hell. Calories are calories. Stuffing my key once again into my pocket, I go in search of snacks. I open my door expecting to see the darkness of night, but am startled to my core to find the woman I saw leaning against the railing earlier now inhabiting my doorway.

"Shit!" I yelp in surprise.

"Hi, hon, saw ya checked in. Need some company?"

My adrenaline is still pumping from my unexpected guest. "What?"

"Do you want a date?" she says slowly, so I understand why she is at my door.

"No!" I say loudly. "Get the hell away from my door."

"Aw, honey," she says, stepping back to lean against the railing. "No need to get your panties in a bunch. Just letting you know I make house calls." She pauses for a second, then with a smirk, "After all, I'm under you."

"You're what?" I ask.

"Under you," she said again. "You're in Nine, I'm in Four — ya know, under you." It reminds me of the bunks at the shelter.

"I'm just getting snacks," I say, not really knowing how to deal with this situation. I push past her, pulling my door locked behind me.

"Snacks?" she says. "Oh, hell babe, that machine has been dead for months. But Rashid has some."

I can't believe I'm having a conversation with her. But after my surprise wears off, I realize she's just a working girl keeping tabs on her neighborhood. Who the hell am I to be offended? She seems perfectly nice. I ask her name, expecting something exotic like "Baby," or "Trixie," or "Diamond." Well, this hooker is named Lisa—just Lisa, nothing fancy and no last name. Lisa looks about how you'd expect a hooker on the edge of town to look. She's white, but her skin is a ruddy pink from acne and winter exposure. Her eyes are blue, but they're submerged behind thick eyeliner and copious amounts of badly applied mascara. She has a simple nose ring and another ring through her lip. Both her ears are loaded with a menagerie of metal and jeweled piercings. Her hair is pulled back, so all her facial adornments are noticeable. Her hair is probably light brown, as that's what's mostly coming through at the roots, even though most of her hair is dyed jet black. It falls below her shoulders. It has a lot of product, creating a stringy, hard rock look reminiscent of Joan Jett in the '80s. Although her eyes are heavily lined with makeup, the rest of her face lacks any painting or spackle. She's probably my age.

It's cold outside, so her hands stay firmly buried in her puffy black coat. The skimpiest of skirts covers her hips and upper thighs. Her legs are slender beneath her black leggings, and she's sporting knock-off Uggs.

After we chat for a few minutes, and she is under no impression that I am looking for a date, I ask Lisa if she wants a drink as I hold up one of the glasses.

"What are we drinking?" she asks.

"I picked up a bottle of Jameson," I say. "It's inside."

"Jameson? And you don't want a blowjob? Promise you aren't a psycho?" she asks, only half-jokingly.

I laugh a little. "No, I'm fine. I don't need your services. I'm just trying not to go nuts tonight."

"OK, hon, what's your name?"

"Caleb."

Well, nice to meet you, Caleb," she says, resigned to my not being a prospective john. "Thanks." She says thanks in a way that indicates she doesn't say it very often. I think the first thing of many I bet we have in common.

"No problem," I answer.

I pour the amber liquid into our tacky cups. I put ice in mine, but she pulls her cup away before I can put ice into hers. She sips the Jameson as if she's testing the water. She likes it and finishes a good two fingers of it in one long pull.

"So, you here on business?"

"Nope, I'm waiting to get into a homeless shelter. I had a few bucks, so I got a room for a few days until it happens." There was a time when I would have made up a story about why I am in such dire straits. It might have been my house had a fire, or I'm in town for a funeral. I'd say anything except the truth. My ego would prevent me from telling the truth because I was always ashamed of the choices I made while manic. I was always trying to cover up the disaster my life had become. One good thing about being homeless is you tend to lose your pride.

"You have money?"

"A little." I'm wary about discussing money with a stranger.

"Then how come you're homeless?" Her husky voice is straining to be clear, but she coughs the cough so many smokers have.

"I ended up in the loony bin last week. I'm spending the last of my work money." I'm not about to tell Lisa that I get disability. I've seen too many guys lose their money to people like Lisa, and if not Lisa, then their pimps. I have a room that is my own, but I'll need to leave it, and there's not a lot of protection once I do.

Lisa looks at me with an examining eye. "You must not ride the horsies," she says. I take notice of her oddly flat upper lip; I'm guessing no top teeth.

"What do you mean?"

"Heroin, darling."

"Hell no. That scares the shit out of me."

Lisa laughs at that prospect. "Scares you?"

"Yeah, just seen too many people in the shelter after drugs have run roughshod over their lives and left them for dead."

"Yeah, I guess that's true. I'm lookin' for some if you know of anyone."

"Sorry, I don't know anyone." I think about the two construction workers who left the shelter while I was there. They shot up plenty. I have the phone number of one of them because he came in high as a kite, promising to put me to work on a job he was putting together. I sat and listened to him as he discussed the huge job that would change everything. He made me put his number in my phone. I thought to myself about a life where you switched between heroin and meth. The poor guy's insides must be falling apart. I think for a fleeting moment about giving his number to Lisa, but I reconsider. I really don't want to be the reason she overdoses or gets arrested. Then I remember, again, that I don't have my phone.

"OK," she says, handing me my glass. "Thanks for the drink, but I gotta get something stronger in me or I'm going to melt."

"OK, Lisa." I think about wishing her good luck, but that concept is too weird. I take her cup, and she walks away toward the stairs leading to the parking lot. I still can't believe she's only wearing leggings. They look terrible on her because she's so skinny that her legs are swimming in the fabric. I guess she's donning an authentic "heroin chic" look.

She disappears for a short while until she re-emerges on the ground floor. She walks across the parking lot, her Uggs scuffing across the asphalt. She swings her bag around and pulls out a pack of cigarettes. Her face brightens up momentarily as her lighter flares. Soon after the smoke curls around her head, the lighter is extinguished. She walks a few more steps to the brick wall and perches herself on top of it. She crosses her thin legs and unzips her coat a bit for what I guess is her "open for business" stance. A thousand things run through my mind: How did she become a prostitute? Is this a normal night for her? Does she have a pimp? How many tricks does she do a night? How much does she cost?

I find myself in that silly position you see in movies where some cop or private investigator needs information, so he pays the hooker for her time. I really wish I had an extra twenty dollars so that I could ask her questions. I'm pondering all this when she swings her bag around again. This time, she pulls out her phone.

She puts it to her ear. I see her nod a few times. Then she stands up. I suspect that she's going off to meet a john. What I didn't expect is that she turns back toward the hotel and heads toward a room here at the Cheap Nite Inn. With fascination, I watch as she walks to a room below me and over two. I can't see her when she reaches the door, but I hear her knock on it twice. I hear the door open and then close.

Just as she goes inside, a car pulls into the driveway. A nice car. It's a near current model of one of the mid-sized Volkswagens. As soon as the engine stops, both car doors open. Two nicely dressed kids get out, or rather, pour themselves out of the doors. There's laughter and a few swear words as the young lady tries to avoid stumbling off her heels. Nice heels. What the hell are these two doing here of all places?

They both stumble up to the front office and disappear inside for a few minutes, returning with one of the ancient door keys. The young, shapely woman, possibly in her late teens or early twenties, takes the key to the room, opens the door, and then disappears inside. The guy, a muscular lad of about the same age, heads toward the bottom floor underneath me. I pull myself onto the railing as I realize he's going to the room where Lisa is. I'm suddenly and unexpectedly protective of her and poise myself on the railing to listen.

I hear him knock on the door. I hear it open. A few words are exchanged, and the door closes. But it closes only for a moment and the young man exits with a baggie in his hand. He heads back to the room where his date entered and knocks. The door opens quickly. A slender arm reaches out and grabs him playfully by the collar, pulling him in. Ah, romance.

After a while, Lisa comes back out and seats herself on the brick retaining wall. Grabbing my key, I leave the room with my glass of whiskey in hand and go to sit with her. When I get there, her bag is not with her. Her head is tilted forward like she might be sleeping but as I approach, she lifts it up slowly. Her eyes are watery, almost like she's been crying, then I realize her eyes aren't watery, they are filled with the comfortable haze that heroin gives people.

"Hey, Lisa," I say, offering her the whiskey.

"Caleb. Hi, baby." Her arm reaches out slowly, touching my arm. "You finally want some sugar now, baby?"

"No, sweetie," I say, sitting on the brick embankment with her. I consider that maybe sitting with me won't be good for business. "Is it OK that I'm sitting with you? Are you working right now?"

"No, baby," she says with a curious slur, not a drunk slur, like someone just waking up. "I'm all set." She says this as she passes her palm from right to left. "Kelly took care of me. I let him go to town on me, and he fixed me up for the night. I don't have to work until tomorrow. I've got all night to chill."

"Right on," I say as I'm figuring out whether this is how I want to chill for the night.

As I say this, the door to the kids' room opens. This catches Lisa's attention in that slow-motion reaction she has to everything right now. "Oh, there are my babies." The two kids are standing in the doorway, eyes blinking slowly, their postures relaxed, just staring out at the parking lot.

"Chaz.... Jenna....hi, babies," Lisa says.

"Hey, Lisa," they both reply from their heroin walking slumber. "We were out with friends, but they were party poopers. They just wanted to drink beer and smoke pot. How stupid is that?"

"Come join us," Lisa says.

Chaz and Jenna seem to hear Lisa. I watch as their minds try to process the invitation. It takes them some time to answer. Jenna answers for them, "OK."

But they remain in their doorway, holding on to the door jamb. They still must be in their euphoria, the feeling of sitting by a fire with a blanket at Christmas time euphoria, which fades quickly, and then you're just kinda sleepy and comfortable. They look sleepy and comfortable.

"Damn rookies," she says. "They can't handle their nod." She giggles slowly to herself and stands up, finding her balance. "I just love those kids." She grabs my hand. "C'mon, let's go see how the other half lives."

CHAPTER TWENTY-EIGHT

Malik — Five Little Dots

A vivid dream about being in the room the night Pops broke Moms' nose is emblazoned on my mind. I learned that night that Venus and the stars didn't visit my house. I learned that night that thunderstorms without rain aren't real. I knew Pops had demons. The church ladies Moms knew would whisper such things to one another. The night Moms had to hide her face from me is the night I learned how much of a monster Pops could be.

It's always hard to imagine your parents as flawed. Parents are people who've experienced their own traumas, insecurities, and setbacks in life. As a kid, you don't see all of that. Some parents rail against all the ills in the world, and their kids grow up being suspicious of the world. Pops was scary, but I still held him in my head as a father capable of caring. Moms did her best to keep the raw reality of my dad's addiction from me, but life happens. I came to realize that, indeed, bad things happen to good people, and bad things had happened to Moms.

It's never easy to lump my dad into the category of being a bad person. People like my mom are good. She seemed to rise to all the occasions Pops put us through. I heard them yelling at one another, but I never heard her speak badly about Pops. As an adult, I can't fathom having that much self-restraint not to disparage my dad in front of me. My aunties were more vocal about it, but Moms always shut down those conversations when I was around.

As a social worker, before I started working at Crossroads, I worked with families. I'll never get the images out of my mind of the parents sitting in the waiting room of social services who were absolutely exhausted. They all had tried their best. Even if their best was lousy, it was the best they could do. Parents of kids from unplanned pregnancies born into unwanted families bring everyone down. Life becomes a day-to-day struggle, and that's for people who were already pretty low on the financial totem pole. It's one thing when an adult finds themselves at rock bottom. They understand they need to climb upward to stability. Being born at rock bottom, the children see it as normal, and their lives unfold, most of the time, repeating the cycle of poverty and the trap set upon them by woeful social skills.

The dream I had last night was painfully vivid. I was standing there in the kitchen with walkie-talkies squawking and lights from cop cars undulating around me. It was amid this scene, at nine years old, that I learned the truth. A lot of kids have their childhood imagination squelched when they discover that someone aside from Santa put presents under a Christmas tree. Kids find out the Easter Bunny doesn't bring the candy baskets on Easter morning. Kids learn these things on their own, in their own time. My childhood fantasies ended without my permission. My life changed after Moms' blood dripped onto my pajamas. I counted five little drops of blood before Moms noticed and began tending to me instead of herself. Even inside Moms' embrace I could see the five little dots. Five little dots. I counted them in my mind. Five little dots.

Five little dots.

The lady cop was nice to both Moms and me. She had a lovely

voice, which I barely heard. I was numb as I looked at the five round, red spots on my sleeve. I remember walking back to my room. Moms tucked me in. She calmly gave me a good night kiss. She didn't sing. She didn't point out Venus or the stars. She just said, "I love you," and shut my door.

The red and blue lights whirled around my room in chaos. No longer did Venus and the stars dance in my room. Instead, the red and blue lights were now angry and ominous. I looked at the five spots on my sleeve. Touching them, I felt the cold moisture of Moms' blood. I wiped my finger on my sleeve, creating a small stripe of red. The lights raged above me as I drew the mark in blood on the sleeve of my Superman pajamas.

My childhood ended that night.

Venus would never shine her light on me again. The stars helping her find her way home would no longer illuminate a path. The thunderstorms, which I learned were the arguing, the shouting, the fighting, and the gunshots, would simply rage, like the confusion in my head. All that remained were the police lights telling me Pops was nearby, waiting to injure my mother. Moms tried to tell her stories, but they were no longer the blanket wrapping me warmly at night. Her stories became silly, like a parent trying to convince a child that Santa still existed after the truth was known. I understand what she was trying to do, but once you know, you know.

If Superman was going to help Moms, Superman had to be watchful. When the lights flashed through my room, I would rush to Moms' side. I remember running to her room, rather than her coming to mine. We would simply hold each other, saying nothing. We would watch the lights together, each keeping the other safe.

When sirens blared while I played in the streets, I would run home to Moms. If sirens rang out while I was at school, I would become ill and ask a nurse to call my mom. Although I was too young to know, Moms recognized the difference in her little boy. Although the bloodstains had long been washed away from my sleeve, the role of Superman was tattooed on my heart.

I couldn't fly like Superman, except to run to Moms as quickly as my feet would take me through the neighborhood. I couldn't leap over buildings either, but I could run through the house to find Moms. My chest would not repel bullets, but I could stand in front of her door, looking down the hallway for Pops to appear.

I understood that Superman was not real, that he was a comic book character on TV. Moms told me time and time again that it was her job to protect me. I told her I knew. Shortly after that night, my pajamas went missing. I looked for them everywhere. I know now that Moms got rid of those pajamas, trying to shake this Superman obsession from her little boy. But what Moms didn't understand was that I didn't need my pajamas to help her. I didn't need to be an imaginary Superman. I was her Clark Kent. Pops was my Kryptonite.

Four years ago, when I was sitting in the front row at the graveside service for my mother, I pulled up my sleeve. I ran my thumb over the glass of my Superman watch. I know it is an odd thing for an adult to wear, but when I saw it in a comic book shop during college, I immediately bought it. The Superman mindset was a memory now. Moms was more than capable of caring for herself and insisted I move forward with my life, even when she was diagnosed with breast cancer. She only showed her vulnerability once it was evident the chemo, radiation, and mastectomy could not capture the spread of the illness. She wasn't scared of dying, she was scared of leaving me. She wanted to see me get married, have kids, and grow into the man she had worked so hard to mold.

During the weeks prior to her death, I spent a lot of time by her side telling her stories about work, about Shonda's progress, and the gossip from the neighborhood. Eventually, when the doctors could do no more for her, she decided to move home with the help of hospice care. I cashed in on my vacation time to be at home with her as much as possible. She constantly told me to go back to work. "I will," I reassured her. As her appetite all but disappeared, I fed her broth with a spoon. She remarked on how she used to do this with me when I was a baby. The morphine she was taking to quell the pain made her sedate. She would often talk to me like I was a young child again. I was happy to play along. She always said being a mother was her best contribution to the world. She always reached for my hand when I sat by her side.

"Malik," she said. "I love you, baby." Her eyes were closed, and her voice was barely audible.

"I love you too, Moms. More than you'll ever know."

She rolled her head toward me and said, "Don't give up, baby. You can do it."

I wasn't sure what she meant. The morphine often made her comments seem out of place. Whatever was in her mind, prompting me not to give up, who could tell? I just replied, "I won't, Moms. I'll never give up."

Her voice was soft and raspy, but she managed to say, "I rise."

I burst into tears. The simple two words were from a poem by Maya Angelou telling everyone to dig down deep and rise up from whatever it was you were facing. I cried knowing that in her last moments on Earth, she was thinking of Maya and her wonderful world of words. The poem took on a new meaning for me. It felt like Moms was telling me not to be afraid because she could feel herself lifting upward toward whatever comes next in life. I wanted her to be out of pain, but I also wanted her here. It's selfish, I know, but it's true. I'd prepared myself for that moment, but I found the notion of life without Moms something for which I could never prepare. Moms had other plans.

Her breathing became faint, irregular, and gravelly. I leaned over, kissing her forehead. And just like that, her breathing stopped. I thought that moment would go on forever. Surely, she would breathe one more breath. But she didn't. She was gone. I was in a world where Moms didn't exist anymore. It felt unnatural that people and events still transpired. *Wasn't the world hurting like I was?*

But the world just kept going, even though my world had just ended.

Moms was gone.

CHAPTER TWENTY-NINE

Caleb — Happy Hour

By all measures, these two kids are beautiful. Jenna has the allure of a multi-ethnic background, giving her high cheekbones, tan skin, and green eyes. Her hair is in an amber-colored pixie cut. A true beauty.

"Who's he, Lisa?" Jenna asks without much assertion.

Chaz, sitting on the bed, looks up with his large brown eyes with a distant look and utters a simple, "Hey."

He has an athletic frame, a blond crew cut, and a youthful face. Jenna makes her way over to Chaz and sits down next to them. As if choreographed, the two of them lie back onto the bed. Chaz's hand meets Jenna's thigh, not in a sexual way, just connected. Jenna puts her hand on top of his.

Lisa walks slowly over to the little table by the window whose curtains are closed. She sits down and puts her hand out, indicating I should take the other chair. I do. What a trip. Lisa closes her eyes for a bit, smiles, and then says, "I remember going out to taverns for a few beers and some pot. Just to hang out. I was about their age too. I wasn't as pretty as Jenna, but I was pretty." Her head drops forward a bit, and she licks her lips. "Well, you can kiss that shit goodbye if you keep riding horses."

"Riding horses?" I ask.

"Horses. It's a nickname for heroin."

Jenna laughs from the bed. "Shut up, Lisa. Life is divine. I hope I never stop getting high." She rolls over, so she is facing Chaz. The two start kissing. Slowly, deeply.

"Miss Society over there," Lisa says to me in a lowered voice. "She'll be on her back in ten years when she ain't so pretty. She'll be here with me. The two of us screwing in motels to get high."

Chaz and Jenna are really getting into one another, like a slow-motion soft porn movie playing out on tacky sheets with bad lighting.

"How much does it cost to get high?" I ask, not knowing how to steer the conversation through this den of iniquity.

"Well, Kelly gives it to me if I give it to him," Lisa says matter-of-factly.

"I mean, like for Chaz and Jenna...or me if I wanted some. How much does it cost?" I ask.

"Twenty bucks a pop. But I ain't getting any for you. You're nice."

"Hey," Jenna says, but turns back to Chaz before finishing her thought.

"Hush up, Jenna. You're nice too, but you're already hooked, babe."

"Twenty bucks? That's it? Wow."

"Yep. Twenty bucks a pop. Pop. Pop pop pop." She giggles as she says the word over and over. "That's a funny word."

"No wonder it's so popular. How long will twenty bucks keep you high?"

"Not long enough." Lisa laughs. After thinking a few moments, she adds, "If you shoot it up, it'll hit you in about twenty seconds. If you smoke it, it takes a bit longer." She puts her hand up to her chest, sort of feeling her heart and enjoying the thought of the rush. "You peak really hard for a few minutes, but the high afterward will last about four or five hours unless you're me. You will need to do more if you want to keep the crash away. The thing I hate about heroin now is that if I don't have it in me, I melt. And it hurts."

"Wow, five hours for twenty bucks?" I say. "I can see why people like that. It's cheaper than going to a movie or out to dinner."

"Well, yeah, it's great for these guys," she says as she looks over at the meshed bodies of Chaz and Jenna on the bed. They are still kissing, but it's like they are both in a dream, each sort of fading in and out of the kiss. They take turns at different levels of wakefulness. "Shit, if I were actually payin' for my drugs, I'd be in bad shape. I'd be running about a hundred bucks a day." She pulls up her sleeve to reveal a forearm and the crook of her elbow. They look like they've been hit with a hammer and drawn on with a Sharpie marker. "And you should see between my toes...just as bad." She thinks for a few moments and says with sincerity, "I'm a junkie."

Her head nods down, diving back into the heroin dream she is doing her best to enjoy. "Once you get started, though, you must constantly use it to stay out of trouble." She pauses, rolling her head around on her neck. "I'm more scared of coming down than getting clean. But I won't get clean. Like I said, I'm a junkie. A real one. She looks at me across the table and seriously says, "You're the best person in my life."

I'm shocked. What a sad and lonesome thing to say. "Oh, man, that's terrible."

"Like I said...junkie. It can hook anyone. Remember that kid from Glee? Or that Phillip Hoffman actor dude. Once you're hooked, you're hooked."

Her insight into her own situation seems clear. She does not have any illusions of how her day-to-day life will transpire. "Have you ever thought about lightening up on what you take? You know, to taper off of it?"

She laughs slowly. "You mean, be a social heroin user? Like on the weekends? Or only after the kids have gone to bed? Oh, sweetie, there ain't no such thing as a social heroin user." She seems to travel away for a few moments. Then, lifting her head, she gathers her thoughts. "These kids are fooling themselves. They've got parents and money. For now, anyway. That won't last long. Soon, when they're out with their pretty friends in their pretty world, that beer and pot won't be near enough. The minute that beer hits their lips, they're going to be yearning for the nod. Heroin will drag them away from their friends and family. Heroin's the girlfriend who will never leave you."

"And you don't want to get clean?"

"I mean, sure. Of course. But it isn't going to happen. I'm not in some after-school movie about getting clean. Nah, I'm a lifer. I got lucky with Kelly. He's nice most of the time. Some dealers are real demons. They enjoy people owing them. They collect desperate people to do their selling." She waves her hand like she is trying to shoo away a bad memory. "Kelly," she says, putting her finger up again as if to punctuate her point, "is decent. Don't get me wrong, he's happy I'm strung out and giving it to him. I don't know why he gives me such a break. Other girls are prettier. But then again, I'll do anything to stay high. Anything."

"Damn." I know I'm going to regret this next question, but I ask it anyway. "Do you have anywhere to sleep tonight that's safe?"

"I'll crash with Kelly, or if Chaz and Jenna move on after they come down, they'll let me stay in their room since it's already paid for."

"OK, good," I say. "I was going to say you could stay in my room, and I can promise I won't try to get in your pants."

She thinks for a minute and then says, "I guess that's a compliment."

"Well, whatever it is, if you need a place to sleep tonight that's safe, you know where my room is."

Lisa looks up at me and says, "Why? You don't know me."

I find it remarkable that out of all the things we discussed tonight, an offer of kindness is the first time she's looked upon me with suspicion. "Nope, I don't, but I know what it's like not to have a place to sleep. It's going to be cold tonight. I don't want you out in the cold." Lisa, sitting in her chair, assesses me. "Seriously, Lisa, it's just a place to sleep."

I look over at Chaz and Jenna. Chaz has his hand deep into Jenna's jeans. Jenna is enjoying the high and being explored by Chaz. Lisa looks at me watching them and says, "Oh, honey, you'll be able to watch them get it on for the next few hours. They'll get naked and do it. That's their thing. They don't care if you watch. Hell, they don't care about anything right now. She reaches into her pocket and then throws me a packet of cheese and crackers with the red stick.

"Dinner and a show, baby," she says, laughing at herself.

I'd like to say I have the good taste to leave. But I don't. And indeed, Lisa and I sit, and watch Chaz and Jenna pull off their clothes and roll over and over one another. Chaz is probably a football player. He is nicely muscled, but with the heroin coursing through his veins, he is unable to perform. So, it really is just an act of going through the motions. Perhaps in their minds they are making love, but from a bystander in the room, it all seems so venal.

I am buzzed from the Jameson. Lisa nods back into a blissful, waking slumber. Chaz and Jenna continue to be both beautiful and tragic. I wonder to myself if, as Lisa said, they'll wind up like her. I wonder if something will happen in their lives to break the arc of their descent into addiction. The absurdity of what is happening sinks in.

"It's happy hour, babe," Chaz says to Jenna.

"It is?" she asks slowly, laboriously.

"Yeah, baby," Chaz says.

"Oh, OK."

I'm not too sure what Happy Hour means, but I don't care. This is too much. I look over to Lisa; she has her hand out with a thumbs-up sign. This display of anodyne hedonism, though, is beyond the pale. When it comes to heroin, I think about what Oscar Wilde wrote, "I can resist everything, except temptation." I wonder if that was an homage to addiction. These two kids are so unaware of their surroundings. They are too high to care. They are literally naked to the world. I think of myself in the admission room of the ER. I was naked there and handled by someone. The vulnerability of Chaz and Jenna reminds me too much of my experience of vulnerability.

Lisa is nodding off in her chair. Chaz is oblivious. Jenna is asleep. A different person could do a lot of damage to these people right now. This is how people end up getting extorted on the Internet. This is how people get raped. This is how people die.

It's too much. I go back to my room. I sit on the edge of the bed.

And the words drop into place:

Creatures of habit, in a world built to consume.
Piercing flesh, pushing poison,
into vulnerable arms held open wide.
Shooting stars, in the cosmos of delusion.
They burn brightly, too brightly,
soaring too close to the sun.

Consumed and drawn by urges
too immense to thwart.
Temptation into desperation into demise into
…oblivion.

CHAPTER THIRTY

Malik — Grounded

I am still thinking about Moms when Moose jumps up and settles himself onto the pillow next to my head as he politely awaits his morning goop. When I fell back to sleep earlier, he snuck off to prowl around the apartment during the night. Sometimes, I can hear the clatter of his mischief as he knocks things off the counter. But when he hears me stirring in my bedroom, he cuts his safari short and comes to see what I'm up to. His soft, rhythmic purring is like a sedative. I reach over and bury my hand in his thick fur. His purring grows louder, and he flips onto his back, stretching his front legs toward me as he yawns.

"Such a good boy," I say to Moose. He returns a short meow. I reach over and scoop him up onto my chest. Moose is more than happy to oblige. I sink into my pillow and ruminate over the past twenty-four hours. It's not been good. I'm stuck between guilt for taking Caleb's things and frustration that I cannot right the wrong immediately. "Respond to need." I keep hearing it in my mind, but I don't know how to respond to this need. I don't know how to conjure a homeless person out of thin air. *How do you find someone who doesn't know they are being sought?* I think of my dad. *Does he even think that I may be wondering where he is? Should I be looking for him? Should I be looking for Caleb?*

I find myself thinking about these lost people. I consider trying to search for Pops on my phone, but decide against it. I just keep getting more and more anxious. It's a vicious cycle. I know it's a vicious cycle. I don't know how to stop thinking about it without coming to some sort of peace with it all. I want to fix it. I want to fix Caleb. I want to fix Pops. I want to fix it all, but I'm just this idiot lying in bed with his damned cat. I know there isn't a peaceful resolution. Well, at least there won't be tonight, lying here in bed.

I grab my phone from the bedside table and use Moose to prop it up. He looks at me with disapproval but settles down anyway. I scroll to the SafeSpace app. It's an online escape when I can't sleep, or like tonight when I can't stop the racing thoughts. I click on the app and log in. It prompts me to either talk to a therapist or join a chat community. I have never used the therapy function. I usually use the chat community to join a conversation with other nut jobs like me. I scroll through the different threads: domestic violence, lgbtq+ safety, AA, NA, Al-Anon, bipolar depression, schizophrenia, and so on. Just looking at all these groups focusing on things that I do not have an issue with helps me, in a small way, realize the depths of my problems are not as bad as a lot of people. I scroll through the various chat groups some more and arrive at the one where I've had some productive conversations. It's entitled: Just neurotic.

I sign in and read the threads available to join: If it's not one thing, it's your mother, Daddy issues, I hate myself, obese AF, and so on. I finally get to the one that's a good combo of crazy mixed with intelligence. It's called, quite quaintly, I Just Need to Talk. Seldom do I actually join in the conversations. I usually just read what everyone else is going through until I find myself thankful that my problems are somewhat under control, at least while people are watching anyway. I talk about my panic attacks sometimes.

Lots of people deal with them in the group, and I've gotten some really good advice. I learned about grounding skills in the group. I learned about accepting the panic when it happens and to sort of guide it back down to earth like I'm landing a plane.

It's a good analogy. The image of a plane landing seems peaceful enough, but most of the time, I'm landing a plane when there's an engine on fire, the pilot has passed out, and all the passengers are drunk. As long as I can get to a space where I'm alone, I can usually ride it out. Sometimes, though, I crash the plane. Sometimes the crew dies, and the fuselage breaks apart into a fiery mess. That's when the Xanax makes an appearance.

I read through the comments of people in tears, needing to talk. Some people are doing well and are just there to provide support. I recognize a few of the usernames. Mine is Luke Cage. It's the name of a Marvel character, a Black guy also known as Power Man. I know it's a name that screams insecure because I'm nothing like the character. But what the hell—this is all anonymous and I don't participate that much. Tonight, however, I decide to jump in the water and post:

[Enter chat]

LUKE CAGE: Hi folks. I screwed things up at work and I can't stop obsessing over it and everything else in my life that's crap.

JYNX: Hi Luke. How can we help?

LUKE CAGE: I don't know. I don't post a lot. Don't really know how to say what I need.

JYNX: That's ok my friend. You're here. Just let it out. Lord knows there's enough of us crying in here about everything!

LUKE CAGE: LOL. Yeah, I don't want to be a snowflake.

STEVE590: Whatever Jynx. Let the poor man vent.

JYNX: Hi Steve–o. I was wondering if you'd be in here tonight.

STEVE590: Hi Jynx.

LUKE CAGE: What do you guys do when you can't shut your mind off at night?

STEVE590: Well, I usually wash down my antipsychotics with a shot of bourbon. LOL!

LUKE CAGE: LOL. I usually do that with my Xanax.

MODERATOR: Please keep the talk of mixing medications with alcohol to a minimum.

JYNX: See!! You pissed mom off! Behave you two.

LUKE CAGE: Yeah, I guess mom is right.

JYNX: I know I sound like a broken record, but grounding yourself as much as possible while it's happening is the best advice I can give.

LUKE CAGE: But what if that doesn't work?

STEVE590: Do you have a therapist?

LUKE CAGE: No.

JYNX: Seriously?

LUKE CAGE: Hahaha...seriously!

JYNX: Jeez, I can't imagine making it through all my crap if I didn't have one.

LUKE CAGE: I think about it all the time. It would probably be in my best interest.

STEVE590: Ya think?

LUKE CAGE: LOL...all right, all right...but like for tonight. Seeing as I don't have a therapist. Any suggestions?

JYNX: Well, try changing your environment. If you're in bed, get in the shower. If you're watching TV, go outside and walk. If you're at work, take a break and ride the elevator. Your mind likes to go places, so you might as well give it some place to go. Otherwise, you go where you don't want to go.

LUKE CAGE: That's actually really helpful.

JYNX: I have my moments.

STEVE590: Yeah, Jynx is pretty smart. Or at least she's smart for a crazy person. LOL.

JYNX: Stop, or you'll hurt my feelings. Wah wah!

LUKE CAGE: You guys are pretty hilarious.

JYNX: I'm brilliant hiding behind a screen name at home with my cat.

LUKE CAGE: Hey, I have a cat. His name is Moose.

STEVE590: You named your cat Moose?

LUKE CAGE: LOL. Yep. Hey, thanks Jynx. I think I'm going to get out of bed and change my scenery. Thanks guys.
STEVE590: You bet. Stay well.
JYNX: Bye Luke. Nice to meet you.
LUKE CAGE: You guys rock. See you around...
[End chat]

I put my phone back on the bedside table. I consider what to do next. It's late, so I don't feel like walking around outside. I could go watch TV, but that doesn't appeal to me, so I decide to take a shower. I gather up Moose and set him on his pillow. He has seemingly forgiven me for using him as a prop for my phone.

I walk toward my bathroom. I take off my underwear and T-shirt, leaving them on the floor. I reach in and turn the nozzle on. The water hits the tub and the shower liner, and it sounds like rain. I like the sound. I don't turn on the light. I like the darkness of the bathroom when I shower.

"Alexa," I say into the air, and the little green and blue light flashes on my Echo. "Play Alicia Keyes." *If I Ain't Got You* fills the air. I love this song. I pull back the curtain and step into the falling water as I sing along with her in my crappy voice. I don't know why I don't think of this more often. I love showering. Living in an apartment complex means I always have good pressure and lots of hot water.

Music has always made a difference in my mindset. Songs lift me up. They transport me in a way unlike anything else. Whitney Houston's *I Will Always Love You* reminds me of Moms. For better or worse, the song *She's a Brick House* will always remind me of Pops. I think back to college when Drake and I spent hours in our tiny dorm bunks listening to music. He was more into rock, and I was more into R&B. We taught each other about music. He introduced me to Iron Maiden and the pulsing songs from their *Number of the Beast* album. I taught him about TLC's *Waterfalls* and Salt-n-Pepa's *Shoop*. We spent our college years steeped in one of the coolest periods of music. Mary J. Blige and Justin Timberlake were on fire. Drake made sure I knew about Linkin Park and Green Day. I made him memorize most of *The Message* by Grand Master Flash and the Furious Five, and Drake made me play air guitar through *In-A-Gadda-Da-Vida* by Iron Butterfly.

As these lyric memories are rushing through my brain, Alexa begins playing Janelle Monae's *Turntables*, and I rap along with the lyrics. It's then that I realize I must have grounded myself. So strange. I'm thinking about good things, listening to music that moves me, and I'm relaxing in the shower. It feels great to stand in peace, which is why it is infuriating when I begin thinking about Caleb again. *With all that has happened, how does he stay grounded?* Without thinking, I turn the nozzle all the way to the right, making the warm water run ice cold. My shocked body lets out a yelp. Goddammit! I'm shocked, but at the same time, I'm laughing. What the hell did I just do? I see an imaginary comment from Jynx in my head. It reads, "You changed your situation." I laugh again, thinking I did something almost subconsciously that was beneficial. I stopped the thinking from bursting in again. The only real negative side effect is that I'm freezing cold now.

I open the curtain. I'm actually a bit refreshed from the blast of cold water. Moose is sitting on the bathroom carpet, looking at me as if trying to figure out what his human is doing. I look at him and say, "Hi, Moose. Yes, your dad is nuts and is taking a shower at three in the morning." He meows back, as if in agreement, and then leaves the bathroom as soon as he is satisfied the guy with the cans of food is ok.

I grab a towel and begin to dry off. I turn the light on and wipe the bathroom mirror with my towel. Through the streaks on the mirror, I check if I need to shave and decide it can wait another day. I'm on the thin side. I flex my arms for a few moments. *Not very impressive*, I think. I never developed a habit of physical exercise or going to the gym. Even when I played basketball and went to workouts, I never seemed to gain weight. I resigned myself to being just a skinny brother a long time ago. I step on the scale in my room. It reads 169 pounds. I've been 169 pounds since college. I'm just under six feet tall, so I'm not overly thin, just "skinny" thin. Moms would make me a plate daily until I got fatter if she were still here.

I look at the large black and white print hanging in the bathroom. It's a photograph of the three women who started the Black Lives Matter movement: Alicia Garza, Patrisse Cullors, and Opal Tometi. The three women stand with stern faces as a young white man with a bullhorn shouts at them. Their faces are so resolved. It's like they are all thinking, *this will be a long and tiresome road, but we can do it.* Their eyes all seem to embody what Martin Luther King Jr once said, that "the arc of the moral universe is long, but it bends toward justice." Every time I take the time to look at those three women, I'm inspired.

CHAPTER THIRTY-ONE

Caleb — Bones on the Desert Floor

With the door closed behind me, I remind myself how quickly life can go awry. I have the image of Chaz and Jenna in mind, naked and vulnerable to the world. The image is not arousing. I think again of myself under the lights in the emergency room, someone taking my clothes off and changing me into a hospital gown. I take drugs to stay under control. Chaz and Jenna take drugs to lose control. That's the difference between having a damaged mind and a mind you damage yourself.

I think about Kate, desperate for attention, probably looking for anyone to love her. It all came to an end for her in a shower stall in a psych ward, awash in her own blood. She was a patient admitted for having passed out from alcohol and becoming combative with the officers who tried to help her. She was on a 72-hour psychiatric hold, but all she needed was fifteen minutes. For so many of us, living is a courageous act unto itself. We've struggled for so long that the thought of happiness is a fantasy. I stand in my room, almost jealous that her troubles are done.

And the words drop into place:

Begone the omnipresent pain,
unseen by prying eyes;
for time can heal all wounds it's said,
but time is rife with lies.
Pain etched on the youthful mind,
disrupts adult-led lives;
the child screams through adult lungs
for that's what time contrives.
Dreams insert their dewy claws
piercing through minds' eyes;
the dreamer walks in anguished tales
waking when he dies.
Ending torment. Slicing long.
Righting what is wrong.

I walk to the table by my little window and pour another glass of Jameson. I'm tipsy. I take a moment to assess. I'm in a room where I can sleep, protected from the elements. I've got clothes in my bags by the window. I have a convenience store nearby where I can get some food. I've got a good bottle of liquor. The heat is on, and it feels good in the room. I sit down on the bed. I lie back down upon it. Looking at the ceiling, I take a moment to breathe. Life at this very moment is good. I try not to think about the future and, more importantly, not about the past. The past is over; it's done. I have to remain steadfast in my blockade of messaging from my failures, my losses, and my wounds. I have to stop listening to the voices of those who took more than I had to give, more than I had to lose.

I'm safe here in my room. The door is locked. No one knows I'm here, especially Craig. I sit back up and then stand, looking at myself in the mirror above the dresser. I'm accustomed to seeing myself as I am, not how I used to be. I spent many years being attractive, being useful, and being engaged with my environment. Now, though, I'm more of a fixture in my environment rather than participating in it. Gone are the days of fruitful contribution. I no longer wear stylish clothing. I no longer think about what others are thinking about me. It's freeing in a way, but it's freeing in a way that means I've given up attempting to join the world. Living on the margins of society has its benefits, but it also has costs that run deep.

In the mirror, I see a man who looks older than his years. And that's OK. I've accepted my limitations, even though I am still subject to the mental war taking place in my head. I begin to take my clothes off in front of the mirror. There was no privacy at the shelter or the BHU, so you slept in your clothing. And being homeless, I don't take my clothes off except in a gas station or laundromat bathroom.

In my underwear, I pull the chair from the table to the mirror and sit down to take my socks off. I stand and pull my shorts down, step out of the leg holes, and walk to the mirror. There is nothing special whatsoever about me. My body carries me from place to place. It's a thing of function, not a thing of desire or passion. I used to be somewhat heavy. I'm no longer heavy. I'm worn down to my core. I'm just a body.

I walk to the bathroom to shower by myself in a safe environment for the first time in months. This is the change that has come to my life. The days of safety. The comfort of this room is almost unnerving. I remind myself that it is temporary. It will be gone soon. That's probably why I got the whiskey. It's easier to be a bit inebriated rather than stay present. The bathroom has a simple white sink and a dingy but relatively clean toilet. The far wall is filled by a single shower curtain, once clear but now tarnished with calcium and use. I pull the curtain back and turn on the water. I can't remember the last time I had a bath, months, maybe years? The room I rented in San Diego had a stand-up shower shared by the other occupants of the house, so this was a true luxury. The water runs hot. I balance it out with a bit of cold, so it isn't scalding. I pull the trip lever, and the water starts filling the tub.

For a moment, I think about running out to get cleanser. But the thought leaves me. Years ago, in another life, I would have scoured the tub with bleach before setting foot in it. But here I am, someone who sleeps in shelters, under highway underpasses, and beneath tall weeds atop broken glass next to freeways. All things are relative now.

The water begins to rise in the tub. I sit on the edge and put my feet one by one into the water. Hot, but tolerable. The feeling of heat and comfort is mesmerizing. I lower my naked body into the tub. I have a fleeting thought of baptisms.

I lean against the tub's back, allowing the water to flow up onto my thighs, over my lower belly, and onto my lower back. *Glorious.* I reach into the chipped ceramic soap dish and retrieve the wrapped soap cake. The bar looks small in my hand. Unwrapping the waxy paper, I let the cake slip into my palm and close it into my hands like a prayer. I put the soap, locked behind my fingers, into the water and slowly wash all parts of my body. I feel a renewal. We were all carried as children in the warmth of a womb, so perhaps that is why it is so rejuvenating.

The sheer joy of knowing there's no one waiting to use the tub after me ripples through my mind. There aren't piles of socks, wrappers, used soap cakes, and detritus in the corner. It's dark in the bathroom aside from the very low light of the sole bedside lamp in the other room. After a few minutes, my eyes adjust. I revel in the dark ambiance, the hot water, and the smell of motel soap. In the darkness, the bathroom seems clean. I'm not going to think about what it might actually look like. It's all part of the façade.

I bend my knees, allowing my back, shoulders, and head to slip under the water. Hushed by the noise of running water, all traces of outside are silenced. The heat from the water envelopes me. The only sound I'm cognizant of is the water still tumbling into the bathtub. I think for a moment about the movie *Altered States* and how they used isolation chambers to unlock parts of the mind. I'm hoping, here beneath the water, I will lock my mind up completely.

I straighten my leg, pushing my head and shoulders above the surface. I breathe. It's strange—being underwater usually means I'm slipping somewhere safe, away from the world. Yet here, in the bathtub, the water is warm and inviting. The only noise in the bathroom is the water flowing from the faucet. I raise my foot and attempt to turn the tub's knob with my toes. After a few attempts, I find success, and the bathroom becomes nearly silent. A distant car horn. Someone whistles. The rumble of a heavy truck on the road outside. All peripheral noises, nothing in the forefront.

For a few moments, I remember this as a lifestyle I once enjoyed and took for granted. I remember what it's like to have things at my disposal: a bath, money in my bank account, a friend calling on the phone, a home to put my things in, and time to spend with loved ones. I roll my head to the side, looking out the bathroom door to the main room. Lit by the pale light are my hefty bags of belongings. Beyond the bed is the small table with the Jameson bottle next to my coat. My boots are by the door.

I turn my head back, trying extremely hard not to go down the path of losses I've tallied over the past decade. I've done that too many times. It never ends well. I do my best to look upward at the bathroom ceiling and return to the thoughts of thankfulness for the warm water, the cleansing soap, and the silence of the tiny bathroom at the Cheap Nite Inn. I understand my scope of prosperity as it is now, not how it was in the past. I am content with my momentary isolation in comfort.

The small bar of soap, guided by my hands, caresses portions of my body slowly and intentionally. I don't recall ever washing myself this purposefully. In my previous life, bathing was expected, so it became perfunctory. Now, here in the tub, cleansing becomes almost ceremonial.

I turn the soap over in my hands. I wash between my toes, the bottoms of my feet, and across my toenails. I can't remember the last time I truly washed my feet. From somewhere deep in the mixed labyrinth of my memory, I remember a Sunday School class about Jesus washing the feet of strangers. If I remember correctly, it's an Old Testament thing from the Bible. But something about the washing of feet sticks with me. I see the image of a basin filled with water, the guest sitting in a chair, and the master of the house washing the feet of someone who has journeyed a long distance. If I remember, Jesus washed the feet of his disciples, too.

My hands clean my other foot. Even though the room is relatively dark, I close my eyes and imagine Jesus washing my feet. *What would it mean to have Jesus wash my feet? Is anything that simple or unconvoluted by ulterior motive or meaning?* My hands let go of the soap, and it disappears into the tub. My chest is tight. I feel like I'm losing track of time somewhat. *Did Jesus hold ill will against those disciples he knew were going to betray him?* My head is swimming.

I can't hold onto the tranquility of taking a bath. My brain always does this to me. It throws up red flags of alarm, replacing the white flags of gentle surrender. My pulse quickens. The relaxing water now begins to feel heavy. My clean body begins to feel saturated by heavy moisture. The solitude of the bathroom begins to feel susceptible to prying eyes through the curtains. I sit up so my arms rest on top of my knees.

Don't let this happen.

My forehead presses down on my forearms. My nakedness, which had just moments before seemed natural and comfortable, begins to feel vulnerable and exposed.

Please don't let this happen.

My pulse is getting quicker still. I feel an intense need to cover myself. I sit up, reaching for a towel. Once in hand, I stand up and begin wiping away the water.

Is Craig here?

I step out of the tub onto the cold tile floor, hurriedly wiping my body. I throw the towel to the floor and take a few steps to the bed. I grab handfuls of covers and pull them back. I roll underneath and pull the blanket and sheet over me. My breathing is labored. My heart rate seems high. I can feel it in my chest. I try to maintain deep breathing, but the anxiety has a severe grip on my mind. Remnants of coping skills flood my mind. Hours of therapy replay in my head in a morbid montage of mixed messaging. I close my eyes tightly, trying to will the confusion out of my mind, but I know I'm too late. The chaos of panic races through my body. My breath quickens, becoming shallower. The dim room grows dimmer. My head is now bright with sweat.

My fists clamp around the blankets as I realize my pills are still rambling around in a paper bag. I need to get them organized. I need to take my meds. Images of Jesus washing the feet of people who would later bring about his earthly death run through my head. The covert, quiet conversations of disciples planning his demise play louder and louder in the bellows of my mind. My face intertwines with Jesus' face as his disciples and my family members toy with provocative conversations about me.

I imagine Jesus washing my feet with cleansers and bleach,

rubbing them raw. Family members now circle me as Jesus claws at my feet with his fingernails. Disciples are laughing. Family members with wild eyes hurl their accusations at me. I pull into a ball beneath the covers. The dim room grows darker. I close my eyes…

•••

I have died a dozen times, maybe more. I lose count, or perhaps more accurately, I have lost interest in the enumeration. Instead, I float in the ether, above the varied tableaus of my past, peering down upon the remnants of lives long lost.

I died in Phoenix. There are no newspaper clippings of my disappearance. No police reports were taken. No outcry of sorrow. I marched, by night, for the next bastion of relief against my demons.

I died in Jackson. When I stopped showing up for work, inquiries were made. There were no friends or acquaintances to provide enlightenment. My landlord knew nothing except his renter skipped town. Once the temp agency that hired me sent a new worker to fill my spot at the warehouse, that was it; my existence was unadorned and unremarkable.

This story was repeated over and over: Reno, Monterrey, or Fresno.

San Diego, Sacramento, Salem.

Boise, Bismarck, Biloxi.

My act of disappearance is hard-wired. Deeply rooted neuroses keep me from relationships. I've learned the cadence of a solitary life. In the arena of mental warfare, I am my own worst enemy. I stand alone, girded by invisible walls, fortified with paranoia.

I slept during the day. My skin was pale from preferring the shadows, much like vampires in lore. I don't rise at night to devour the sanguine blood of innocent victims; rather, the only thing I consume is regret. I am the mundane phenomenon of depression, anxiety, and trauma left unchecked.

Baltimore, Poughkeepsie, Wilkes-Barre.

Twenty years awash on shores where waters cling to the land only to recede back into the body from which they came. Over and over again, like cycles amid the waves. Waters so deep and vast that to be caught in their pull is to be forever reaching for air, gasping for something to buoy myself.

St. Louis, Salt Lake City, and Oakland.

My deaths were not corporeal in nature; they were psychic. The seed of anxiety was deposited in my thinking, nourished by the frenetic energy of my troubled cognition. The only thing that has ever stopped the mental infestation was my absence. I must walk away from whatever life I have. Each time I did, my psychical mind descended into bleak malaise. It was an affliction from which I could not escape. So, I died inside from the exquisite pain of madness running rampant. It is a pain that suffocates one's life until fleeing is the only remedy.

That's why now, as the vulture's beak, strong with practice, pulls the remaining sinews from my skull. I am surprised at my sadness. It's an emotion I thought I'd forgotten. Looking down upon my deteriorating body, I find myself unexpectedly sad. I find myself wanting to live. I have died so many times in the minds of others that I thought naught what it would feel like when I did depart from this plane.

I don't like it.

I find myself pining to try again in life, to find a reason not to die away. I am struck by the irony of my seeking death as an escape, only to suddenly want to escape from a death I have so long sought.

I don't remember anything from when the semi hit me. I had walked along the side of US Route 95. I was headed North, away from the heat and insular culture of Yuma. I had enjoyed the sound of passing traffic, the white noise present during my northward trek. The truck had drifted a few feet to the right onto the shoulder without the driver's knowledge. The moment of impact registered as a bright, white light.

Then nothing.

Nothing until I realized the yawn of morning and the presence of sunlight sufficient to see myself lying on the hardpan dirt of the Sonoran Desert. There I lay. My legs contorted unnaturally. My face is immersed in the Earth. My backpack resting a good distance away, seemingly unmolested. My body, just far enough away from traffic to lie unseen among the sage and stones, crumpled and still.

Time takes on a different role after death. It is no longer linear. The view I see of myself from wherever I am is constant. I can see today, yesterday, and tomorrow.

Today I see the vulture harvesting the final nutrients beneath my tattered clothing. The protuberance of a humerus bone clutching onto its radius counterpart with a weathered ligament poking through my clothing. My sun-soaked skull revealing my occipital bone.

I find myself in a perpetual orbit above the body I knew, a body that had been given the chance to live but whose mind never allowed it to thrive. I have truly died. I am now departed from myself, watching my body slowly become part of the lonely desert. My broken phalanges are but small stones on the desert floor, scattered without intention or purpose, akin to the lives I used to live.

Looking down now, I recognize my future is extinguished. Yet here I am, still awash in the memories of lives I lived. To what end have I come? For so long, I sought to die and be released from life. And now, in a place absent of pain and anxiety, I mourn myself, my fettered existence. Death, I realize, was not an answer; it is a premature conclusion without remedy. In life, I understood death like the Tarot card placed in front of me, time and time again, depicting a skeleton with an arm raised toward the seeker, is not about death; it is about change. My life repeatedly sought change, not death, but a hungered change, a change I was unable to affect with my aberrant mental faculty. I see that now, as plainly as I see my bones on the desert floor, discharged among the sage and boulders.

Because, at long last, I died...

CHAPTER THIRTY-TWO

Malik — We're All Mad Here

The next morning, the alarm comes on as usual, broadcasting the Too Live Crew carrying on about local politics. The quips and jokes fill my bedroom, and Snoop's *Drop It Like It's Hot* plays behind their banter. The library doesn't open until nine o'clock. It's six now.

Today I must rectify a mistake. My mistake. I must roll back the effects of playing God.

Tap. Tap. Tap. Tap. Tap.

I drop my feet over the side of the bed and lean forward with my hands on my thighs, breathing in a few deep breaths. My eyes close shut as I acknowledge the day ahead. I walk into the living area and pick up my phone. I know no one is at work, so I message my boss to let them know I'm taking a sick day. That won't be a problem. I have tons of sick days accrued. I think about my boss telling us that they aren't considered sick days; they're considered mental health days. Sometimes, you need a day to adjust your outlook on things. Today is one of those days.

Tap. Tap. Tap. Tap. Tap.

I play in my mind about how this morning is going to happen.

I'll get there before opening, so I'm first in line. Maybe I'll see him there. *Crap. What if he isn't there?* I walk into the kitchen and grab my French press. I pull the gourmet, pre-ground coffee bag from the cabinet and set it on the granite countertop. I turn the flame up underneath the kettle and wait for the water to boil. I heap a good third cup of coffee grounds into the bottom of the press.

Waiting for the water to boil, I think about Caleb's reaction. *Will he think about how badly I intruded on his life? Will he be mad? Happy? Indifferent?*

Tap. Tap. Tap. Tap. Tap.

I hope that the return of his laptop will overshadow any ill feelings he might have toward me. The kettle starts to whistle. I retrieve it from the heat and pour the boiling water over the aromatic grounds in the press. I let it steep for a minute or two, thinking about how to tell Caleb that I ended up with his stuff. I send the plunger on its way down the decanter, bringing the blessed fluid into being. The scent brings a modicum of happiness. The plunger reaches the bottom. I pluck a mug from the hook on the backsplash and pour the coffee.

This is one thing I count as approaching a religious experience: The first cup of coffee from the press. Coffee can retrieve me from down the rabbit hole, like in *Alice in Wonderland*. The "Drink Me" potion returns me to reality.

As I stand here slowly sipping my first taste of coffee for the day, I say softly to myself, "We're all mad here. I'm mad, you're mad." It's a line from *Alice in Wonderland*. Nothing could be further from the truth. For some reason, my issues, no matter how thinly veiled, still allow me to have a life. I know PTSD can be triggered by growing up in a violent neighborhood, and it can manifest itself in things that I do, but at least I have control of things in my life. No matter how bad the panic attacks are, I know they will end.

Poor Caleb. Seeing things. Hearing things. Being tackled by police in a library. Having people steal his computer. "There but for the grace of God, go I," I mutter, knowing full well a physiological tweak of dopamine, serotonin, or noradrenaline in my brain could have rendered me just like Caleb.

More of God's work.

The image of Hurricane Katrina survivors comes to mind. The ones whose houses were spared have spray-painted on their roofs, "Thank you, God." That would be me: The one who got saved by God. Caleb would be in the submerged house, a total loss. What do you spray paint on that rooftop, "Where did God go?" I sip the coffee, coming back to life from my mental field trip, wondering when I will hear back from Drake.

As if on cue, my phone rings.

"Drake?" I ask.

"Hello, asshole," Drake answers.

"Yeah. Sorry about texting so early."

"Another panic attack?"

"No," I answer. "Well, maybe...shit, I don't know. I, uh, had another idea that I wanted to talk to you about."

"At four in the morning?" he says, laughing.

"Yeah," I say again. "Sorry, uh, you still got that vacancy on Sullivan?"

"Hell yeah," he says. "Been open for over two months. This time of year is a crappy time to have a vacancy. No one wants to move when it's cold outside. And those who've expressed an interest in it, so far, have been disasters."

"What if I had a tenant for you?"

"Seriously?" Drake says. "That would be awesome. Do you know..." He pauses. "Wait a minute. Is this about your psycho dude friend from the other night?"

"Well, 'psycho dude' might be a little harsh. How about 'artfully crazy'?"

"Aw, man," he says. "I've got three pretty normal guys in there now who all get along. I can't introduce an unknown quantity like a crazy dude into the mix."

"What if I had an idea that would limit any of the crazy stuff to a minimum?"

"Oh God," he says. "Don't start your bleeding-heart crap on me."

"I wouldn't think of it, Drake, my man." There's a pregnant pause. "You haven't hung up the phone yet, so can I keep talking?"

There's a sigh. "Go ahead. What's crawling through that fever swamp of a brain of yours?"

"I met with him the other day. I want you to meet him if I can find him today. He's the best kind of crazy."

"Does he have an income?"

"Yes. He receives disability with enough to pay his rent and share of utilities."

"But will he be around the house all day bugging the crap out of everyone since he's on disability?"

"No, man. Homeboy works through temp agencies and spends most of his time at the library working on writing projects."

"Writing projects?"

"Yes, the guy's got a good functioning brain. And to be honest, I looked at his file, and his meltdowns aren't that often. And chances are he's getting hooked up with therapy now, too."

"Yeah, about those meltdowns..." I could feel Drake shaking his head through the phone.

"He's back on his medication. He is starting therapy. He is motivated to get out of the shelter. He's one of the few who seem out of place at the shelter. He's always reading and likes to stay busy."

"Ok..."

"It will take some coordination, for sure, but thankfully, you know someone who is a social worker who could help Caleb integrate with your tenants. I can sit down with them and answer all their questions. You could come, too, so they know this is something that you back."

"Well, I'm still thinking about it. There's such liability at stake if I knowingly take on a resident who is volatile."

"Well, you know as well as I do that even though someone looks great on paper, they can still be a disaster. You've had tenants blow up in your face, and they were the saner ones."

"So, you'll vouch for this guy." It wasn't a question. It was a statement, as in, I'm assuming responsibility for anything should it blow up in his face. I take a moment to think about what Drake just asked. I hesitate for a minute, thinking about how I may be interfering again in someone's life.

Tap. Tap. Tap. Tap. Tap.

"Yes, Drake," I say. "I will vouch for Caleb. I feel like all he needs is a break and some support." Tap. Tap. Tap. Tap. Tap.

"Aw, jeez," Drake says.

"Look, man. I have a whole community project I could start around this. The Four Corners Neighborhood Initiative. Your house is a perfect place to start something like this. It's something that is so desperately needed, getting homeless people into real living situations, not these slum apartments overrun with cockroaches and crack." I pause. "I know this is a risk for you, Drake. I understand that, but this could really work."

"What's your community project?" he asks. I can almost hear him putting air quotes around the community project.

"So, in a nutshell, people like you with rental properties partner with people like me, a social worker with links to housing programs. I pre-qualify individuals for income and background, and then put them in touch with people like you. Right now, we can only place people in apartments. We can't rent someone just a room in a house. But I plan to create a new type of housing for people like Caleb."

"Ok," he says. "I get how you are involved, but what's the community aspect of this? Are you starting a colony for people with disabilities?" He chuckles a bit at that thought.

"No, man, I'm starting a shared housing placement program that I know the admins at Crossroads will help develop. All the pieces are here: the houses from the Land Bank, do-gooders like you, social workers like me, and crazy dudes like Caleb. I'd get the backing of the police CIT, the Crisis Intervention Team. Columbus PD is really starting to move manpower and dollars to assist people in crisis." I remind him about Caleb's episode at the library. "This morning, I connected with Sergeant Gabriel Santos at Columbus PD. He's been doing training within the department about CIT. He's open to connecting Caleb with a CIT team."

I can tell Drake is thinking about it. He says, "So if anything went haywire and the tenants had to call the cops, there would be a CIT response instead of a regular police response."

"Right," I say.

"Ok," he says. "Well, the idea doesn't suck."

"If you agree to do this, it could become a program," I say, knowing that the community programming aspect appeals to Drake. He, unlike Adam, Keith, and me, went into administration rather than the client side of social services. I think he'll like the idea of a private nonprofit footing the bill instead of waiting on tenants to pay. "Gabriel also alerted me to one more tool. Caleb would wear a Medic ID bracelet, too. This way if he is arrested, or sedated, those attending to him will know he is most likely having a psychiatric event and is not someone out to do harm."

There is a pause in the conversation. Drake is contemplating it. I know his pragmatic reasoning can go either way. He, at his core, does want to help people. But he is a stickler for rules, and ultimately, he is introducing a risk factor into a business rental he created.

"Hey, man, remember how many hours I rode that damned floor sander getting your floors in order?" I say.

"Yeah," Drake says.

He is considering it.

Tap. Tap. Tap. Tap. Tap.

"Besides," I say, "if this program gets off the ground, you'd be a new social outreach program founder. More feathers in your cap." Drake loves accolades. I can hear the wheels turning in his head.

"If it worked, I could buy another house from the Land Bank. We could help folks and create a revenue stream to fund the project."

He's in! I thought to myself. "Well, for now," I say, "let's just try one tenant in one house." More pauses. "Well, what do you think?"

"What the hell," he says. "Let's give it a try. Do you still have a key to show the place to him?"

"I do," I say.

"Well then, things look promising. Now, all you have to do is find the guy."

CHAPTER THIRTY-THREE

Caleb — Resolved

The dreams and anxiety I experienced last night have fallen away from my mind. I wake up today feeling...good? *What a change.* The motel, in all its depravity, has been a godsend. I'm not sure what time it is, but it doesn't matter. The aches of hauling my life around are minimal. My head is clearer. And I'm going to do my best to get my laptop back today.

Such a strange event, to wake up hopeful. *Is this how the world should be?* I walk over to the window, pull back the curtain, and slide open the glass. It's still crisp and cold. Lisa has taken up her usual spot on the street by the brick wall. Chaz and Jenna's car is gone, and there is no telltale sign of their ever having been here. The few cars from yesterday are replaced by other cars. I don't see any children, but I hear an infant crying.

I push the window closed, leaving the curtain open for some natural light, and busy myself in the bathroom getting cleaned up for the day. The shower feels great—the soap is fragrant, and the water is hot. I have one change of clothes left. If I can get change, I'll do the laundry in my Hefty bags.

The clock radio informs me it is eight o'clock in the morning. I'm going to the library today, hoping there is someone there who can tell me where my laptop might be. I feel motivated. Once I know more about when I can get back into the shelter, I can start looking for another job. I don't even bother calling the old one back. I'm sure I was replaced by some other junkie or homeless guy by the following morning. Now that I'm clean, shaven, and dressed, I make my way downstairs to the street where I will pick up the bus to take me to the library. I have just enough money to buy another pass.

The diversity on a bus never ceases to fascinate me. Young kids are sitting right behind the driver on their way to school. There are moms with babies on their way to daycare. There's a nurse, two guys in what I think are janitors' uniforms, two older ladies clutching their bags, and, of course, the signature riffraff. There are a couple of teenagers sitting on the back bench, sort of entangled with one another. I think about Chaz and Jenna, the way their bodies commingled with each other. I can see a bare midriff with several belly button piercings. Their fingernails are painted with chipped black polish, and their hair is matted and unkempt. I wonder if they are trying to look homeless.

There are two kids with developmental delays. Their mouths hang open. Their stocking caps are tied below their chins. They hold hands. A few wraith-like meth heads are talking with lots of animation toward one another a few seats back. They are planning to receive a substantial amount of money if they are involved in an accident and are hit by a car. And then there's me. I look different today. I'm bathed, shaven, and dressed in clean clothes. I wonder if there are other people-watchers on the bus. *Are they looking at me, trying to figure out my story? Would they know that a couple of weeks ago, I was sleeping under an overpass?*

The bus turns left on Grant Street. Just a mile or so to go and I'll be at the library. I think about the words that dropped into place in the past few days but had nowhere to land. Having my laptop pacifies me. It reminds me at any moment I may have a thought that will resound across many readers; that is, if I ever get something published.

The act of writing something profound exhilarates me. I know I have a lot to learn, but I think I've come a long way in the last few years in creating enough content that someday might make its way to an agent or publisher. I think about Sylvia Plath and her book *The Bell Jar* or Susanna Kaysen and her book *Girl, Interrupted.* These women led lives punctuated with mental illness and their books got to press. Someday, maybe, I can make the same sort of impact.

My story is convoluted. It started in the most unassuming of suburbs, yet it slithered downward to find its place among the loners, junkies, and hookers living in seedy motel rooms. I know this is not the end of my story, just a transition. I feel like I'm constantly pulling the Death card from a Tarot deck. The Tarot is for the spiritually attuned to divine information from a certain array of cards. I don't believe in all that, but I do like that Death not only means the end of something but, more importantly, it means the beginning of something new, like a butterfly emerging from its chrysalis. I'm hoping that this motel is some sort of Death card. I would love for things to take a drastic change right now, for the better.

The bus pulls up on the north side of the library. The main entrance is on the east side, but I prefer the west side entrance. It's right by the coffee shop and is generally less crowded. I'm not a big fan of the taste of their coffee, but I love sitting for a few minutes surrounded by the freshly perking aroma. I miss being able to make fresh, good coffee each morning. Those are the types of things that get me. When I'm waking up and can't get that brew of ground beans, turning water into an onyx elixir that sustains me. Instead, I've been drinking the decaf Folgers at the shelter, nothing at all in the psych ward, or since I got to the motel. There aren't too many Starbucks in the ghetto.

The bell chimes, signifying the library is opening, and I enter through the large glass doors into the coffee shop. I sit at a table. Usually, I take my laptop out and begin working on whatever project is percolating inside my head. Today I just sit. I try to people-watch, but I'm too nervous about approaching the lost and found area over at the circulation desk. *What if it isn't there? What if, because of my behavior, they handed it over to the police? What if they call the police when they see me?* I try not to think about it. I linger a few more minutes in the caffeinated, aromatic splendor before sliding off my chair and making my way over to the circulation desk. This is my Shangri-la, refuge from a life unnecessary.

And the words drop into place:

> Words, puzzles of letters,
> making mountains from mole hills.
> Words, sharp, blunt, and terse,
> puncture minds and change hearts.
> Twenty-six options,
> millions of possibilities.

CHAPTER THIRTY-FOUR

Malik — Trust Me

There's a small but lovely statue in front of the library. I've passed by it multiple times in my journeys around town, but I must admit I never stopped to consider it. I'm surprised to find out it is a statue of Peter Pan. He looks down State Street, so if you cross the street toward the library, he seems to watch you as you pass by. I loved it when Moms would read the Peter Pan story to me. Tinkerbell allowed a kid to fly away whenever he wanted. I would have loved to have flown away when the lights whirled around my bedroom, or when Pops had one of his nights. But my body always stayed rooted in my panic. I remember the line from Peter Pan when he said, "The moment you doubt whether you can fly, you cease forever to be able to do it." *When did I lose my ability? Maybe I never had it to begin with.*

It's eight forty-five, and on the steps leading up to the large wrought iron doors on the east side of the library is a smattering of people waiting to enter. Most of the folks look like they could be clients of the shelter. Libraries have become neighborhood community centers. Many of our guys spend their time here. It makes sense. They can charge their phones, escape the weather, use a clean bathroom, and drink fresh water. There are people at the library who treat them with respect. I wonder how much training the librarians get in social work because they seem to have become the default caretakers of many homeless people. Some libraries employ social workers because the line between being an open public space and a space for homeless people to spend their time is fraught with difficulties beyond the average librarian's skill set.

It's a cold morning, and several of the folks waiting to enter the library should have better clothing, although they don't act distressed. There are also several young people, perhaps college students, waiting to enter, and a few folks like me, dressed casually in khaki pants, button-down shirts, and insulated coats. I notice we are all waiting away from the group by the doors. We've placed a buffer between ourselves and the rest without realizing we are doing so.

I check my phone to see if Drake has texted back any questions or, God forbid, to let me know he's changed his mind.

Tap. Tap. Tap. Tap. Tap.

There's no message from him.

Tap. Tap. Tap. Tap. Tap.

I click the Weather Channel app. It reads 39° and indicates a chance of snow showers. I pull my hat down firmly onto my ears. I watch the folks around the door and, like the guys outside of the shelter during the day who smoke, the cold doesn't seem to bother them. Perhaps it does, but they've become inured to it; theoretically, it's above freezing, so they aren't in danger of frostbite. I can't fathom how uncomfortable it must be to be chronically cold. My thermostat is set at 70°. Homeless people, for all their faults, are made of stern stuff.

The sound of a bell chimes, and the large, heavy doors swing open. The crowd begins to enter the library. Those of us who have stood back waiting for others to enter walk forward, climbing the steps to the doors. Walking into the foyer, I'm met with warm, comfortable air. There are large, dark, metallic orbs suspended from the ceiling. They resemble a darkly shaded solar system of sorts. As I step farther inside the lobby, it opens into a wide-open, impressive space. There is an intricate model train display. It features snowy mountains, numerous pine trees, and winding tracks that traverse villages and mountain passes.

Librarians off to the left welcome us all as we enter. I smile back and keep walking. There is a coffee bar ahead, and since I didn't see Caleb anywhere in the open space, I decide to get a coffee and wait. I'm hoping to speak to someone at the circulation desk to find out if it is possible to make an announcement over the PA to bring Caleb down to the lobby. I rethink that, though. If I send a message that he is wanted at the front desk, he may leave the library thinking he might be in trouble.

Tap. Tap. Tap. Tap. Tap.

As I walk to the coffee bar and order my Americano with an extra shot, I realize there is a second entrance at the back. I scan the crowd quickly, adjusting my backpack filled with Caleb's things. I don't see him. The aroma from the coffee bar is intense. It smells a bit like over-roasted beans. I like my coffee bitter, but not so much that I need to put milk into it. I decide to risk getting a latte as I watch for Caleb. Standing in line, I keep peering toward both entrances, something akin to watching a tennis match. The barista slides the coffee cup across the counter to me.

"Two fifty-five," the frail-looking kid says. I hand him a five-dollar bill and notice how starkly different our hands are. My dark skin, his light skin. *I wonder how our differing skin tones have impacted our lives. Does he ever get stopped out of the blue? Have security guards ever followed him through a store? How is it that an infinitesimal difference of pigmentation changes the course of many lives?*

"Malik?" I hear from behind me. I'm surprised to hear my name called. I turn around and am flooded with relief.

"Caleb!" I nearly shout as I recognize him beneath his gray hoodie, standing several feet away. The coffee lurches through its small, perforated hole in the lid and stings my skin. I put the cup down and shake my hand in pain.

"You OK?"

"Uh, yeah," I say quickly as I wipe my hand free of spilled coffee. I go to meet him, but the barista interrupts me, saying he has my change. I grab the two bills and the collection of coins, shoving them into my pocket.

"Do you have a minute, Caleb?" I ask clumsily.

"I, uh, yes," Caleb says, taking a small step back.

"I apologize," I say, noting his reticence. "I'm actually here to talk to you." I let out a big breath of air.

Seemingly confused by the past few moments of activity, Caleb asks, "You are?"

"Yes," I say, taking a moment to catch my breath and compose myself. A quarter falls from my pocket where I'm still trying to put the change from the coffee counter. "I really need to talk to you."

"You do?" he responds, standing, still evaluating what is happening.

"Yes," I answer, once again taking a breath to calm down and talk to Caleb. I'm sure my presence so soon after being put out from the shelter is weird for him. My having to speak to him is probably sending out alarm bells, as if I'm following him. "But I promise it's a good thing."

"A good thing?" he repeats, not understanding.

"Let's sit over there," I say, pointing to a high-top table with two chairs.

"I, uh, I'm actually here to talk to, to see someone about..."

Caleb doesn't finish. I can tell this whole scenario is starting to freak him out.

"I'm here to talk to you about your computer." I realize I have been tapping this entire time. He looks at me with a practiced face, trying to make sense of things without giving away his fear. "You were arrested here. You had a crisis and were taken to the hospital." I pause, letting my assessment sink into Caleb's thoughts. "You were taken to the ER. They called me because you had some paperwork on you from the shelter. I think it was a form from your intake interview for the housing program or something like that." Caleb's face shows a moment of brief emotion. "After you were admitted to the BHU, I couldn't find you, so I came here to see if there was any information they could give me."

"You did?" Caleb asked.

"I did," I replied.

"I see. What did they say?" I can't tell whether he's curious or getting angry. I suspect anger because I overstepped.

"They didn't tell me much," I said. "But Caleb, they had your computer, phone, paperwork, chargers, and backpack." Caleb's eyes focus on me, and a slight pink hue creeps across his cheeks. "I took them." Caleb's face registers alarm. "I took your things to make sure they got back to you." I'm nearly stammering as I say this, awaiting his angry response.

"You have my computer?" he asks bluntly. I'm suddenly aware of Caleb's size. We're not at the shelter where rules keep the clients in order. Instead of answering, I slip the backpack off my shoulder, set it down on the floor, and unzip the top compartment. I reach in and pull out his well-worn HP Chromebook laptop. I set it on top of the table.

Caleb simply stands there. He looks at the computer, and all of what I have been talking about seems to fall into place. "My computer," he says softly. "May I have it?"

"What? Oh, yes. Of course you can have it!" I say in a tone to match his own. He takes the laptop in both hands and looks at it. "I took the liberty of charging it before I came here. Let's go over to the table, and you can see if everything is here that you left behind." Caleb says nothing. I keep wondering if he's angry. He has to be angry. I took his belongings. "I didn't know how to get a hold of you once you left the shelter, and when I got the call from the ER, I missed you by the time I could get down to the hospital. Once you were in the BHU, you may as well have been Amelia Earhart for how difficult it was to find you. I know I shouldn't have taken your stuff, Caleb. I know that. But I was just so concerned that it might not get back to you." I unload the charging cord, the chargers, and a collection of notecards. At last, folded up in my own backpack is his backpack. "I know that I overstepped here by taking your things. I apologize for that. I'm very sorry; I just wanted to make sure that you got them."

"I don't care," Caleb says. His words are firm.

I know he doesn't care what I have to say. He probably just wants me to leave. Leave him and his electronics alone.

Tap. Tap. Tap. Tap. Tap.

"I'm sorry, Caleb," I say.

Tap. Tap. Tap. Tap. Tap.

"I really am." I am standing here next to him, just a few yards away from the same place where he was arrested. It took several guards to get him under control, and now, here I am, the guy who stole his electronics. He could probably toss me across the lobby if he wanted.

"What I mean is," Caleb says, "I don't care that you took my stuff. It's here. That's all I care about."

"Really? You swear?"

"I swear."

"OK," I say, mostly because I am relieved not to become a decoration on the wall. "So...we're cool?" I don't feel the need to tap.

"Of course," Caleb says. "Thank you." And at that moment, Caleb, this giant mixed-up guy who stands a good eight inches taller than me, who also outweighs me by a good fifty pounds, becomes the person I remember. A quiet, respectful person greatly in need of the benefit of the doubt. We both sit at the table. He opens the laptop. It blinks and starts to warm up. It clicks and whirs like the fan might be a bit hinky. The screen gives a few bright flashes and then starts to glow.

"It works," he says.

"Good," I say.

"Right," he says quietly.

Here Caleb sits, after who knows what he's been through since he left the shelter. He is wearing the same clothes I see him wearing each day in the shelter: boots, jeans, and a gray hoodie. I pretty much had the entirety of his property. I think about my apartment, my electronics, clothing, furniture, and all the rest. Caleb's life fits into a backpack.

I have change from the barista: two dollars and some change in my pocket; chump change for me but this could be a meal for Caleb. I know he works from time to time, but still, this is a man reduced to the basics. I look over at his screen. There is a crack extending about halfway across it.

"Looks like your screen is broken."

"Yeah," he answers. "That happened on my way out here."

"Out here? You're not from around here?"

"No, I came here from San Diego."

"Really? I've never even left Columbus."

"Wow. Wish I could say the same."

"What do you mean?" I realize that may be a loaded question as Caleb drops his head a bit, thinking about his statement.

"Never mind. Long story."

Picking up on Caleb diverting away from his long story, I say, "Ok, so is everything in shape with your computer?"

"Yeah, looks like it's as good as it's going to get."

"What do you mean?"

"Well, this machine is pretty old. You must have realized that because of how heavy it is."

"I did notice that."

"The power jack is almost shot, and the screen has this stupid crack now," he says. "But it's still good for what I need it for."

"For gaming?"

He chuckles a bit. "No, I'm not into gaming. I am trying to be a writer. I need to finish a project I've been working on for quite some time. Then I'll actually have something to publish."

"A writer? Now, why does that not surprise me? You seem like quite the intelligent person. Knowing what little I do about you, it fits."

"Yeah," he says. "It's about the only thing I'm good at nowadays."

"Would you like to write?" I ask. "I mean, like become an actual author?" Caleb looks up at me. I think it's the first time he has met my gaze or that I've actually looked into his face.

"It's about the only thing that keeps me going, Malik."

His comment hits me like a punch in the gut. I ponder whether to tell him about my plan with Drake to find him a room at the rental property. I think rather than tell him about it, I'll take him to the house and see if it interests him. I think it would be easier for Caleb to answer if he has an idea of where we are talking about.

"Caleb, do you trust me?"

Tap. Tap. Tap. Tap. Tap.

“Tell you what, look through all your stuff. Make sure everything is there. Then, let me take you to wherever you’re staying?”

“OK,” he says.

“Good, I’ll buy us lunch too.”

We leave the library together. We stop at Subway on our way to Caleb’s motel. Caleb gets a veggie sub. I ask if he wants something with meat, thinking he’s being polite and not ordering an expensive sandwich.

“No,” Caleb says. “I’m a vegetarian.”

I laugh. I don’t know why it strikes me as funny. “You’re full of surprises.” He gives me a somewhat puzzled look, and I realize it’s my own preconception about homeless people. Of course, they can be vegetarian. “Hey, would you mind if I make a stop?” I’m both nervous and excited about showing Caleb what Drake and I have put together. Drake’s house is located near the neighborhood where the shelter is situated.

“Are we going back to the shelter?” Caleb asks.

“We’ll be near there, but no, we’re not going to the shelter.” I can tell that Caleb is a little let down. Maybe he was thinking that I’d be taking him back to the shelter, that a space opened up.

“I don’t exactly have a pressing work schedule right now, so no problem about making a stop.”

“Great, thanks.”

After about a ten-minute drive, I pull over and stop before Drake’s renovated home near the shelter. He really did a great job with it. It’s painted a butterscotch color with nutmeg trim. The front porch sweeps across the entire front of the house. The planters hung on the railing are bare, but I can imagine them full of sweet peas and lobelia vines during the summer. We get out of the car in front of the house. I watch Caleb’s face, wondering if he’s figured out what’s happening.

"Well, here it is. What do you think of it?"

"What do I think of what?" Caleb asks.

"The house."

"It's nice."

"A friend of mine owns it. His name is Drake. He can be a jerk, but he's generally a good guy. I helped him fix it up. I come over and do yard work from time to time. I have a key in case of emergencies."

Caleb looks at me and then at the house. "Is this an emergency?"

"No, there's no emergency. I just want your opinion on the house."

"Don't you think that's a funny question to ask a homeless person? The house is fine, but I'd say the same thing about a garden shed if it had a space heater. You do remember I was sleeping underneath a highway a few weeks ago..."

I chuckle. "Hey, man, just because you're homeless doesn't mean that you don't have taste. You haven't always been homeless."

"True, but why are we here?"

"Seriously, we've renovated it. What's your opinion?"

Looking at the house for a moment, Caleb says, "I think you have something here to be very proud of. It looks quite comfortable."

"Well, thanks. I appreciate it."

The porch floorboards and ceiling are painted the same nutmeg as the trim color. Normally, a dark color would make things seem smaller, but in the case of this porch, it just makes it seem rich. There is some light brown exterior patio furniture from a big box store. It's designed to look like wicker, but it is made of industrial plastic to withstand the elements. There are chains from each piece of furniture leading to an eye hook in the floorboard, protection against late-night rummagers in the neighborhood.

"I'm going to ring the doorbell, but I don't think the tenants are home at this hour." Caleb stands on the sidewalk as I walk toward the door. "C'mon, I want to show you the inside." Caleb looks at me with a bit of trepidation. I press the doorbell to the side of the door. A chime rings inside, something soft and pleasant. No one answers. "That's what I thought."

I fumble with my keychain until I find the key. After I slide it into the lock, the door opens inward, revealing a wooden floor leading directly to a staircase in the middle of the foyer. There is a living area to the left and a bathroom to the right; a kitchen lies ahead beyond the staircase.

On the wall inside the foyer, there are a half-dozen hooks. Most are taken up with coats. An assortment of men's boots lay in pairs below the jackets. Next to the bathroom, a mountain bike rests against the wall.

"Here's the living room with the couch, oversized loveseat, and a flat screen."

"Nice," Caleb says, still taking it all in with a bit of reticence. I walk out of the living room and down to the kitchen. It's nicely equipped with a big gas-burning stove and oven, a side-by-side fridge, a stainless-steel sink with two basins, and butcher-block countertops. "The countertops were a mistake. They take a lot of care, but the guys seem to do a pretty good job. Drake, the guy who owns the place, will have to sand them down and refinish them each year."

"They're pretty," Caleb says.

"Yeah, it was tricky finishing off the kitchen," I say. "Everything was here except the side-by-side fridge, so we decided to splurge and do the butcher-block countertops. Wouldn't you know, the one thing left to our decision; we screwed up."

I show him the dining area to the right of the kitchen area. It is painted white mostly, with beadboard running around the walls. There is a table that seats four comfortably. What is most impressive about both rooms are the windows running along them that face out onto the backyard. It makes the two regular-sized rooms seem enormous.

"If you go back down the hallway and turn right at the staircase, there's a small downstairs bathroom."

"Yes, I saw that on the way in."

"It's only a half bath," I say. "But it's nice to have if you have guests."

We walk back to the staircase and make our way up the wide treads. "I had to fight the other guys to keep this staircase. It's almost twice as wide as normal staircases."

"I thought so too," Caleb says. "It really makes the place seem grand."

"Grand," I repeat, thinking about the language I hear around the shelter. Caleb really is different from most of the guys. "You have a way with words."

"Thanks," Caleb says, and after a few moments, he asks, "Malik, what am I doing here?"

"I just had some time to kill, so I thought I could show you what my friends and I work on,"

Caleb looks down at his feet. I can tell that he's getting uncomfortable for some reason. Getting to the top of the stairs, more hardwood floors run the length of the open hallway of the interior top floor. The hallways lead off to four separate bedrooms, two on each side of the stairway. There is a large bathroom at the top of the stairway.

"The upstairs bathroom would have been perfect for a huge claw-foot bathtub," I say, pushing open the door. "Unfortunately, as you can see, we had to go with a bathtub insert with a shower."

"It's still very nice," Caleb says.

"Yeah, it is. Maybe if Drake goes to sell one day, I'll buy it."

"Isn't that odd?" Caleb says. "People fixing their homes up for someone else to enjoy."

"I never thought about it that way, but yeah, it is a bit weird." I look at Caleb again, considering his way of thinking.

He notices me looking at him and says, "What?"

"Nothing, man," I say. "You just always catch me off guard with how you describe things."

"I like words."

"I bet you're going to be a serious writer."

Caleb stands still.

"You ok?" I say after a few moments.

"Yeah," Caleb says. "I just get glimpses of poems sometimes. Something gets said, and I see the words swirling around it. I try to write them down when they happen. It's my chronicle of things."

"Cool," I answer. "Do you have a title for it?"

"Chronicles of a Loser," he says.

"Why do you call it that? You might be down and out right now, but you're not a loser."

"Sure I am," he says, looking down at his feet. "I've lost integrity. I've lost my family. I've lost friends. I've lost jobs. I've lost places to live. Hell, I even lost my mind, repeatedly. The title isn't an indictment, it's a play on words. Everyone does what you're doing now, thinking about it as a judgment. It's not. It's a statement of fact. I have lost a lot. The poems describe how that happened."

I pause, taking in what Caleb is saying. The guys at the shelter are in a constant state of loss, like him. As people, they've lost, so in that sense, they are losers. But even though they've had substantial losses, they go on. And in going on, they're not losers, they're achievers. I'm blown away with how this guy's mind operates.

"Having losses doesn't equate to being a loser, is that what you mean?"

"They're just two different things. We all lose things. If we start thinking about the actual loss, it is different than thinking about someone being a loser. If we fall, we're not called fallers. If we grieve, we're not grievers. We are someone who has fallen or someone who is grieving. Those aren't derogatory terms. Someone who has lost something doesn't automatically make them a loser. It makes them someone who has lost. It's not the entirety of their character."

"Dude. You're some kind of genius, I think."

"Yeah." Caleb laughs a bit. "A genius who lives under bridges."

"Well, maybe not for much longer."

Caleb looks at me with caution. "So, Malik, again, why am I here?"

"Look, I know you don't have many things right now, and I don't presume to know what you need."

"OK," Caleb says. "Are we getting to the part where you let me in on the secret of this impromptu excursion?"

"Yeah, something like that."

Caleb stands waiting for my answer. He's not curious like I thought he might be. Instead, he looks uncomfortable.

"I asked you if you liked the place when we got out of the car."

"Right. The place is lovely. You've done a good job with it. But why am I here?"

I smile a bit at him.

He looks at his shoes again. "Malik, what's this leading to?" His cheeks are a bit flushed, and I grow a little concerned for him. He seems to be shutting down. He's not moving. He can't hold eye contact.

"Leading to? Something good, I hope." I'm trying to be

reassuring. "I'd like to show you the empty room here." Caleb seems to hold his shoulders tight. I'm not sure what's happening in Caleb's mind. "Is something wrong?" I put a hand on his shoulder. To my surprise, he smacks my hand away. "Whoa, man, what's up?"

"Look, I can't do that!" Caleb yells, pushing me away so I almost fall.

"Do what?" I ask, really alarmed.

"That!" he says resolutely.

"That what?" For the life of me, I cannot think what he's talking about. And then it dawns on me. Someone's taken advantage of him in the past. *Does he think I'm looking for sex?*

"Dude, no, man. That's not at all why I brought you here."

Caleb looks at me, red-faced. "It's not?"

I soften my voice. "No, man. I brought you to see if you'd be interested in living here."

Caleb's face remains strained with anger. "Living here?"

"Drake has a room open. It's yours if you'd like it." Caleb keeps his feet in place. "You ok?" I ask.

"I, uh..." Caleb stammers a bit, still looking at his feet. "I don't understand. How could that happen?"

"Well, like I said, my friend Drake owns the place. He's got an opening, this room right here."

"He'd rent to me?" Caleb asks.

"He would if I asked him to," I say. "And I did ask him."

"I...I'm sorry, Malik," Caleb says quietly.

"You've got nothing to be sorry about. I really screwed that up. I guess I should have been more straightforward about what was going on, especially before taking you to an empty bedroom in an empty house." We both chuckle a little nervously. "I'd never take advantage of you like that. Neither would Drake. I promise. I'm offering you the choice of being a tenant here, no strings attached.

Except for rent."

"No strings attached?" Caleb asks again, letting his guard down. "It's just been a long time since someone has gone out of their way for me, without strings attached. Why would you do this?"

"Look, you got screwed by losing your bed when you went to the hospital. You keep track of your meds. You have a job, or had one, which means you can get another one. And you're not a creep like a lot of the guys at the shelter."

"Well, I got screwed at the shelter because I screwed things up," Caleb said. "I always screw things up."

"You got screwed because the system isn't set up to deal with guys like you. I've worked at the shelter for a long time. Not many guys like you come through. I'm aware of what you deal with. I also know you're a nice guy who probably has a history of not-so-nice things happening in your life."

"There have been a lot of strings."

"Look, I had this idea. We have a lot of homeless people all jockeying for the same crappy apartments. If we expand our housing inventory by adding rooms for rent in established homes owned by people like Drake, we can really put a dent in the homeless population. I've got connections to help you out if you'd be willing to be a guinea pig to see if we can get this program up and running. I think you'd make a great first candidate."

"No strings attached?"

"No. No strings attached. I promise." I carefully put my hand on his shoulder and repeat, "I promise." I'm just about to ask him if he wants to stay at the house a little longer to get situated when my phone disrupts the moment with a notification. I take my hand from Caleb's shoulder and look down at the screen. It reads: Fairfield County Prison. Alert notification for Walter Clarence

Arons.

Am I really seeing this?

Is this real?

I realize I'm holding my breath. I exhale. Caleb is looking at me, but I'm transfixed to the screen on my phone. "Um, I'll be right back."

I leave Caleb in the house and walk outside to sit in one of the chairs on the porch. My hands tremble slightly as I do my best to navigate the prompts to open the notification. It comes from the maximum security Fairfield County Prison.

He's in prison.

Why send a notification now?

I have searched the prison website for inmate locations dozens of times, and then I remember. The FCP had been updating the paper files to digital files. The progress was slow but steady. I'd been in their records room. It's a large basement storage facility that looked as disorganized as my work office. Maybe they finally got to the timeline where my father was incarcerated. As much as I wanted him to be alive and well, living his life somewhere peaceful, I can accept the fact that he is in prison. His past would certainly have been prologue for such an event.

I click the link to the Department of Corrections website and open the Offender Search tab. It prompts me for his name and some other details. I enter as much as I can. I click search. It comes back with a number: A247382. I stare at the number: A247382. It was a number replacing his name in the prison system, no longer a person, just a number to manage. *How well did he manage? If he couldn't find control over his life on the outside, maybe on the inside, in prison, he found some semblance of a life.*

I click through the information about his parole dates and how he never showed up for his parole hearings. *Strange.* I click further into the system and see that he had been admitted to the psychiatric facility within the prison. *Was he getting help? Would he want to see me? How would I go about arranging that kind of a meeting?*

I click further into the system and notice that for the past several years, there are no notations.

Then I read it.

It was written as plain as day: A247382. Deceased, April 27, 2019. Fairfield County Coroner.

In the split second it took to read that my father was dead, my heart breaks. I always knew this was a possibility, but it still didn't prepare me for the shock of reading, for certain, that my dad was gone.

Should I tell Moms? Should I reach out to find where he was buried, and take Moms there? How will I break the news to her? What should I...

Stop.

I'm jumping right back into trying to help my way out of an emotional situation. I strain my thinking to stop worrying about Moms for just a moment and focus on the news that Pops is dead. He's really dead. There would be no reunion. There would be no catharsis. There was just the simple fact that after a life of addiction, crime, bullying, and misdeeds, he's dead.

I thought I would feel it somehow if he were dead.

Was it my own superhero complex bullshit that led me to believe he could still be alive and helped onto a better path in life?

That's when I felt it. The moisture on my cheek. Tears from a different part of my mind. From when I was a kid, when things were calm between the numerous storms. From when Pops would take me on his shoulders into Smitty's and buy me a candy bar. From when he picked me up off the street when I crashed as I learned to ride the second-hand bicycle he gave me. Those memories are there, despite the trauma of the later episodes. The shouting, the threats, and the violence always punctuated the good times. *Always.* Even as I clung to the memories of when he wasn't addicted or abusive.

I wipe my cheeks.

Staring at that damned word: deceased, is like looking into the sun. I can't bear it. It hurts to see it. I log out of the website. What more is there to do? The search that had held sway over so much of my adult life ends with a few clicks on my phone. *What do I do when something that looms so large in my life is suddenly over, without warning or fanfare? It's just...over.*

That's when I notice something else. This huge event has happened, and I haven't tapped. I don't recite my mantra. I don't feel panic. It all just feels numb. He won't be walking back into my life. I won't find him in some shelter. I won't get closure, like saying goodbye. Closure will have to come from my own mind. Superman won't need to fly anymore. Pops was my kryptonite, and now he's gone.

I make a call to the prison to find out information about where my father might be buried. I am told that he is buried at the Institution Cemetery, a place where inmates are buried when no one claims the body.

Still numb, I walk back inside and tell Caleb what has transpired in the past few minutes. I feel a little sick to my stomach that my father is buried in some random field without a funeral or someone to mourn his loss. I ask Caleb if he needs a ride somewhere, and he answers, "No, I'm fine, but you look like you could use some company. Are you ok?"

"Yes, I think. I mean, no." I realize I'm stammering.

"C'mon. Let's go."

"Let's go where?" I ask, thinking there's no way he's suggesting what I think he is suggesting. "Let's go find your father," he says matter-of-factly. "Malik, you've given me a home. The least I can do is go with you to the cemetery. I can at least do that much for you."

Caleb is a constant source of surprise, and I am grateful for the company. "Ok, let's go."

Google Maps takes us to the cemetery. It looks more like a vacant lot, covered with sparse patches of crabgrass. The tombstones are flat and unassuming. We walk through the graveyard and realize the graves are organized chronologically. It takes about twenty minutes, but we finally find it. His headstone was simple. It included his name, his inmate number, and the date of his death. That's it. The totality of a person's life on a twelve-by-sixteen concrete headstone.

I took a picture of the headstone. I'll show Moms if she wants to see it. I can't guess if she would or wouldn't want to see it, or if she'd want to visit the grave. Pops represented so much of our struggle in life, and Moms may just want it to be over. Then again, if the person who caused her the most pain in her life is deceased, maybe it will be a relief to see the headstone. The bandwidth in my brain is overloaded.

"I'm going to call my mother," I tell Caleb. He nods his head and walks away to a nearby section of the cemetery to give me privacy on the phone. I get Mom's answering machine. Maybe this is the best way. She can hear the news and react privately. She can call back when she's ready for more information.

"Hey Moms, it's me. I, uh, I have some news..."

CHAPTER THIRTY-SEVEN

Caleb — Home

After Malik speaks briefly to his mother, he and I return to the house. He is lost in thought. I ask him if he's going to be ok. He shrugs his shoulder and says, "I guess we'll find out, won't we." He gets out of his car and walks back to the trunk. He opens it and gets out something wrapped in a large shopping bag. "I, uh, I'm just leaving something for Drake inside." He uses his key to enter the house, is inside for just a few moments, and then reappears, walking down to the street.

I thank him again for making the connection between Drake and myself. He thanks me for coming out to the cemetery. We look at one another, each of us in such different places, yet we both share unique pain and adversity in our lives. As he drives away, I'm holding the key he gave to me. The key in my hand signifies something transformative to someone who has spent lengthy periods without a home. This key has a counterpart in a door. A door that leads to where belongings are kept, where a person sleeps, and where someone can return whenever they need or want. I've had keys to lockers where I stored my stuff during the day as I walked the streets. I had a key to a broken-down car, owned by a friend, where I stayed until it got towed. I've even had keys to apartments, whose doors opened to me until my brain chemistry dictated otherwise. This key is to a house. From what is starting to evolve, it may become a home, more so than the shelter, more so than the motel, and much more than the freeway underpass. I turn the key over and over in my hand.

A lot is riding on me and whether I happen. If I happen, how will the new people in my life react to it? Malik told me that he would attend a monthly house meeting with the other guys and me. He also is going to introduce me to a cop who patrols the neighborhood regularly. She knows how to deal with people like me, people who find themselves in mental health crises from time to time. He explains that the guys in the house may call this officer if they feel I'm heading toward trouble. I'm encouraged that, should I happen, should I go underwater, should the volcano explode, there will be people in place to help.

I'm going to be honest with my housemates. Honesty takes a lot of doing. I live in a depth of shame about my circumstances. The police reports and hospital records tell the story of a very volatile person. Versions of the truth tend to trickle back to me if I allow it. It sounds as though when I lose time or lose control, I may now have people who know how to react to the events. I will have a history to learn from, not just a past from which I run.

I put my music to shuffle and *I'm Changing* sung by Jennifer Hudson fills my ears. It's a poignant theme for me today. As I take in the neighborhood, the street where the house is seems normal for the neighborhood, maybe a bit more cared for by the residents. There are a few vacant lots with some trash blown onto them, but there are also signs of real recovery. Homes purchased by folks in the neighborhood, either as rentals or for themselves. These homes are fixed up nicely. There is a neighborhood watch group that mows the lawns on vacant lots, plants shrubs and flowers along the sidewalks, and tries to stay on top of the litter.

Christmas is coming. I remember the large red bow my mother used to affix to the post below our yard light. It was made of a fabric that was weather-resistant. I remember it seemed regal. Christmas time was a good time growing up. We always did holiday things with families other than Craig's. Mom always had copious amounts of comforting food. I was attached to her knees as a kid, and later I would watch as she cooked, decorated, and sewed. My mom was a soft person, but not one to hug or show affection. I watched and learned things from her. I miss her. I miss those days. At least the days when Craig wasn't around.

So many thoughts go through my head as I look at the house.

Am I ready to reconnect with people?

Will they be willing to connect with a nut job like me?

I'm not sure how long I've been standing in front of the house. A man, apparently a guy who lives next door to the house, is watching me. I return his gaze. He lifts an arm and waves back and forth a few times. He is holding a portable shopping cart on his porch. His pants are baggy and a bit ill-fitted. He wears a dark jacket over a tie-dyed shirt. His head is capped by a red stocking cap with an enormous pom-pom on top. A new, colorful neighbor. I admire him. He is eccentric, showing his unique take on the world. He looks joyful, if not a bit goofy.

A simple silver key doesn't mean a lot to many folks. But to me, it means a transformation, an evolution. The Tarot is drawn and I get the Death card. *Am I on the precipice of change* That's when it really hits me. *I think I want to be a part of the world again.*

As the revelation of this thought takes hold, I see once again my serendipitous friend, growing in the cracks of the steps, bobbing up and down on the light breeze.

And the words drop into place:

Soft and subtle, growing sweet from sour,
so is the blossom of the chicory flower.
From grounds of regret, lacking in hope,
finding traction upon the concrete slope.
Blooming from fractured, rocky parts,
is the periwinkle dream for broken hearts.
Soft and subtle growing sweet from sour,
so is the blossom of the chicory flower.

Beautiful things can grow from the most unlikely of places, like me holding a key to a home. It's a circumstance I could not have foreseen as I picked debris from my clothing when I emerged from the underpass all those weeks ago. The guys in AA talk about not quitting before the miracle happens. For them, sobriety is their miracle. For me, it's...what?...the simple chance to start over? No, that's not it. I've started over dozens of times. I'm on the cusp of inventing a life of some sort. And that's when I realize my miracle: the possibility that good things can happen.

Thoughts of futility and suicide are waning. Could those thoughts truly be a thing of my past? And if they are a thing of the past, I reckon I must now look forward to a future where indeed good things may happen. Here I am, with a key and the possibility of unlocking not just a house, but a life. A light snowfall floats down as I walk up the steps to the porch. A pair of mourning doves take flight from near the walkway.

The house seems quiet, but it doesn't feel empty. Someone's newspaper sits rolled up on one of the chairs on the porch. An ashtray holds the butts of someone who sat there smoking, thinking. Malik said the guys usually start showing up here about five or five thirty after their days at work. I have time to walk around the house by myself before I make introductions. I put the key into the lock, listening to the deadbolt slide back. No buzzer letting me in.

No one patting me down before entering. No smell of sanitizer or bleach. No one is taking the strings out of my hoodies or pulling the belt off my pants. I turn the doorknob. And as easy as that, I'm walking into a home.

It's quiet. Everything is where it was when I walked through with Malik, except the bicycle by the downstairs bathroom is now gone. My housemates are out leading lives. Perhaps I will be leading a life someday soon too. Perhaps I'll be writing about my life. Maybe I won't be losing anymore. Maybe I need a new title for my poetry collection, or to start a new book altogether.

I put a hand on the stair rail and slowly ascend. A few planks issue a slow creak, as if the house is speaking to me, urging me to my room. I feel the words coming to mind. It's been a while since calm thoughts have frequented my mind and stayed.

I push the door open and look around the room. There is a set of new sheets for the full-sized bed, a new towel, a box fan, and a few other useful things for a new room. I am so thankful that Malik has gone above and beyond for me. My eyes fall on the table that is set up as my desk. I see the package that Malik retrieved from his trunk. He said it was for Drake, so I'm a bit confused about why it's in my room. I hold the package, wondering if I should open it. I decide to open the shopping bag, and in doing so, my heart skips a beat as to what is inside.

It's a laptop. A new laptop. A laptop with a simple yellow Post-it stuck to the top. I press my finger upon the note. It reads:

Caleb, We hope this helps. – Malik & Drake

I sit down in the chair, overwhelmed with emotion. No more twigs stuck in my clothing. No more black plastic bags as luggage. Gone are the wet socks and the sore shoulders. The hospital and Kate seem like distant memories now. Lisa and her friends at the motel fade into memory. Life may actually be different now.

I will have roommates, not happenstance characters pushing heroin into their veins. No more concrete pillows. No more sketchy motel rooms. It's not a guarantee that this will remain, I mean, it's possible that I will happen again. But it's a good first step toward stability, toward becoming something more than the totality of my symptoms. And, momentarily, the beast is nowhere to be found.

I rest my palm on the surface of the laptop. It is cool and reassuring, like my cinderblock wall at the shelter. I close my eyes. The tears flow as the words, no, not the words, but the *word* drops into place:

Home.

Acknowledgments

My appreciation goes out to Heather Chouinard and her wonderful photographs through Enchanted Evermore Photography. I would also like to thank Paula Lester at Polaris Editing, polarisediting.com. She guided me through the editing process. Editing is such a vulnerable time in a manuscript's life; she made it easy, and her insight was invaluable. Lastly, I want to thank Kate at Beta Reading Bookings LLC. Her input helped hone the arc of the novel in the best possible way.

About the Author

Joseph resides along the shores of Lake Superior in Michigan's Upper Peninsula, where the long winters offer plenty of quiet time for writing. When the weather warms, he can often be found hiking the region's rugged trails or tending his garden. He hosts *Walking in America*, a podcast devoted to open conversations about overcoming mental health challenges, and is a passionate advocate for mental health awareness. With a background in Montessori education and a degree in business management, Joseph brings both insight and empathy to his work. Having personally faced the complexities of persistent mental health conditions, he is grateful that the right combination of medication and therapy has allowed him to live a fulfilling, productive life. Beyond writing and recording, Joseph enjoys cooking and spending time with DJ, his outspoken orange tabby.

Apprentice House is the country's only campus-based, student-staffed book publishing company. Directed by professors and industry professionals, it is a nonprofit activity of the Communication Department at Loyola University Maryland.

Using state-of-the-art technology and an experiential learning model of education, Apprentice House publishes books in untraditional ways. This dual responsibility as publishers and educators creates an unprecedented collaborative environment among faculty and students, while teaching tomorrow's editors, designers, and marketers.

Eclectic and provocative, Apprentice House titles intend to entertain as well as spark dialogue on a variety of topics. Financial contributions to sustain the press's work are welcomed. Contributions are tax deductible to the fullest extent allowed by the IRS.

To learn more about Apprentice House books or to obtain submission guidelines, please visit www.apprenticehouse.com.

Apprentice House Press
Communication Department
Loyola University Maryland
4501 N. Charles Street
Baltimore, MD 21210
Ph: 410-617-5265
info@apprenticehouse.com • www.apprenticehouse.com

www.ingramcontent.com/pod-product-compliance
Lightning Source LLC
LaVergne TN
LVHW010602100826
845148LV00014B/2817

* 9 7 8 1 6 2 7 2 0 6 1 9 8 *